Various Miracles

'Shields's outlines of lives, witty and generous, are alive with this provisional happiness, a fragile incandescence glowing against the dark.' – *Independent on Sunday*

'Shields's stories are spiked by moments of supernatural transcendence.' – Victoria Glendinning, *Daily Telegraph*

'Carol Shields manages in a particularly original way to turn water into wine, transfiguring the mundane with meaning.' – *The Times*

'The tales in Carol Shields's *Various Miracles* are united by a common fascination with the giddy euphorics of chance . . . A loving testimony to the slow, unspoken bargains of lasting marriage, Shields's work here is shot through with honest awe.' – *Financial Times*

'Carol Shields's short stories are full of sentences you could almost sing . . . her sentences transmute base metal into gold.' – *Independent*

'Good writing has nothing to fear from sentimentality and Shields writes with that big heart of hers ablaze.' – *Sunday Times*

'Shields takes the everyday and makes it extraordinary through the quality of attention she gives it.' – *Observer*

'While Shields is a buoyant and generously comic writer, she conveys in this collection, more than previously, the pain of knowing that, whatever patterns our existence may have, they cannot be seen or controlled.' – *Times Literary Supplement*

'As always with the most cleverly crafted fiction, Shields appears to have stumbled into the heart of it naturally and accidentally. The description applied by one of Shields's characters to the scenes in her life sums up the simple beauty of her stories: ". . . sometimes she thinks of them as little keys on a chain, keys that will open nothing but simply exist for the beauty of their toothed edges and the way they chime in her pocket".' – *London Review of Books*

'Reading Shields's work makes you look at the person sitting next to you on the bus with renewed sympathy and curiosity: she's an antidote to indifference.' – *Tatler*

'One of the best writers around.' – *U Magazine*

'Shields brilliantly illuminates life coincidences in these tales . . . Wonderful, inspired writing.' – *Midweek*

Various Miracles

Born and brought up in suburban Chicago, Carol Shields has lived in Canada for more than three decades. Her novels include *Mary Swann* (1990), *Happenstance* (1991) and *The Republic of Love* (1992). *The Stone Diaries*, also published by Fourth Estate, was short-listed for the 1993 Booker Prize, and was awarded the Pulitzer Prize for Fiction in 1995.

ALSO BY CAROL SHIELDS

Small Ceremonies

The Box Garden

Mary Swann

Happenstance

The Republic of Love

The Stone Diaries

Various Miracles

Carol Shields

FOURTH ESTATE · *London*

This paperback edition first published 1995
This collection first published in Great Britain in 1994 by
Fourth Estate Limited
6 Salem Road
London W2 4BU

A catalogue record for this book is available from the British Library.

ISBN 978-0-00-729126-7

The author and publisher wish to acknowledge with thanks previous publication of the following stories: 'Various Miracles', *Canadian Forum/Double Bond*; 'Home', 'The Journal', *Fiddlehead*; 'Times of Sickness and Health', *A Room of One's Own*; 'Mrs. Turner Cutting the Grass', *Arts Manitoba*; 'Accidents', 'Love So Fleeting', *The Malahat Review*; 'Hinterland', *Prairie Fire*; 'Dolls, Dolls, Dolls, Dolls', *Aurora/CBC Anthology*; 'Fuel for the Fire', *Border Crossings*; 'Milk Bread Beer Ice', *Saturday Night*.

Typeset by York House Typographic Ltd
Printed in Great Britain by Cox & Wyman Ltd, Reading

For my daughter Meg

Contents

Hazel

AFTER A MAN has mistreated a woman he feels a need to do something nice which she must accept.

In line with this way of thinking, Hazel has accepted from her husband, Brian, sprays of flowers, trips to Hawaii, extravagant compliments on her rather ordinary cooking, bracelets of dull-coloured silver and copper, a dressing gown in green tartan wool, a second dressing gown with maribou trim around the hem and sleeves, dinners in expensive revolving restaurants and, once, a tender kiss, tenderly delivered, on the instep of her right foot.

But there will be no more such compensatory gifts, for Brian died last December of heart failure.

The heart failure, as Hazel, even after all these years, continues to think of it. In her family, the family of her girlhood that is, a time of gulped confusion in a place called Porcupine Falls, all familiar diseases were preceded by the horrific article: *the* measles, *the* polio, *the* rheumatism, *the* cancer, and – to come down to her husband Brian and his final thrashing with life – *the* heart failure.

He was only fifty-five. He combed his uncoloured hair smooth and wore clothes made of gabardinelike materials, a silky exterior covering a complex core. It took him ten days to die after the initial attack, and during the time he lay there, all his minor wounds healed. He was a careless man who bumped into things, shrubbery, table legs, lighted cigarettes, simple kerbstones. Even the making of love seemed to him a labour and a recovery, attended by scratches, bites, effort, exhaustion and, once or twice, a mild but humiliating infection. Nevertheless, women found him attractive. He had an unhurried, good-humoured persistence about him and could be kind when he chose to be.

The night he died Hazel came home from the hospital and sat propped up in bed till four in the morning, reading a trashy, fast-moving New York novel about wives who lived in spacious duplexes overlooking Central Park, too alienated to carry on properly with their lives. They made salads with rare kinds of lettuce and sent their apparel to the dry cleaners, but they were bitter and helpless. Frequently they used the expression 'fucked up' to describe their malaise. Their mothers or their fathers had fucked them up, or jealous sisters or bad-hearted nuns, but mainly they had been fucked up by men who no longer cared about them. These women were immobilised by the lack of love and kept alive only by a reflexive bounce between new ways of arranging salad greens and fantasies of suicide. Hazel wondered as she read how long it took for the remembered past to sink from view. A few miserable tears crept into her eyes, her first tears since Brian's initial attack, that shrill telephone call, that unearthly hour. Impetuously she wrote on the book's flyleaf the melodramatic words 'I am alone and suffering unbearably'. Not her best handwriting, not her usual floating morning-glory tendrils. Her fingers cramped at this hour. The cheap ball-point pen held back its ink, and the result was a barely legible scrawl that she nevertheless underlined twice.

By mid-January she had taken a job demonstrating kitchenware in department stores. The ad in the newspaper promised on-the-job training, opportunities for advancement and contact with the public. Hazel submitted to a short, vague, surprisingly painless interview, and was rewarded the following morning by a telephone call telling her she was to start immediately. She suspected she was the sole applicant, but nevertheless went numb with shock. Shock and also pleasure. She hugged the elbows of her dressing gown and smoothed the sleeves flat. She was fifty years old and without skills, a woman who had managed to avoid most of the arguments and issues of the world. Asked a direct question, her voice wavered. She understood nothing of the national debt or the situation in Nicaragua, nothing. At ten-thirty most mornings she was still in her dressing gown and had the sense to know this was shameful. She possessed a softened, tired body and rubbed-looking eyes. Her posture was only moderately good. She often touched her mouth with the back of her hand. Yet someone, some person with a downtown commercial address and an official letterhead and a firm telephone manner had seen fit to offer her a job.

Only Hazel, however, thought the job a good idea.

Brian's mother, a woman in her eighties living in a suburban retirement centre called Silver Oaks, said, 'Really, there is no need, Hazel. There's plenty of money if you live reasonably. You have your condo paid for, your car, a good fur coat that'll last for years. Then there's the insurance and

Brian's pension, and when you're sixty-five – now don't laugh, sixty-five will come, it's not that far off – you'll have your social security. You have a first-rate lawyer to look after your investments. There's no need.'

Hazel's closest friend, Maxine Forestadt, a woman of her own age, a demon bridge player, a divorcée, a woman with a pinkish powdery face loosened by too many evenings of soft drinks and potato chips and too much cigarette smoke flowing up toward her eyes, said, 'Look. You're not the type, Hazel. Period. I know the type and you're not it. Believe me. All right, so you feel this urge to assert yourself, to try to prove something. I know, I went through it myself, wanting to show the world I wasn't just this dipsy pushover and hanger-oner. But this isn't for you, Haze, this eight-to-five purgatory, standing on your feet, and especially *your* feet, your arches, your arches act up just shopping. I know what you're trying to do, but in the long run, what's the point?'

Hazel's older daughter, Marilyn, a pathologist, and possibly a lesbian, living in a women's co-op in the east end of the city, phoned and, drawing on the sort of recollection that Hazel already had sutured, said, 'Dad would not have approved. I know it, you know it. I mean, Christ, flogging pots and pans, it's so public. People crowding around. Idle curiosity and greed, a free show, just hanging in for a teaspoon of bloody quiche lorraine or whatever's going. Freebies. People off the street, bums, anybody. Christ. Another thing, you'll have to get a whole new wardrobe for a job like that. Eye shadow so thick it's like someone's given you a punch. Just ask yourself what Dad would have said. I know what he would have said, he would have said thumbs down, nix on it.'

Hazel's other daughter, Rosie, living in British Columbia, married to a journalist, wrote: 'Dear Mom, I absolutely respect what you're doing and admire your courage. But Robin and I can't help wondering if you've given this decision enough thought. You remember how after the funeral, back at your place with Grandma and Auntie Maxine and Marilyn, we had that long talk about the need to lie fallow for a bit and not rush headlong into things and making major decisions, just letting the grieving process take its natural course. Now here it is, a mere six weeks later, and you've got yourself involved with these cookware people. I just hope you haven't signed anything. Robin says he never heard of Kitchen Kult and it certainly isn't listed on the boards. We're just anxious about you, that's all. And this business of working on commission is exploitative to say the least. Ask Marilyn. You've still got your shorthand and typing and, with a refresher course, you probably could find something, maybe Office Overload would give you a sense of your own independence and some spending money besides. We just don't want to see you hurt, that's all.'

At first, Hazel's working day went more or less like this: at seven-thirty her alarm went off; the first five minutes were the worst; such a steamroller of sorrow passed over her that she was left as flat and lifeless as the queen-size mattress that supported her. Her squashed limbs felt emptied of blood, her breath came out thin and cool and quiet as ether. What was she to do? How was she to live her life? She mouthed these questions to the silky blanket binding, rubbing her lips frantically back and forth across the stitching. Then she got up, showered, did her hair, made coffee and toast, took a vitamin pill, brushed her teeth, made up her face (going easy on the eye shadow), and put on her coat. By eight-thirty she was in her car and checking her city map.

Reading maps, the tiny print, the confusion, caused her headaches. And she had trouble with orientation, turning the map first this way, then that, never willing to believe that north must lie at the top. North's natural place should be toward the bottom, past the Armoury and stockyards where a large cold lake bathed the city edges. Once on a car trip to the Indian River country early in their married life, Brian had joked about her lack of map sense. He spoke happily of this failing, proudly, giving her arm a squeeze, and then had thumped the cushioned steering wheel. Hazel, thinking about the plushy thump, wished she hadn't. To recall something once was to remember it forever; this was something she had only recently discovered, and she felt that the discovery might be turned to use.

The Kitchen Kult demonstrations took her on a revolving cycle of twelve stores, some of them in corners of the city where she'd seldom ventured. The Italian district. The Portuguese area. Chinatown. A young Kitchen Kult salesman named Peter Lemmon broke her in, *familiarising* her as he put it with the Kitchen Kult product. He taught her the spiel, the patter, the importance of keeping eye contact with customers at all times, how to draw on the mood and size of the crowd and play, if possible, to its ethnic character, how to make Kitchen Kult products seem like large beautiful toys, easily mastered and guaranteed to win the love and admiration of friends and family.

'That's what people out there really want,' Peter Lemmon told Hazel, who was surprised to hear this view put forward so undisguisedly. 'Lots of love and truckloads of admiration. Keep that in mind. People can't get enough.'

He had an aggressive pointed chin and ferocious red sideburns, and when he talked he held his lips together so that the words came out with a soft zitherlike slur. Hazel noticed his teeth were discoloured and badly crowded, and she guessed that this accounted for his guarded way of talking. Either that or a nervous disposition. Early on, to put him at his ease, she told him of her small-town upbringing in Porcupine Falls, how her elderly parents had never quite recovered from the surprise of having a child. How at eighteen she came to Toronto to study stenography. That she was now a widow with two daughters, one of whom she suspected of being unhappily married and one who was undergoing a gender crisis. She told Peter Lemmon that this was her first real job, that at the age of fifty she was out working for the first time. She talked too much, babbled in fact – why? She didn't know. Later she was sorry.

In return he confided, opening his mouth a little wider, that he was planning to have extensive dental work in the future if he could scrape the money together. More than nine thousand dollars had been quoted. A quality job cost quality cash, that was the long and short of it, so why not take the plunge. He hoped to go right to the top with Kitchen Kult. Not just sales, but the real top, and that meant management. It was a company, he told her, with a forward-looking sales policy and sound product.

It disconcerted Hazel at first to hear Peter Lemmon speak of the Kitchen Kult product without its grammatical article, and she was jolted into the remembrance of how she had had to learn to suppress the article that attached to bodily ailments. When demonstrating product, Peter counselled, keep it well in view, repeating product's name frequently and withholding product's retail price until the actual demo and tasting has been concluded.

After two weeks Hazel was on her own, although Peter Lemmon continued to meet her at the appointed 'sales venue' each morning, bringing with him in a company van the equipment to be demonstrated and helping her 'set up' for the day. She slipped into her white smock, the same one every day, a smooth permapress blend with grommets down the front and Kitchen Kult in red script across the pocket, and stowed her pumps in a plastic bag, putting on the white crepe-soled shoes Peter Lemmon had recommended. 'Your feet, Hazel, are your capital.' He also produced, of his own volition, a tall collapsible stool on which she could perch in such a way that she appeared from across the counter to be standing unsupported.

She started each morning with a demonstration of the Jiffy-Sure-Slicer, Kitchen Kult's top seller, accounting for some sixty per cent of total sales. For an hour or more, talking to herself, or rather to the empty air, she shaved hillocks of carrots, beets, parsnips and rutabagas into baroque curls or else she transformed them into little star-shaped discs or elegant matchsticks. The use of cheap root vegetables kept the demo costs down, Peter Lemmon said, and presented a less threatening challenge to the average shopper, Mrs. Peas and Carrots, Mrs. Corn Niblets.

As Hazel warmed up, one or two shoppers drifted toward her, keeping her company – she learned she could count on these one or two who were elderly women for the most part, puffy of face and bulgy of eye. Widows, Hazel decided. The draggy-hemmed coats and beige tote bags gave them away. Like herself, though perhaps a few years older, these women had taken their toast and coffee early and had been driven out into the cold in search of diversion. 'Just set the dial, ladies and gentlemen,' Hazel told the discomfited two or three voyeurs, 'and press gently on the Jiffy lever. Never requires sharpening, never rusts.'

By mid-morning she generally had fifteen people gathered about her, by noon as many as forty. No one interrupted her, and why should they? She was free entertainment. They listened, they exchanged looks, they paid attention, they formed a miniature, temporary colony of good will and consumer seriousness waiting to be instructed, initiated into Hazel's rituals and promises.

At the beginning of her third week, going solo for the first time, she looked up to see Maxine in her long beaver coat, gawking. 'Now this is just what you need, madam,' Hazel sang out, not missing a beat, an uncontrollable smile on her face. 'In no time you'll be making more nutritious, appealing salads for your family and friends and for those bridge club get-togethers.'

Maxine had been offended. She complained afterwards to Hazel that she found it embarrassing being picked out in a crowd like that. It was insulting, especially to mention the bridge club, as if she did nothing all day long but shuffle cards. 'It's a bit thick, Hazel, especially when you used to enjoy a good rubber yourself. And you know I only play cards as a form of social relaxation. You used to enjoy it, and don't try to tell me otherwise because I won't buy it. We miss you, we really do. I know perfectly well it's not easy for you facing Francine. She was always a bit of a you-know-what, and Brian was, God knows, susceptible, though I have to say you've put a dignified face on the whole thing. I don't think I could have done it, I don't have your knack for looking the other way, never have had, which is why I'm where I'm at, I suppose. But who are you really cheating, dropping out of the bridge club like this? I think, just between the two of us, that Francine's a bit hurt, she thinks you hold her responsible for Brian's attack, even though we all know that when our time's up, it's up. And besides, it takes two.'

In the afternoon, after a quick pick-up lunch (leftover grated raw vegetables usually or a hard-boiled egg), Hazel demonstrated Kitchen Kult's all-purpose non-stick fry pan. The same crowds that admired her julienne carrots seemed ready to be mesmerised by the absolute roundness of her crepes and omelettes, their uniform gold edges and the ease with which they came pulling away at a touch of her spatula. During the early months, January, February, Hazel learned just how easily people could be hypnotised, how easily, in fact, they could be put to sleep. Their mouths sagged. They grew dull-eyed and immobile. Their hands went hard into their pockets. They hugged their purses tight.

Then one afternoon a small fortuitous accident occurred: a crepe, zealously flipped, landed on the floor. Because of the accident, Hazel discovered how a rupture in routine could be turned to her advantage. 'Whoops-a-daisy,' she said that first day, stooping to recover the crepe. People laughed out loud. It was as though Hazel's mild exclamation had a forgotten period fragrance to it. 'I guess I don't know my own strength,' she said, shaking her curls and earning a second ripple of laughter.

After that she began, at least once or twice a day, to misdirect a crepe. Or overcook an omelette. Or bring herself to a state of comic tears over her plate of chopped onions. 'Not my day,' she would croon. Or 'good grief' or 'sacred rattlesnakes' or a shrugging, cheerful, 'who ever promised perfection on the first try'. Some of the phrases that came out of her mouth reminded her of the way people talked in Porcupine Falls back in a time she could not possibly have remembered. Gentle, unalarming expletives calling up wells of good nature and neighbourliness. She wouldn't have guessed she had this quality of rubbery humour inside her.

After a while she felt she could get away with anything as long as she kept up her line of chatter. That was the secret, she saw – never to stop talking. That was why these crowds gave her their attention: she could perform miracles (with occasional calculated human lapses) and keep right on talking at the same time. Words, a river of words. She had never before talked at such length, as though she were driving a wedge of air ahead of her. It was easy, *easy*. She dealt out repetitions, little punchy pushes of emphasis, and an ever growing inventory of affectionate declarations directed towards her vegetable friends. 'What a devil!' she said, holding aloft a head of bulky cauliflower. 'You darling radish, you!' She felt foolish at times, but often exuberant, like a semi-retired, slightly eccentric actress. And she felt, oddly, that she was exactly as strong and clever as she need be.

But the work was exhausting. She admitted it. Every day the crowds had to be wooed afresh. By five-thirty she was too tired to do anything more than drive home, make a sandwich, read the paper, rinse out her Kitchen Kult smock and hang it over the shower rail, then get into bed with a thick paperback. Propped up in bed reading, her book like a wimple at her chin, she seemed to have flames on her feet and on the tips of her fingers, as though she'd burned her way through a long blur of a day and now would burn the night behind her too. January, February, the first three weeks of March. So this was what work was: a two-way bargain people made with the world, a way to reduce time to rubble.

The books she read worked braids of panic into her consciousness. She'd drifted towards historical fiction, away from Central Park and into the Regency courts of England. But were the queens and courtesans any happier than the frustrated New York wives? Were they less lonely, less adrift? So far she had found no evidence of it. They wanted the same things more or less: abiding affection, attention paid to their moods and passing thoughts, their backs rubbed and, now and then, the tender grateful application of hands and lips. She remembered Brian's back turned toward her in sleep, well covered with flesh in his middle years. He had never been one for pyjamas, and she had often been moved to reach out and stroke the smooth mound of flesh. She had not found his extra weight disagreeable, far from it.

In Brian's place there remained now only the rectangular softness of his allergy-free pillow. Its smooth casing, faintly puckered at the corners, had the feel of mysterious absence.

'But why does it always have to be one of my *friends*!' she had cried out at him once at the end of a long quarrel. 'Don't you see how humiliating it is for me?'

He had seemed genuinely taken aback, and she saw in a flash it was only laziness on his part, not express cruelty. She recalled his solemn promises, his wet eyes, new beginnings. She fondly recalled, too, the resonant pulmonary sounds of his night breathing, the steep climb to the top of each inhalation and the tottery stillness before the descent. How he used to lull her to sleep with this nightly music! Compensations. But she had not asked for enough, hadn't known what to ask for, what was owed her.

It was because of the books she read, their dense complications and sharp surprises, that she had applied for a job in the first place. She had a sense of her own life turning over page by page, first a girl, then a young woman, then married with two young daughters, then a member of a bridge club and a quilting club, and now, too soon for symmetry, a widow. All of it fell into small childish paragraphs, the print over-large and blocky like a school reader. She had tried to imagine various new endings or turnings for herself – she might take a trip around the world or sign up for a course in ceramics – but could think of nothing big enough to fill the vacant time left to her – except perhaps an actual job. This was what other people did, tucking in around the edges those little routines – laundry, meals, errands – that had made up her whole existence.

'You're wearing yourself out,' Brian's mother said when Hazel arrived for an Easter Sunday visit, bringing with her a double-layered box of chocolate almond bark and a bouquet of tulips. 'Tearing all over town every day, on your feet, no proper lunch arrangements. You'd think they'd give you a good hour off and maybe a lunch voucher, give you a chance to catch your breath. It's hard on the back, standing. I always feel my tension in my back. These are delicious, Hazel, not that I'll eat half of them, not with my appetite, but it'll be something to pass round to the other ladies. Everyone shares here, that's one thing. And the flowers, tulips! One or the other would have more than sufficed, Hazel, you've been extravagant. I suppose now that you're actually earning, it makes a difference. You feel differently, I suppose, when it's your own money. Brian's father always saw that I had everything I needed, wanted for nothing, but I wouldn't have minded a little money of my own, though I never said so, not in so many words.'

One morning Peter Lemmon surprised Hazel, and frightened her too, by saying, 'Mr. Cortland wants to see you. The big boss himself. Tomorrow at ten-thirty. Downtown office. Headquarters. I'll cover the venue for you.'

Mr. Cortland was the age of Hazel's son-in-law, Robin. She couldn't have said why, but she had expected someone theatrical and rude, not this handsome curly-haired man unwinding himself from behind a desk that was not really a desk but a gate-legged table, shaking her hand respectfully and leading her toward a soft brown easy chair. There was genuine solemnity to his jutting chin and a thick brush of hair across his quizzing brow. He offered her a cup of coffee. 'Or perhaps you would prefer tea,' he said, very politely, with a shock of inspiration.

She looked up from her shoes, her good polished pumps, not her nurse shoes, and saw a pink conch shell on Mr. Cortland's desk. It occurred to her it must be one of the things that made him happy. Other people were made happy by music or flowers or bowls of ice cream – enchanted, familiar things. Some people collected china, and when they found a long-sought piece, *that* made them happy. What made *her* happy was the obliteration of time, burning it away so cleanly she hardly noticed it. Not that she said so to Mr. Cortland. She said, in fact, very little, though some dragging filament of intuition urged her to accept tea rather than coffee, to forgo milk, to shake her head sadly over the proffered sugar.

'We are more delighted than I can say with your sales performance,' Mr. Cortland said. 'We are a small but growing firm and, as you know' – Hazel did not know, how could she? – 'we are a family concern. My maternal grandfather studied commerce at McGill and started this business as a kind of hobby. Our aim, the family's aim, is a reliable product, but not a hard sell. I can't stress this enough to our sales people. We are anxious to avoid a crude hectoring approach or tactics that are in any way manipulative, and we are in the process of developing a quality sales force that matches the quality of our product line. This may surprise you, but it is difficult to find people like yourself who possess, if I may say so, your gentleness of manner. People like yourself transmit a sense of trust to the consumer. We've heard very fine things about you, and we have decided, Hazel – I do hope I may call you Hazel – to put you on regular salary, in addition of course to an adjusted commission. And I would like also to present you with this small brooch, a glazed ceramic K for Kitchen Kult, which we give each quarter to our top sales person.'

'Do you realise what this means?' Peter Lemmon asked later that afternoon over a celebratory drink at Mr. Duck's Happy Hour. 'Salary means you're on the team, you're a Kitchen Kult player. Salary equals professional, Hazel. You've arrived, and I don't think you even realise it.'

Hazel thought she saw flickering across Peter's guarded, eager face, like a blade of sunlight through a thick curtain, the suggestion that some privilege had been carelessly allocated. She pinned the brooch on the lapel of her good spring coat with an air of bafflement. Beyond the simple smoothness of her pay cheque, she perceived dark squadrons of planners and decision makers who had brought this teasing irony forward. She was being rewarded – a bewildering turn of events – for her timidity, her self-effacement, for what Maxine called her knack for looking the other way. She was a shy, ineffectual, untrained, neutral looking woman, and for this she was being kicked upstairs, or at least this was how Peter translated her move from commission to salary. He scratched his neck, took a long drink of his beer, and said it a third time, with a touch of belligerence it seemed to Hazel, 'a kick upstairs.' He insisted on paying for the drinks, even though Hazel pressed a ten-dollar bill into his hand. He shook it off.

'This place is bargain city,' he assured her, opening the orange cave of his mouth, then closing it quickly. He came here often after work, he said, taking advantage of the two-for-one happy hour policy. Not that he was tight with his money, just the opposite, but he was setting aside a few dollars a week for his dental work in the summer. The work was mostly cosmetic, caps and spacers, and therefore not covered by Kitchen Kult's insurance scheme. The way he saw it, though, was as an investment in the future. If you were going to go to the top, you had to be able to open your mouth and project. 'Like this brooch, Hazel, it's a way of projecting. Wearing the company logo means you're one of the family and that you don't mind shouting it out.'

That night, when she whitened her shoes, she felt a sort of love for them. And she loved, too, suddenly, her other small tasks, rinsing out her smock, setting her alarm, settling into bed with her book, resting her head against Brian's little fibre-filled pillow with its stitched remnant of erotic privilege and reading herself out of her own life, leaving behind her cut-out shape, so bulky, rounded and unimaginably mute, a woman who swallowed her tongue, got it jammed down her throat and couldn't make a sound.

Marilyn gave a shout of derision on seeing the company brooch pinned to her mother's raincoat. 'The old butter-up trick. A stroke here, a stroke there, just enough to keep you going and keep you grateful. But at least they had the decency to get you off straight commission, for that I have to give them some credit.'

'Dear Mother,' Rosie wrote from British Columbia. 'Many thanks for the waterless veg cooker which is surprisingly well made and really very attractive too, and Robin feels that it fulfils a real need, nutritionally speaking, and also aesthetically.'

'You're looking better,' Maxine said. 'You look as though you've dropped a few pounds, have you? All those grated carrots. But do you ever get a minute to yourself? Eight hours on the job plus commuting. I don't suppose they even pay for your gas, which adds up, and your parking. You want to think about a holiday, people can't be buying pots and pans three hundred and sixty-five days a year. JoAnn and Francine and I are thinking seriously of getting a cottage in Nova Scotia for two weeks. Let me know if you're interested, just tell those Kitchen Kult moguls you owe yourself a little peace and quiet by the seaside, ha! Though you do look more relaxed than the last time I saw you, you looked wrung out, completely.'

In early May Hazel had an accident. She and Peter were setting up one morning, arranging a new demonstration, employing the usual cabbage, beets and onions, but adding a few spears of spring asparagus and a scatter of chopped chives. In the interest of economy she'd decided to split the asparagus lengthwise, bringing her knife first through the tender tapered head and down the woody stem. Peter was talking away about a new suit he was thinking of buying, asking Hazel's advice – should he go all out for a fine summer wool or compromise on wool and viscose? The knife slipped and entered the web of flesh between Hazel's thumb and forefinger. It sliced further into the flesh than she would have believed possible, so quickly, so lightly that she could only gaze at the spreading blood and grieve about the way it stained and spoiled her perfect circle of cucumber slices.

She required twelve stitches and, at Peter's urging, took the rest of the day off. Mr. Cortland's secretary telephoned and told her to take the whole week off if necessary. There were insurance forms to sign, but those could wait. The important thing was – but Hazel couldn't remember what the important thing was; she had been given some painkillers at the hospital and was having difficulty staying awake. She slept the afternoon away, dreaming of green fields and a yellow sun, and would have slept all evening too if she hadn't been wakened around eight o'clock by the faint buzz of her doorbell. She pulled on a dressing gown, a new one in flowered seersucker, and went to the door. It was Peter Lemmon with a clutch of flowers in his hand. 'Why Peter,' she said, and could think of nothing else.

The pain had left her hand and moved to the thin skin of her scalp. Its remoteness as much as its taut bright shine left her confused. She managed to take Peter's light jacket – though he protested, saying he had only come for a moment – and steered him toward a comfortable chair by the window. She listened as the cushions subsided under him, and hurried to put the flowers, already a little limp, into water, and to offer a drink – but what did she have on hand? No beer, no gin, and she knew better than to suggest sherry. Then the thought came: what about a glass of red wine?

He accepted twitchily. He said, 'You don't have to twist my arm.'

'You'll have to uncork it,' Hazel said, gesturing at her bandaged hand. She felt she could see straight into his brain where there was nothing but rags and old plastic. But where had *this* come from, this sly, unpardonable superiority of hers?

He lurched forward, nearly falling. 'Always happy to do the honours.' He seemed afraid of her, of her apartment with its settled furniture, lamps and end tables and china cabinet, regarding these things first with a strict, dry, inquiring look. After a few minutes, he resettled in the soft chair with exaggerated respect.

'To your career,' Peter said, raising his glass, appearing not to notice how the word career entered Hazel's consciousness, waking her up from her haze of painkillers and making her want to laugh.

'To the glory of Kitchen Kult,' she said, suddenly reckless. She watched him, or part of herself watched him, as he twirled the glass and sniffed its contents. She braced herself for what would surely come.

'An excellent vin–' he started to say, but was interrupted by the doorbell.

It was only Marilyn, dropping in as she sometimes did after her self-defence course. 'Already I can break a collarbone,' she told Peter after a flustered introduction, 'and next week we're going to learn how to go for the groin.'

She looked surprisingly pretty with her pensive, wet, youthful eyes and dusty lashes. She accepted some wine and listened intently to the story of Hazel's accident, then said, 'Now listen, Mother, don't sign a release with Kitchen Kult until I have Edna look at it. You remember Edna, she's the lawyer. She's sharp as a knife; she's the one who did our lease for us, and it's airtight. You could develop blood poisoning or an infection, you can't tell at this point. You can't trust these corporate entities when it comes to–'

'Kitchen Kult,' Peter said, twirling his glass in a manner Hazel found silly, 'is more like a family.'

'Balls.'

'We've decided,' Maxine told Hazel a few weeks later, 'against the cottage in Nova Scotia. It's too risky, and the weather's only so-so according to Francine. And the cost of air fare and then renting a car, we just figured it's too expensive. My rent's going up starting in July and, well, I took a look at my bank balance and said, Maxine kid, you've got to tighten the old belt. As a matter of fact, I thought – now this may surprise you – I'm thinking of looking for a job.'

Hazel set up an interview for Maxine through Personnel, and in a week's time Maxine did her first demonstration. Hazel helped break her in. As a result of a dimly perceived office shuffle, she had been promoted to Assistant Area Manager, freeing Peter Lemmon for what was described as 'Creative Sales Outreach.' The promotion worried her slightly and she wondered if she were being compensated for the nerve damage in her hand, which was beginning to look more or less permanent. 'Thank God you didn't sign the release,' was all Marilyn said.

'Congrats,' Rosie wired from British Columbia after hearing about the promotion. Hazel had not received a telegram for some years. She was surprised that this austere printed sheet went by the name of telegram. Where was the rough grey paper and the little pasted together words? She wondered who had composed the message, Robin or Rosie, and whose idea it had been to abbreviate the single word and if thrift were involved. *Congrats*. What a hard little hurting pellet to find in the middle of a smooth sheet of paper.

'Gorgeous,' Brian's mother said of Hazel's opal-toned silk suit with its scarf of muted pink, pearl and lemon. Her lips moved appreciatively. 'Ah, gorgeous.'

'A helluva improvement over a bloody smock,' Maxine sniffed, looking sideways.

'Most elegant!' said Mr. Cortland, who had called Hazel into his office to discuss her future with Kitchen Kult. 'The sort of image we hope and try to project. Elegance and understatement.' He presented her with a small box in which rested, on a square of textured cotton, a pair of enamelled earrings with the flying letter K for Kitchen Kult.

'Beautiful,' said Hazel, who never wore earrings. The clip-on sort hurt her, and she had never got around to piercing her ears. 'For my sake,' Brian had begged her when he was twenty-five and she was twenty and about to become his wife, 'don't ever do it. I can't bear to lose a single bit of you.'

Remembering this, the tone of Brian's voice, its rushing, foolish sincerity, Hazel felt her eyes tingle. 'My handbag,' she said, groping blindly.

Mr. Cortland misunderstood. He leaped up, touched by his own generosity, a Kleenex in hand. 'We simply wanted to show our appreciation,' he said, or rather sang.

Hazel sniffed, more loudly than she intended, and Mr. Cortland pretended not to hear. 'We especially appreciate your filling in for Peter Lemmon during his leave of absence.'

At this Hazel nodded. Poor Peter. She must phone tonight. He was finding the aftermath of his dental surgery painful and prolonged, and she had been looking, every chance she had, for a suitable convalescent card, something not too effusive and not too mocking – Peter took his teeth far too seriously. Perhaps she would just send one of her blurry impressionistic hasty notes, or better yet, a jaunty postcard saying she hoped he'd be back soon.

Mr. Cortland fingered the pink conch shell on his desk. He picked it up between his two hands and rocked it gently to and fro, then said, 'Mr. Lemmon will not be returning. We have already sent him a letter of termination and, of course, a generous severance settlement. It was decided that his particular kind of personality, though admirable, was not quite in line with the Kitchen Kult approach, and we feel that you yourself have already demonstrated your ability to take over his work and perhaps even extend the scope of it.'

'I don't believe you're doing this,' Marilyn shouted over the phone to Hazel. 'And Peter doesn't believe it either.'

'How do you know what Peter thinks?'

'I saw him this afternoon. I saw him yesterday afternoon. I see him rather often if you want to know the truth.'

Hazel offered the Kitchen Kult earrings to Maxine who snorted and said, 'Come off it, Hazel.'

Rosie in Vancouver sent a short note saying, 'Marilyn phoned about your new position, which is really marvellous, though Robin and I are wondering if you aren't getting in deeper than you really want to at this time.'

Brian's mother said nothing. A series of small strokes had taken her speech away and also her ability to leave her bed. Nothing Hazel brought her aroused her interest, not chocolates, not flowers, not even the fashion magazines she used to love.

Hazel phoned and made an appointment to see Mr. Cortland. She invented a pretext, one or two ideas she and Maxine had worked out to tighten up the demonstrations. Mr. Cortland listened to her and nodded approvingly. Then she sprang. She had been thinking about Peter Lemmon, she said, how much the sales force missed him, missed his resourcefulness and his attention to details. He had a certain imaginative flair, a peculiar usefulness. Some people had a way of giving energy to others, it was uncanny, it was a rare gift. She didn't mention Peter's dental work; she had some sense.

Mr. Cortland sent her a shrewd look, a look she would not have believed he had in his repertoire. 'Well, Hazel,' he said at last, 'in business we deal in hard bargains. Maybe you and I can come to some sort of bargain.'

'Bargain?'

'That insurance form, the release. The one you haven't got round to signing yet. How would it be if you signed it right now on the promise that I find some slot or other for Peter Lemmon by the end of the week? You are quite right about his positive attributes, quite astute of you, really, to point them out. I can't promise anything in sales though. The absolute bottom end of management might be the best we can do.'

Hazel considered. She stared at the conch shell for a full ten seconds. The office lighting coated it with a pink, even light, making it look like a piece of unglazed pottery. She liked the idea of bargains. She felt she understood them. 'I'll sign,' she said. She had her pen in her hand, poised.

On Sunday, a Sunday at the height of summer in early July, Hazel drives out to Silver Oaks to visit her ailing mother-in-law. All she can do for her now is sit by her side for an hour and hold her hand, and sometimes she wonders what the point is of these visits. Her mother-in-law's face is impassive and silken, and occasionally driblets of spittle, thin and clear as tears, run from the corners of her mouth. It used to be such a strong, organised face with its firm mouth and steady eyes. But now she doesn't recognise anyone, with the possible exception of Hazel.

Some benefit appears to derive from these hand-holding sessions, or so the nurses tell Hazel. 'She's calmer after your visits,' they say. 'She struggles less.'

Hazel is calm too. She likes sitting here and feeling the hour unwind like thread from a spindle. She wishes it would go on and on. A week ago she had come away from Mr. Cortland's office irradiated with the conviction that her life was going to be possible after all. All she had to do was bear in mind the bargains she made. This was an obscene revelation, but Hazel was excited by it. Everything could be made accountable, added up and balanced and fairly, evenly, shared. You only had to pay attention and ask for what was yours by right. You could be clever, dealing in sly acts of surrender, but holding fast at the same time, negotiating and measuring and tying up your life in useful bundles.

But she was wrong. It wasn't true. Her pride had misled her. No one has that kind of power, no one.

She looks around the little hospital room and marvels at the accident of its contents, its bureau and tumbler and toothbrush and folded towel. The open window looks out on to a parking lot filled with rows of cars, all their shining roofs baking in the light. Next year there will be different cars, differently ordered. The shrubs and trees, weighed down with their millions of new leaves, will form a new dark backdrop.

It is an accident that she should be sitting in this room, holding the hand of an old, unblinking, unresisting woman who had once been sternly disapproving of her, thinking her countrified and clumsy. 'Hazel!' she had sometimes whispered in the early days. 'Your slip strap! Your salad fork!' Now she lacks even the power to wet her lips with her tongue; it is Hazel who touches the lips with a damp towel from time to time, or applies a bit of Vaseline to keep them from cracking. But she can feel the old woman's dim pulse, and imagines that it forms a code of acknowledgement or faintly telegraphs certain perplexing final questions – how did all this happen? How did we get here?

Everything is an accident, Hazel would be willing to say if asked. Her whole life is an accident, and by accident she has blundered into the heart of it.

Mrs. Turner Cutting the Grass

OH, MRS. TURNER is a sight cutting the grass on a hot afternoon in June! She climbs into an ancient pair of shorts and ties on her halter top and wedges her feet into crepe-soled sandals and covers her red-grey frizz with Gord's old golf cap – Gord is dead now, ten years ago, a seizure on a Saturday night while winding the mantel clock.

The grass flies up around Mrs. Turner's knees. Why doesn't she use a catcher, the Saschers next door wonder. Everyone knows that leaving the clippings like that is bad for the lawn. Each fallen blade of grass throws a minute shadow which impedes growth and repair. The Saschers themselves use their clippings to make compost which they hope one day will be ripe as the good manure that Sally Sascher's father used to spread on his fields down near Emerson Township.

Mrs. Turner's carelessness over the clippings plucks away at Sally, but her husband Roy is far more concerned about the Killex that Mrs. Turner dumps on her dandelions. It's true that in Winnipeg the dandelion roots go right to the middle of the earth, but Roy is patient and persistent in pulling them out, knowing exactly how to grasp the coarse leaves in his hand and how much pressure to apply. Mostly they come up like corks with their roots intact. And he and Sally are experimenting with new ways to cook dandelion greens, believing as they do that the components of nature are arranged for a specific purpose – if only that purpose can be divined.

In the early summer Mrs. Turner is out every morning by ten with her sprinkling can of chemical killer, and Roy, watching from his front porch, imagines how this poison will enter the ecosystem and move by quick capillary surges into his fenced vegetable plot, newly seeded now with green beans and lettuce. His children, his two little girls aged two and four – that they should be touched by such poison makes him morose and angry. But he and Sally so far have said nothing to Mrs. Turner about her abuse of the planet because they're hoping she'll go into an old-folks home soon or maybe die, and then all will proceed as it should.

High-school girls on their way home in the afternoon see Mrs. Turner cutting her grass and are mildly, momentarily repelled by the lapped, striated flesh on her upper thighs. At her age. Doesn't she realise? Every last one of them is intimate with the vocabulary of skin care and knows that what has claimed Mrs. Turner's thighs is the enemy called cellulite, but they can't understand why she doesn't take the trouble to hide it. It makes them queasy; it makes them fear for the future.

The things Mrs. Turner doesn't know would fill the Saschers' new compost pit, would sink a ship, would set off a tidal wave, would make her want to kill herself. Back and forth, back and forth she goes with the electric lawn mower, the grass flying out sideways like whiskers. Oh, the things she doesn't know! She has never heard, for example, of the folk-rock recording star Neil Young, though the high school just around the corner from her house happens to be the very school Neil Young attended as a lad. His initials can actually be seen carved on one of the desks, and a few of the teachers say they remember him, a quiet fellow of neat appearance and always very polite in class. The desk with the initials N.Y. is kept in a corner of Mr. Pring's homeroom, and it's considered lucky – despite the fact that the renowned singer wasn't a great scholar – to touch the incised letters just before an exam. Since it's exam time now, the second week of June, the girls walking past Mrs. Turner's front yard (and shuddering over her display of cellulite) are carrying on their fingertips the spiritual scent, the essence, the fragrance, the aura of Neil Young, but Mrs. Turner is as ignorant of that fact as the girls are that she, Mrs. Turner, possesses a first name – which is Geraldine.

Not that she's ever been called Geraldine. Where she grew up in Boissevain, Manitoba, she was known always – the Lord knows why – as Girlie Fergus, the youngest of the three Fergus girls and the one who got herself in hot water. Her sister Em went to normal school and her sister Muriel went to Brandon to work at Eatons, but Girlie got caught one night – she was nineteen – in a Boissevain hotel room with a local farmer, married, named Gus MacGregor. It was her father who got wind of where she might be and came banging on the door, shouting and weeping. 'Girlie, Girlie, what have you done to me?'

Girlie had been working in the Boissevain Dairy since she'd left school at sixteen and had a bit of money saved up, and so, a week after the humiliation in the local hotel, she wrote a farewell note to the family, crept out of the house at midnight and caught the bus to Winnipeg. From there she got another bus down to Minneapolis, then to Chicago and finally New York City. The journey was endless and wretched, and on the way across Indiana and Ohio and Pennsylvania she saw hundreds and hundreds of towns whose unpaved streets and narrow blinded houses made her fear some conspiratorial, punishing power had carried her back to Boissevain. Her father's soppy-stern voice sang and sang in her ears as the wooden bus rattled its way eastward. It was summer, 1930.

New York was immense and wonderful, dirty, perilous and puzzling. She found herself longing for a sight of real earth which she assumed must lie somewhere beneath the tough pavement. On the other hand, the brown flat-roofed factories with their little windows tilted skyward pumped her full of happiness, as did the dusty trees, when she finally discovered them, lining the long avenues. Every last person in the world seemed to be outside, walking around, filling the streets, and every corner breezed with noise and sunlight. She had to pinch herself to believe this was the same sunlight that filtered its way into the rooms of the house back in Boissevain, fading the curtains but nourishing her mother's ferns. She sent postcards to Em and Muriel that said, 'Don't worry about me. I've got a job in the theatre business.'

It was true. For eight and a half months she was an usherette in the Lamar Movie Palace in Brooklyn. She loved her perky maroon uniform, the way it fit on her shoulders, the way the strips of crinkly gold braid outlined her figure. With a little flashlight in hand she was able to send streams of light across the furry darkness of the theatre and onto the plum-coloured aisle carpet. The voices from the screen talked on and on. She felt after a time that their resonant declarations and tender replies belonged to her.

She met a man named Kiki her first month in New York and moved in with him. His skin was as black as ebony. *As black as ebony* – that was the phrase that hung like a ribbon on the end of his name, and it's also the phrase she uses, infrequently, when she wants to call up his memory, though she's more than a little doubtful about what *ebony* is. It may be a kind of stone, she thinks, something round and polished that comes out of a deep mine.

Kiki was a good-hearted man, though she didn't like the beer he drank, and he stayed with her, willingly, for several months after she had to stop working because of the baby. It was the baby itself that frightened him off, the way it cried probably. Leaving fifty dollars on the table, he slipped out one July afternoon when Girlie was shopping, and went back to Troy, New York, where he'd been raised.

Her first notion was to take the baby and get on a bus and go find him, but there wasn't enough money, and the thought of the baby crying all the way on the hot bus made her feel tired. She was worried about the rent and about the little red sores in the baby's ears – it was a boy, rather sweetly formed, with wonderful smooth feet and hands. On a murderously hot night, a night when the humidity was especially bad, she wrapped him in a clean piece of sheeting and carried him all the way to Brooklyn Heights where the houses were large and solid and surrounded by grass. There was a house on a corner she particularly liked because it had a wide front porch (like those in Boissevain) with a curved railing – and parked on the porch, its brake on, was a beautiful wicker baby carriage. It was here she placed her baby, giving one last look to his sleeping face, as round and calm as the moon. She walked home, taking her time, swinging her legs. If she had known the word *foundling* –

which she didn't – she would have bounded along on its rhythmic back, so airy and wide did the world seem that night.

Most of these secrets she keeps locked away inside her mottled thighs or in the curled pinkness of her genital flesh. She has no idea what happened to Kiki, whether he ever went off to Alaska as he wanted to or whether he fell down a flight of stone steps in the silverware factory in Troy, New York, and died of head injuries before his 30th birthday. Or what happened to her son – whether he was bitten that night in the baby carriage by a rabid neighbourhood cat or whether he was discovered the next morning and adopted by the large, loving family who lived in the house. As a rule, Girlie tries not to think about the things she can't even guess at. All she thinks is that she did the best she could under the circumstances.

In a year she saved enough money to take the train home to Boissevain. She took with her all her belongings, and also gifts for Em and Muriel, boxes of hose, bottles of apple-blossom cologne, phonograph records. For her mother she took an embroidered apron and for her father a pipe made of curious gnarled wood. 'Girlie, my Girlie,' her father said, embracing her at the Boissevain station. Then he said, 'Don't ever leave us again,' in a way that frightened her and made her resolve to leave as quickly as possible.

But she didn't go so far the second time around. She and Gordon Turner – he was, for all his life, a tongue-tied man, though he did manage a proper proposal – settled down in Winnipeg, first in St. Boniface where the rents were cheap and then Fort Rouge and finally the little house in River Heights just around the corner from the high school. It was her husband, Gord, who planted the grass that Mrs. Turner now shaves in the summertime. It was Gord who trimmed and shaped the caragana hedge and Gord who painted the little shutters with the cut-out hearts. He was a man who loved every inch of his house, the wide wooden steps, the oak door with its glass inset, the radiators and the baseboards and the snug sash windows. And he loved every inch of his wife, Girlie, too, saying to her once and only once that he knew about her past (meaning Gus MacGregor and the incident in the Boissevain Hotel), and that as far as he was concerned the slate had been wiped clean. Once he came home with a little package in his pocket; inside was a diamond ring, delicate and glittering. Once he took Girlie on a picnic all the way up to Steep Rock, and in the woods he took off her dress and underthings and kissed every part of her body.

After he died, Girlie began to travel. She was far from rich, as she liked to say, but with care she could manage one trip every spring.

She has never known such ease. She and Em and Muriel have been to Disneyland as well as Disney World. They've been to Europe, taking a sixteen-day trip through seven countries. The three of them have visited the south and seen the famous antebellum houses of Georgia, Alabama and Mississippi, after which they spent a week in the city of New Orleans. They went to Mexico one year and took pictures of Mayan ruins and queer shadowy gods cut squarely from stone. And three years ago they did what they swore they'd never have the nerve to do: they got on an airplane and went to Japan.

The package tour started in Tokyo where Mrs Turner ate, on her first night there, a chrysanthemum fried in hot oil. She saw a village where everyone earned a living by making dolls and another village where everyone made pottery. Members of the tour group, each holding up a green flag so their tour leader could keep track of them, climbed on a little train, zoomed off to Osaka where they visited an electronics factory, and then went to a restaurant to eat uncooked fish. They visited more temples and shrines than Mrs. Turner could keep track of. Once they stayed the night in a Japanese hotel where she and Em and Muriel bedded down on floor mats and little pillows stuffed with cracked wheat, and woke up, laughing, with backaches and shooting pains in their legs.

That was the same day they visited the Golden Pavilion in Kyoto. The three-storeyed temple was made of wood and had a roof like a set of wings and was painted a soft old flaky gold. Everybody in the group took pictures – Em took a whole roll – and bought postcards; everybody, that is, except a single tour member, the one they all referred to as the Professor.

The Professor travelled without a camera, but jotted notes almost continuously into a little pocket scribbler. He was bald, had a trim body and wore Bermuda shorts, sandals and black nylon socks. Those who asked him learned that he really was a professor, a teacher of English poetry in a small college in Massachusetts. He was also a poet who, at the time of the Japanese trip, had published two small chapbooks based mainly on the breakdown of his marriage. The poems, sadly, had not caused much stir.

It grieved him to think of that paltry, guarded nut-like thing that was his artistic reputation. His domestic life had been too cluttered; there had been too many professional demands; the political situation in America had drained him of energy – these were the thoughts that buzzed in his skull as he scribbled and scribbled, like a man with a fever, in the back seat of a tour bus travelling through Japan.

Here in this crowded, confused country he discovered simplicity and order and something spiritual, too, which he recognised as being authentic. He felt as though a flower, something like a lily, only smaller and tougher, had unfurled in his hand and was nudging along his fountain pen. He wrote and wrote, shaken by catharsis, but lulled into a new sense of his powers.

Not surprisingly, a solid little book of poems came out of his experience. It was published soon afterwards by a well-thought-of Boston publisher who, as soon as possible, sent him around the United States to give poetry readings.

Mostly the Professor read his poems in universities and colleges where his book was already listed on the Contemporary Poetry course. He read in faculty clubs, student centres, classrooms, gymnasiums and auditoriums, and usually, part way through a reading, someone or other would call from the back of the room, 'Give us your Golden Pavilion poem.'

He would have preferred to read his Fuji meditation or the tone poem on the Inner Sea, but he was happy to oblige his audiences, though he felt 'A Day At the Golden Pavilion' was a somewhat light piece, even what is sometimes known on the circuit as a 'crowd pleaser'. People (admittedly they were mostly undergraduates) laughed out loud when they heard it; he read it well, too, in a moist, avuncular amateur actor's voice, reminding himself to pause frequently, to look upward and raise an ironic eyebrow.

The poem was not really about the Golden Pavilion at all, but about three midwestern lady tourists who, while viewing the temple and madly snapping photos, had talked incessantly and in loud, flat-bottomed voices about knitting patterns, indigestion, sore feet, breast lumps, the cost of plastic raincoats and a previous trip they'd made together to Mexico. They had wondered, these three – noisily, repeatedly – who back home in Manitoba should receive a postcard, what they'd give for an honest cup of tea, if there was an easy way to remove stains from an electric coffee maker, and where they would go the following year – Hawaii? They were the three furies, the three witches, who for vulgarity and tastelessness formed a shattering counterpoint to the Professor's own state of transcendence. He had been affronted, angered, half-crazed.

One of the sisters, a little pug of a woman, particularly stirred his contempt, she of the pink pantsuit, the red toenails, the grapefruity buttocks, the overly bright souvenirs, the garish Mexican straw bag containing Dentyne chewing gum, aspirin, breath mints, sun goggles, envelopes of saccharine, and photos of her dead husband standing in front of a squat, ugly house in Winnipeg. This defilement she had spread before the ancient and exquisitely proportioned Golden Pavilion of Kyoto, proving – and here the Professor's tone became grave – proving that sublime beauty can be brought to the very doorway of human eyes, ears and lips and remain unperceived.

When he comes to the end of 'A Day At The Golden Pavilion' there is generally a thoughtful half-second of silence, then laughter and applause. Students turn in their seats and exchange looks with their fellows. They have seen such unspeakable tourists themselves. There was old Auntie Marigold or Auntie Flossie. There was that tacky Mrs. Shannon with her rouge and her jewellery. They know –

despite their youth they know – the irreconcilable distance between taste and banality. Or perhaps that's too harsh; perhaps it's only the difference between those who know about the world and those who don't.

It's true Mrs. Turner remembers little about her travels. She's never had much of a head for history or dates; she never did learn, for instance, the difference between a Buddhist temple and a Shinto shrine. She gets on a tour bus and goes and goes, and that's all there is to it. She doesn't know if she's going north or south or east or west. What does it matter? She's having a grand time. And she's reassured, always, by the sameness of the world. She's never heard the word *commonality*, but is nevertheless fused with its sense. In Japan she was made as happy to see carrots and lettuce growing in the fields as she was to see sunlight, years earlier, pouring into the streets of New York City. Everywhere she's been she's seen people eating and sleeping and working and making things with their hands and urging things to grow. There have been cats and dogs, fences and bicycles and telephone poles, and objects to buy and take care of; it is amazing, she thinks, that she can understand so much of the world and that it comes to her as easily as bars of music floating out of a radio.

Her sisters have long forgotten about her wild days. Now the three of them love to sit on tour buses and chatter away about old friends and family members, their stern father and their mother who never once took their part against him. Muriel carries on about her children (a son in California and a daughter in Toronto) and she brings along snaps of her grandchildren to pass round. Em has retired from school teaching and is a volunteer in the Boissevain Local History

Museum, to which she has donated several family mementos: her father's old carved pipe and her mother's wedding veil and, in a separate case, for all the world to see, a white cotton garment labelled 'Girlie Fergus' Underdrawers, handmade, trimmed with lace, circa 1918'. If Mrs. Turner knew the word *irony* she would relish this. Even without knowing the word irony, she relishes it.

The professor from Massachusetts has won an important international award for his book of poems; translation rights have been sold to a number of foreign publishers; and recently his picture appeared in the *New York Times*, along with a lengthy quotation from 'A Day At The Golden Pavilion'. How providential, some will think, that Mrs. Turner doesn't read the *New York Times* or attend poetry readings, for it might injure her deeply to know how she appears in certain people's eyes, but then there are so many things she doesn't know.

In the summer as she cuts the grass, to and fro, to and fro, she waves to everyone she sees. She waves to the high-school girls who timidly wave back. She hollers hello to Sally and Roy Sascher and asks them how their garden is coming on. She cannot imagine that anyone would wish her harm. All she's done is live her life. The green grass flies up in the air, a buoyant cloud swirling about her head. Oh, what a sight is Mrs. Turner cutting her grass and how, like an ornament, she shines.

Various Miracles

SEVERAL OF THE miracles that occurred this year have gone unrecorded.

Example: On the morning of January 3, seven women stood in line at a lingerie sale in Palo Alto, California, and by chance each of these women bore the Christian name Emily.

Example: On February 16 four strangers (three men, one woman) sat quietly reading on the back seat of the number-10 bus in Cincinnati, Ohio; each of them was reading a paperback copy of *Smiley's People*.

On March 30 a lathe operator in a Moroccan mountain village dreamed that a lemon fell from a tree into his open mouth, causing him to choke and die. He opened his eyes, overjoyed at being still alive, and embraced his wife who was snoring steadily by his side. She scarcely stirred, being reluctant to let go of a dream she was dreaming, which was that a lemon tree had taken root in her stomach, sending its pliant new shoots upwards into her limbs. Leaves, blossoms and finally fruit fluttered in her every vein until she began to tremble in her sleep with happiness and intoxication. Her husband got up quietly and lit an oil lamp so that he could watch her face. It seemed to him he'd never really looked at her before and he felt how utterly ignorant he was of the spring that nourished her life. Now she lay sleeping, dreaming, her face radiant. What he saw was a mask of happiness so intense it made him fear for his life.

On May 11, in the city of Exeter in the south of England, five girls (aged fifteen to seventeen) were running across a playing field at ten o'clock in the morning as part of their physical-education programme. They stopped short when they saw, lying on the broad gravel path, a dead parrot. He was grassy green in colour with a yellow nape and head, and was later identified by the girls' science mistress as *Amazona ochrocephala*. The police were notified of the find, and later it was discovered that the parrot had escaped from the open window of a house owned by a Mr. and Mrs. Ramsay, who claimed, while weeping openly, that they had owned the parrot (Miguel by name) for twenty-two years. The parrot, in fact, was twenty-five years old, one of a pair of birds sold in an open market in Marseilles in the spring of 1958. Miguel's twin brother was sold to an Italian soprano who kept it for ten years, then gave it to her niece Francesca, a violinist who played first with the Netherlands Chamber Orchestra and later with the Chicago Symphony. On May 11 Francesca was wakened in her River Forest home by the sound of her parrot (Pete, or sometimes Pietro) coughing. She gave him a dish of condensed milk instead of his usual whole-oats-and-peanut mixture, and then phoned to say she would not be able to attend rehearsal that day. The coughing grew worse. She looked up the name of a vet in the Yellow Pages and was about to dial when the parrot fell over, dead in his cage. A moment before Francesca had heard him open his beak and pronounce what she believed were the words, *'Ça ne fait rien.'*

On August 26 a man named Carl Hallsbury of Billings, Montana, was wakened by a loud noise. 'My God, we're being burgled,' his wife, Marjorie, said. They listened, but when there were no further noises, they drifted back to sleep. In the morning they found that their favourite little watercolour – a pale rural scene depicting trees and a winding road and the usual arched bridge – had fallen off the living-room wall. It appeared that it had bounced onto the cast-iron radiator and then ricocheted to a safe place in the middle of the living-room rug. When Carl investigated he found that the hook had worked loose in the wall. He patched the plaster methodically, allowed it to dry, and then installed a new hook. While he worked he remembered how the picture had come into his possession. He had come across it hanging in an emptied-out house in the French city of St. Brieuc, where he and the others of his platoon had been quartered during the last months of the war. The picture appealed to him, its simple lines and the pale tentativeness of the colours. In particular, the stone bridge caught his attention since he had been trained as a civil engineer (Purdue, 1939). When the orders came to vacate the house late in 1944, he popped the little watercolour into his knapsack; it was a snug fit, and the snugness seemed to condone his theft. He was not a natural thief but already he knew that life was mainly a matter of improvisation. Other returning soldiers brought home German helmets, strings of cartridge shells and flags of various sorts, but the little painting was Carl's only souvenir. And his wife, Marjorie, is the only one in the world who knows it to be stolen goods; she and Carl belong to a generation that believes there should be no secrets between married couples. Both of them, Marjorie as much as Carl, have a deep sentimental attachment to the picture, though they no longer believe it to be the work of a skilled artist.

It was, in fact, painted by a twelve-year-old boy named Pierre Renaud who until 1943 had lived in the St. Brieuc house. It was said that as a child he had a gift for painting and drawing; in fact, he had a gift merely for imitation. His little painting of the bridge was copied from a postcard his father had sent him from Burgundy where he'd gone to conduct some business. Pierre had been puzzled and ecstatic at receiving a card from his parent who was a cold, resolute man with little time for his son. The recopying of the postcard in watercolours – later Pierre saw all this clearly – was an act of pathetic homage, almost a way of petitioning his father's love.

He grew up to become not an artist but a partner in the family leather-goods business. In the late summer he likes to go south in pursuit of sunshine and good wine, and one evening, August 26 it was, he and Jean-Louis, his companion of many years, found themselves on a small stone bridge not far from Tournus. 'This is it,' he announced excitedly, spreading his arms like a boy, and not feeling at all sure what he meant when he said the words, 'This is it.' Jean-Louis gave him a fond smile; everyone knew Pierre had a large capacity for nostalgia. 'But I thought you said you'd never been here before,' he said. 'That's true,' Pierre said, 'you are right. But I feel, *here*' – he pointed to his heart – 'that I've stood here before.' Jean-Louis teased him by saying, 'Perhaps it was in another life.' Pierre shook his head, 'No, no, no,' and then, 'well, perhaps.' After that the two of them stood on the bridge for some minutes regarding the water and thinking their separate thoughts.

On October 31 Camilla LaPorta, a Cuban-born writer, now a Canadian citizen, was taking the manuscript of her new novel to her Toronto publisher on Front Street. She was nervous; the publisher had been critical of her first draft, telling her it relied too heavily on the artifice of coincidence. Camilla had spent many months on revision, plucking apart the faulty tissue that joined one episode to another, and then, delicately, with the pains of a neurosurgeon, making new connections. The novel now rested on its own complex microcircuitry. Wherever fate, chance or happenstance had ruled, there was now logic, causality and science.

As she stood waiting for her bus on the corner of College and Spadina that fall day, a gust of wind tore the manuscript from her hands. In seconds the yellow typed sheets were tossed into a whirling dance across the busy intersection. Traffic became confused. A bus skittered on an angle. Passersby were surprisingly helpful, stopping and chasing the blowing papers. Several sheets were picked up from the gutter where they lay on a heap of soaked yellow leaves. One sheet was found plastered against the windshield of a parked Pontiac half a block away; another adhered to the top of a lamp-post; another was run over by a taxi and bore the black herringbone of tyre prints. From all directions, ducking the wind, people came running up to Camilla and bringing her the scattered pages. 'Oh, this is crazy, this is crazy,' she cried into the screaming wind.

When she got to the publisher's office he took one look at her manuscript and said, 'Good God Almighty, don't tell me, Camilla, that you of all people have become a post-modernist and no longer believe in the logic of page numbers.'

Camilla explained about the blast of wind, and then the two of them began to put the pages in their proper order. Astonishingly, only one page was missing, but it was a page Camilla insisted was pivotal, a keystone page, the page that explained everything else. She would have to try to reconstruct it as best she could. 'Hmmmmm,' the publisher said – this was late in the afternnnon of the same day and they sat in the office sipping tea – 'I truly believe, Camilla, that your novel stands up without the missing page. Sometimes it's better to let things be strange and to represent nothing but themselves.'

The missing page – it happened to be page 46 – had blown around the corner of College Street into the open doorway of a fresh-fruit and vegetable stand where a young woman in a red coat was buying a kilo of zucchini. She was very beautiful, though not in a conventional way, and she was also talented, an actress, who for some months had been out of work. To give herself courage and cheer herself up she had decided to make a batch of zucchini-oatmeal muffins, and she was just counting out the change on the counter when the sheet of yellow paper blew through the doorway and landed at her feet.

She was the kind of young woman who reads everything, South American novels, Russian folk tales, Persian Poetry, the advertisements on the subway, the personal column in the *Globe and Mail*, even the instructions and precautions on public fire extinguishers. Print is her way of entering and escaping the world. It was only natural for her to bend over and pick up the yellow sheet and begin to read.

She read: *A woman in a red coat is standing in a grocery store buying a kilo of zucchini. She is beautiful, though not in a conventional way, and it happens that she is an actress who –*

Home

IT WAS SUMMER, the middle of July, the middle of this century, and in the city of Toronto 100 people were boarding an airplane.

'Right this way,' the lipsticked stewardess cried. 'Can I get you a pillow? A blanket?'

It was a fine evening, and they climbed aboard with a lightsome step, even those who were no longer young. The plane was on its way to London, England, and since this was before the era of jet aircraft, a transatlantic flight meant twelve hours in the air. Ed Dover, a man in his mid-fifties who worked for the Post Office, had cashed in his war bonds so that he and his wife, Barbara, could go back to England for a twenty-one-day visit. It was for Barbara's sake they were going; the doctor had advised it. For two years she had suffered from depression, forever talking about England and the village near Braintree where she had grown up and where her parents still lived. At home in Toronto she sat all day in dark corners of the house, helplessly weeping; there was dust everywhere, and the little back garden where rhubarb and raspberries had thrived was overtaken by weeds.

Ed had tried to cheer her first with optimism, then with presents – a television set, a Singer sewing machine, boxes of candy. But she talked only about the long, pale Essex twilight, or a remembered bakeshop in the High Street, or sardines on toast around the fire, or the spiky multicoloured lupins that bloomed by the back door. If only she could get lupins to grow in Toronto, things might be better.

Ed and Barbara now sat side by side over a wing, watching the propellers warm up. She looked out the window and dozed. It seemed to her that the sky they travelled through was sliding around the earth with them, given thrust by the fading of the sun's colour. She thought of the doorway of her parents' house, the green painted gate and the stone gateposts that her father polished on Saturday mornings.

Then, at the same moment, and for no reason, the thought of this English house fused perfectly with the image of her own house, hers and Ed's, off Keele Street in Toronto, how snug it was in winter with the new fitted carpet and the work Ed had done in the kitchen, and she wondered suddenly why she'd been so unhappy there. She felt something like a vein reopening in her body, a flood of balance restored, and when the stewardess came around with the supper tray, Barbara smiled up at her and said, 'Why, that looks fit for a king.'

Ed plunged into his dinner with a good appetite. There was duckling with orange sauce and, though he wasn't one for fancy food, he always was willing to try something new. He took one bite and then another. It had a sweet, burned taste, not unpleasant, which for some reason reminded him of the sharpness and strangeness of sexual desire, the way it came uninvited at queer moments – when he was standing in the bathroom shaving his cheeks, or when he hurried across Eglinton Avenue in the morning to catch his bus. It rose bewilderingly like a spray of fireworks, a fountain that was always brighter than he remembered, going on from minute to minute, throwing sparks into the air and out onto the coolness of grass. He remembered, too, something almost forgotten: the smell of Barbara's skin when she stepped out of the bath and, remembering, felt the last two years collapse softly into a clock tick, their long anguish becoming something he soon would be looking back upon. His limbs seemed light as a boy's. The war bonds, their value badly nibbled away by inflation, had been well-exchanged for this moment of bodily lightness. Let it come, let it come, he said to himself, meaning the rest of his life.

Across from Ed and Barbara, a retired farmer from Rivers, Manitoba, sat chewing his braised duckling. He poked his wife in the knees and said, 'For God's sake, for God's sake,' referring, in his withered tenor voice, to the exotic meal and also to the surpassing pleasure of floating in the sky at nine o'clock on a fine summer evening with first Quebec, then the wide ocean skimming beneath him.

His wife was not a woman who appreciated being poked in the knees, but she was too busy thinking about God and Jesus and loving mercy and the colour of the northern sky, which was salmon shading into violet, to take offence. She sent the old man, her husband for forty years, a girlish, new-minted smile, then brought her knuckles together and marvelled at the sliding terraces of grained skin covering the backs of her hands. Sweet Jesus our Saviour – the words went off inside her ferny head like popcorn.

Not far from her sat a journalist, a mole-faced man with a rounded back, who specialised in writing profiles of the famous. He went around the world phoning them, writing to them, setting up appointments with them, meeting them in hotels or in their private quarters to spy out their inadequacies, their tragedies, their blurted fears, so that he could then treat them – and himself – to lavish bouts of pity. It was hard work, for the personalities of the famous vanish into their works, but always, after one of his interviews, he was able to persuade himself that it was better, when all was said and done, to be a nobody. In Canada he had interviewed the premier of a large eastern province, a man who had a grey front tooth, a nervous tremor high up on one cheek and a son-in-law who was about to go to jail for a narcotics offence. Now the journalist was going home to his flat in Notting Hill Gate; in twenty-four hours he would be fingering his collection of tiny glass animals and thinking that, despite his relative anonymity, his relative loneliness, his relatively small income and the relatively scanty degree of recognition that had come his way – despite this, his prized core of neutrality was safe from invaders. And what did that mean? – he asked himself this with the same winning interrogation he practised on the famous. It meant happiness, or something akin to happiness.

Next to him sat a high school English teacher, a woman of forty-odd years, padded with soft fat and dressed in a stiff shantung travel suit. Once in England, she intended to take a train to the Lake District and make her way to Dove Cottage where she would sign her name in the visitors' book as countless other high school teachers had done. When she returned to Toronto, a city in which she had never felt at home, though she'd been born there, and when she went back to her classroom in September to face unmannerly adolescents who would never understand what *The Prelude* was about, it would be a comfort for her to think of her name inscribed in a large book on a heavy oak table – as she imagined it – in the house where William Wordsworth had actually lived. The world, she suddenly saw, was accessible; oceans and continents and centuries could be spryly overleapt. From infancy she'd been drawn towards those things that were transparent – glass, air, rain, even the swimmy underwaterness of poetry. The atmosphere on the plane, its clear chiming ozone, seemed her true element, rarified, tender, discovered. Thinking this, she put back her head and heard the pleasurable crinkle of her new perm, a crinkle that promised her safe passage – or anything else she desired or could imagine.

They were all happy, Ed and Barbara Dover, the lip-smacking farmer and his prayerful wife, the English journalist, and the Toronto teacher – but they were far from being the only ones. By some extraordinary coincidence (or cosmic dispensation or whatever), each person on the London-bound flight that night was, for a moment, filled with the steam of perfect happiness. Whether it was the oxygen-enriched air of the fusiform cabin, or the duckling with orange sauce, or the soufflé-soft buttocks of the stewardess sashaying to and fro with her coffeepot, or the unchartable currents of air bouncing against the sides of the vessel, or some random thought dredged out of the darkness of the aircraft and fuelled by the proximity of strangers – whatever it was, each of the 100 passengers – one after another, from rows one to twenty-five, like little lights going on – experienced an intense, simultaneous sensation of joy. They were for that moment swimmers riding a single wave, tossed upwards by infection or clairvoyance or a slant of perception uniquely heightened by an accident of altitude.

Even the pilot, a Captain Walter Woodlock, a man plagued by the most painful and chronic variety of stomach ulcers, closed his eyes for the briefest of moments over Greenland and drifted straight into a fragment of dream. It couldn't have lasted more than thirty seconds, but in that short time he felt himself falling into a shrug of relaxation he'd almost forgotten. Afloat in his airy dimension, he became a large wet rose nodding in a garden, a gleaming fish smiling on a platter, a thick slice of Arctic moon reaching down and tenderly touching the small uplifted salty waves. He felt he could go on drifting forever in this false loop of time, so big and so blue was the world at that moment.

It must have been that the intensity and heat of this gathered happiness produced a sort of gas or ether or alchemic reaction – it's difficult to be precise – but for a moment, perhaps two, the walls of the aircraft, the entire fuselage and wings and tail section became translucent. The layers of steel, the rivets and bracing and ribwork turned first purple, then a pearly pink, and finally metamorphosed to the incandescence of pure light.

This luminous transformation, needless to say, went unnoticed by those in the aircraft, so busy was each of them with his or her private vision of transcendence.

But there was, it turned out, one witness: a twelve-year-old boy who happened to be standing on a stony Greenland beach that midsummer night. His name was Piers and he was the son of a Danish Lutheran clergyman who had come to the tiny Greenland village for a two-year appointment. The boy's mother had remained behind in Copenhagen, having fallen in love with a manufacturer of pharmaceuticals, and none of this had been adequately explained to the boy –

which may have been why he was standing, lonely and desperately confused, on the barren beach so late at night.

It was not very dark, of course. In Greenland, in the middle of the summer, the sky keeps some of its colour until eleven o'clock and even after that there are traces of brightness, much like the light that adheres to small impurities suspended in wine. The boy heard the noise of the motors first, looked up frowningly and saw the plane, shiningly present with its chambered belly and elegant glassy wings and the propellers spinning their milky webs. He was too dazzled to wave, which was what he normally did when a plane passed overhead. What could it be? he asked himself. He knew almost nothing of science fiction, a genre scorned by his father, and the church in which he had been reared strictly eschewed angelic hosts or other forms of bodily revelation. A trick of the atmosphere? – he had already seen the aurora borealis and knew this was different. The word *phenomenon* had not yet entered his vocabulary, but when it did, a few years later, dropping like a ripe piece of fruit into his consciousness, he found that it could usefully contain something of the spectacle of that night.

Such moments of intoxication, of course, quickly become guilty secrets – this is especially true of children – so it is not surprising that he never told anyone about what he had seen.

Like his father, he grew up to become a man of God, though like others of his generation he wore the label with irony. He went first to Leiden to study, and there lost his belief in the Trinity. After that he received a fellowship to the Union Theological Seminary in New York where his disbelief grew, as did his reputation for being a promising young theologian. Before long he was invited to join the faculty; he became, in a few short years, the author of a textbook and a sought-after lecturer, and in his late thirties he fell in love with a nervous, intelligent woman who was a scholar of medieval history.

One night, when wrapped in each other's arms, she told him how women in the Middle Ages had pulled their silk gowns through a golden ring to test the fineness of the cloth. It seemed to him that this was the way in which he tested his belief in God, except that instead of determining the fineness of faith, he charted its reluctance, its lumpiness, its ultimate absurdity. Nevertheless, against all odds, there were days when he was able to pull what little he possessed through the ring; it came out with a ripply whoosh of surprise, making him feel faint and bringing instantly to mind the image of the transparent airplane suspended in the sky of his childhood. All his life seemed to him to have been a centrifugal voyage around that remembered vision – the only sign of mystery he had ever received.

One day, his limbs around his beloved and his brain burning with pleasure, he told her what he had once been privileged to see. She pulled away from him then – she was a woman with cool eyes and a listening mouth – and suggested he see a psychiatrist.

Thereafter, he saw less and less of her, and finally, a year later, a friend told him she had married someone else. The same friend suggested he should take a holiday.

It was summertime, the city was sweltering, and it had been some time since he had been able to pull anything at all through his gold ring. He considered returning to Greenland for a visit, but the flight schedule was unbelievably complicated and the cost prohibitive; only wealthy bird-watchers working on their life lists could afford to go there now. He found himself one afternoon in a travel agent's office next to a pretty girl who was booking a flight to Acapulco.

'Fabulous place,' she said. Glorious sun. Great beaches. And grass by the bushel.

Always before, when the frivolous, leisured world beckoned, he had solemnly refused. But now he bought himself a ticket, and by the next morning he was on his way.

At the airport in Acapulco, a raw duplicity hangs in the blossom-sweet air – or so thinks Josephe, a young woman who works as a baggage checker behind the customs desk. All day long fresh streams of tourists arrive. From her station she can see them stepping off their aircraft and pressing forward through the wide glass doors, carrying with them the conspiratorial heft of vacationers-on-the-move. Their soft-sided luggage, their tennis rackets, their New York pallor and anxious brows expose in Josephe a buried vein of sadness, and one day she notices something frightening; 109 passengers step off the New York plane, and each of them – without exception – is wearing blue jeans.

She's used to the sight of blue jeans, but such statistical unanimity is unnerving, as though a comic army has grotesquely intruded. Even the last passenger to disembark and step onto the tarmac, a man who walks with the hesitant gait of someone in love with his own thoughts, is wearing the ubiquitous blue jeans.

She wishes there had been a single exception – a woman in a bright flowered dress or a man archaic enough to believe that resort apparel meant white duck trousers. She feels oddly assaulted by such totality, but the feeling quickly gives way to a head-shaking thrill of disbelief, then amusement, then satisfaction and, finally, awe.

She tries hard to get a good look at the last passenger's face, the one who sealed the effect of unreality, but the other passengers crowd around her desk, momentarily threatened by her small discoveries and queries, her transitory power.

In no time it's over; the tourists, duly processed, hurry out into the sun. They feel lighter than air, they claim, freer than birds, drifting off into their various inventions of paradise as though oblivious to the million invisible filaments of connection, trivial or profound, which bind them one to the other and to the small green planet they call home.

Times of Sickness and Health

KAY'S MOTHER HAD ideas, notions of refinement. One of these notions was that young girls benefited from the experience of ballet classes, and so all three of her daughters were enrolled – Kay's sister Joan, a second sister Dorrie, and Kay herself who was the youngest in the class, the youngest by far, being not quite five years old.

The lessons were held in a large mirrored room on the second floor of a commercial building. Kay remembers the long unbroken stairway, lit at the top and bottom, but dark in the middle. Their dance shoes they carried in their hands, soft-toed satiny slippers, not the hard-nosed shoes of classical ballet. The teacher was a thin, darkish woman. She wore a kind of short-skirted costume. Fancy, shiny. Another woman played the piano. One-two-three jump was the way they started off each week.

The older girls seemed able to remember the order of the dance steps. Kay watched them hard, baffled by their ease and earnestness, trying to copy what their arms and feet did, but she was unable to shake off a sense of dazed confusion. There was dust on the mirror walls and on the hardwood floor. What was she doing here? It seemed to go on for a very long time, over and over again, one-two-three-jump.

There was mention of a recital. It filtered through to Kay, that charmed, important word. *Recital.* Like ice in a pitcher of water. The class was perfecting a dance routine called 'The Wedding,' and Kay's sister, Joan, was appointed the bride, a deserved tribute it seemed. Everyone else was to be a bridesmaid, except for Kay who was given the role of flower girl. She had no idea what this meant. She'd seen her mother cover her hands with flour when she made pie crust, smooth it on her fingers and palms, rub it into the rolling pin and on the pastry board.

A small berry basket filled with torn-up bits of newspaper was put in Kay's hands. These she was to scatter on the floor during the course of the wedding dance. This crude, stained basket with its improvised string handle and its rubbishy contents spelled out the fullness of her disgrace. Clearly she was being punished, but why? She did as she was told, shuffled and kicked and turned, always a shameful half-second behind the others, and threw paper on the floor, knowing she was doomed and powerless. Something was wrong, but she didn't know what. Who would she have asked? And what would she have said?

Kay, who is fifty, has no children of her own, but is interested in the way children think and the questions they like to ask. For example: is a tomato a fruit or a vegetable? (Which is it? – Kay's looked it up but can't remember.) Do these querying children, she wonders, really want an answer? Or is there a kind of hopeful rejoicing at the overlapping of categories, a suggestion that the material and immaterial world spills out beyond its self-imposed classifications? What is the difference between sand and gravel? Between weeds and flowers? Between liking and loving?

It occurs to her that these children may be bluffing with their bright, winning curiosity, being playful and sly, and masking a deeper, more abject and injurious sense of bewilderment. There is, after all, so much authentic chaos to sort out, so much seething muddle and predicament that it is a wonder children survive their early ignorance. How do they bear it? You would think they would hold their breath out of sheer rage or hurl themselves down flights of stairs. You would think they'd get sick and die.

'Do you know Philip Halliwell?' a woman asked Kay.

Kay was a young woman, barely more than a girl, standing in a public washroom applying lipstick, the ruby red putty people wore in those days.

'Slightly,' she answered carefully.

'I wouldn't trust him further than I could throw him,' the woman said.

Kay slipped quickly past a row of women who were saying things women had always said. The same things their mothers and grandmothers have said, shaking the same powder across their broad or narrow noses and peering at their dabbed, genetically condemned faces or at a broken nail, probably bitten, held up and examined in the weak light. No, she did not trust Philip Halliwell. But she had fallen under his spell. That's what it felt like, being under a spell. She had, in fact, after a two-week courtship, married him. It was a secret marriage because she was still a student, working in the field of early English manuscripts. She lived in a women's residence and held a prestigious scholarship which would have been jeopardised, or so they reasoned. All this was years and years ago.

Recently she was in the hospital for a week (tests, bone scans, which turned out negative, thank God) and Philip sent a basket of hydrangeas. She hadn't seen him for six months, and so the gift surprised her. But she didn't know how to look after these particular flowers, and the nurses were too rushed off their feet to lend a hand. She took the nearly dead plant home, and on the way through the hospital corridor two people stopped her and instructed her in the care of hydrangeas. 'Never let the roots go dry,' one said. The other said, 'Water daily, but don't allow the roots to actually stand in water.'

Many people resent advice, and Kay has never been able to understand this. A man she knows, Nils Almquist, a cataloguer in the museum where she works, tells her that this resistance to advice is a Teutonic failing, that people from Mediterranean countries – Greece, Italy, Spain – routinely ask the advice of their friends and relatives before making a major decision. It is a sign of courtesy to seek counsel. People whose opinion is sought are flattered, and at the same time no one is strictly bound to accept what is offered. This arrangement strikes Kay as having a good deal of human flexibility to it, and a crafty balance of consolation and hoarded-up responsibility.

'Never wear white pumps after Labor Day,' her mother used to say, 'or before the twenty-fourth of May.' Kay believed this. It made a kind of sense, these permissive bracketing holidays and the broad field of liberty that lay between. 'If you lose something,' a girl named Patsy Tobin told her when she was about seven or eight, 'just shut your eyes and pray to St. Anthony.' Patsy Tobin's family was

Roman Catholic, which was why she knew of the secret and specialised powers of St. Anthony. The advice worked. After uttering a short, breathy prayer ('Dear St. Anthony, please help me find . . . '), Kay almost always came across her lost shoe or doll or handkerchief or whatever. 'When you have the growing pains in your legs,' her Auntie Ruth said during one of her prolonged summer visits, 'lie very still in bed, not moving a muscle, and count to one hundred.' This proved excellent advice, practical to the point of magic, for not only did the pains ease as she counted, but she was almost always fast asleep before reaching a hundred.

'Happiness is capability.' A woman Kay knows has written this sentence on a slip of paper and stuck it to her refrigerator door with one of those little magnets. 'Oh, I know it sounds simplistic,' she said, reading Kay's expression, 'but it works. And it's the only thing that does work.'

'There must be something you can do for him,' Kay said to the doctor when her father lay dying – bedridden, bored, kept from his pinochle and poker cronies – in terrible pain. She had arranged the postponement of her comprehensive exams and come home for a few weeks.

'Aside from boiling up a deck of cards and feeding him the broth, we can't do a thing,' the doctor said.

She liked this brand of non-advice. She found it ironic, indirect, cocky and kindly meant. It seemed like the sort of folksy palliative you might hear from a grunty old family practitioner. But this was a young doctor speaking. A very tall, good looking man with exceptionally blue eyes. Kay had only just met him that morning. His name, he told her, was Philip. They shook hands and then he helped her on with her coat. She looked tired, he said, especially her eyes.

For some reason – self-pity or injured vanity – this made her want to lean up against him and cry, but she remembers that she resisted.

Her father did not die, not then. Instead he made something of a limited recovery, getting out of bed eventually, getting himself dressed, taking short walks in the neighbourhood, going as far as the corner for a newspaper or a loaf of bread. His clothes hung loosely on him, looked clownish and poor, and Kay wondered at that time why her mother didn't do something about those miserable clothes. He had given up smoking at the start of his illness; now he gave up cards. If he came upon a group of men hunched over a game, he shook his head in a puzzled but unreproachful way as though powerless to understand why grown men would idle away valuable time.

He started to read a thick book about butterflies. Kay remembers that her mother bought this book in a second-hand store; she was always haunting such places. She loved a bargain. The book was old, its cover damaged, but the colour plates were in beautiful condition. Better still, here and there, preserved in the pages close to the spine, were the dried pressed bodies of real butterflies, captured by some previous reader. They were exceedingly fragile but had kept their colour and, like thin sheets of mica, glinted with metallic richness. When her father came across one of these flattened creatures, he left it where it was, untouched, as if it were a sign of good luck.

About this time Kay and Philip went to Sardinia. This was their so-called honeymoon, delayed nearly two years because of her father's condition and also because of revisions to her thesis. It was a terrible day when they left, an afternoon in late January. It was necessary to land in Toronto in order to de-ice the plane. They taxied into a hangar where the whole of the plane – the wings, body and nose – was covered with pink foam. Kay remembers it took more than an hour to restore the plane's silvery sides, and even then they rose with a shudder into a grey, torn-up looking sky. It seemed not all that improbable that they would perish. Philip ordered a bottle of champagne somewhere over Quebec, Kay's first taste of champagne, though she was twenty-five years old at the time, a tall, loping, solemn girl with a head full of roughly filed facts and opinions.

Crossing the Atlantic, Philip ignored her. He had struck up an acquaintance with a Belgian priest across the aisle, and the two of them were soon trading anecdotes – miracles and blessings of a medical and spiritual nature. Half-dozing, Kay listened to Philip describe the spontaneous recovery of one of his patients. It took a minute or two to realise it was her father's case he was recounting, the story was that full of echoes, pauses and resonance; her father with his flapping, shabby clothes became a kind of golden fabulation, a character in a rich folktale who had burst through to reality and health.

She has only a few memories of that time in Sardinia, and even the half-dozen, utterly faded, stiff-edged Polaroid snaps that remain seem to bear no relation to the two of them or what they hoped to find there: he sitting on a large rock with his hands stretched skyward; she in the doorway of a hotel; he stepping gracefully through the arch of an ancient chapel; she climbing into a little hump-backed rental car; he standing in the morning surf and wearing a pair of exotically printed swimming trunks; and another of him crouched on a hillside examining a small plant.

An odd thing happened. During the weeks in Sardinia they stayed in three different hotels, and in each of these places they were given the same room number, number five. Kay was the one who pointed this out to Philip, who might otherwise not have noticed. As a coincidence it seemed to her mildly amusing and, perhaps, even an omen of good luck, not that her instincts leaned toward omens. Philip, on the other hand, found it thrilling and also alarming. He brooded about the numbers and even quizzed the desk clerk in the third hotel about the way in which rooms were allotted. Though their time was running out, he insisted on registering in a fourth hotel in order to test the pattern, then changed his mind at the last minute. One night he worked out the probability figures on the back of a menu, allowing each hotel fifteen rooms. The numbers were overwhelmingly against such a coincidence. He rechecked the figures. 'Look at this,' he demanded. Kay could see that he felt threatened and at the same time exhilarated. He discussed it with anyone who would listen including, one evening, a British couple they met in the hotel dining room. His voice grew implausibly overpitched, and the English pair exchanged sharp looks of apprehension – or so Kay thought. The next morning he woke up saying, 'I'm making too much of this. I'm letting it get to me.'

In Kay's memory the two of them took picnic lunches every day to lonely little beaches, but it may have been only two or three times that they did this. Probably they bought what they needed in the village shops, bread and sausage and a bottle of cheap wine. Kay remembers that one day – this was perhaps the same day Philip was cured of his obsession with the room numbers – they lay on their backs on the warm sand and she felt something brush her knee. It was a butterfly, not large, but quite brilliantly coloured in shades of red and yellow and amber. She thought of her father's book and its brightly illustrated pages. Between the windows of colour on the wings were tiny transparent panes edged in black. She held perfectly still, wondering what this creature made of the roundness of her knee, wondering if it perceived its own ephemeral grace. 'Maybe it's a rare mutation,' she said to Philip who had fallen asleep. 'Maybe it's the world's rarest butterfly.'

This seemed possible. She was not just being whimsical. Almost anything she could imagine seemed possible and, for the moment at least, she felt she knew everything she needed to know to stay alive in the world.

'The world's yours, honey, if you want it,' Kay's Auntie Ruth used to say. Auntie Ruth was her mother's younger sister. She arrived every June for a visit and stayed until the first of August, sometimes longer if she judged she was not getting on her brother-in-law's nerves. For his part he was fond of her, but found her noisy chattering tiresome, and objected in a mild, manly way to her many toiletries lined up along the toilet tank. Kay's mother defended this array of lotions and powders; Auntie Ruth suffered from eczema, also heat rash and various unidentified allergies. Besides, she got it all for free since her husband, Uncle Nat, was a pharmacist.

Uncle Nat was left at home in Brandon. He was too tied down with the drugstore, Auntie Ruth maintained, to go for a vacation. He wasn't one for travel anyway, being older than Auntie Ruth, twenty years older, and suffering from piles and also backache. She, and Kay's mother too, referred to him as The Old Poke. 'I'd better drop a few lines to The Old Poke,' she would say a week or so into her visit.

Auntie Ruth's visits had an effect on Kay's mother; they made her girlish. The two of them set up folding cots on the screened porch so they could talk half the night away. They made themselves twin cotton dresses with wide circular skirts and wore them downtown. Once they dipped gum-drops in lemon extract, arranged them on top of a chiffon cake and set them alight at the table. Another day they dropped in on an old friend of Kay's mother who told them she had had an exhausting morning – she had rinsed out her shoe laces and brushed her teeth. They couldn't stop laughing at this, repeating it time and again and inventing variations. 'I'm so tired, I just washed my feet and ironed a hanky.' 'I'm just done in, I've blown my nose and changed my underpants.' On and on they went. Afternoons in the backyard, drinking glasses of iced tea, they speculated on their niece Ethel's hurry-up marriage. 'You only have to put two and two together,' Kay's mother said knowingly. 'You only have to put *one* and *one* together,' Auntie Ruth hooted, pitching them into spasms of hilarity.

At the end, though, there was trouble between them. Kay's mother lay in the hospital for four months with cancer of the lungs, this despite the fact that she had never smoked a cigarette in her life. Her sister Ruth sent her a card every single day, but in all those months she never once came to visit. 'I can't, honey,' she said to Kay on the telephone, speaking up because of the long distance. 'Since your Uncle Nat passed on I just can't face hospitals, they get me down so.' Kay's mother refused at last to open the cards. She was bitter. She made her daughters promise they would have nothing to do with Auntie Ruth in the future, and they did promise. But, in fact, it was a promise that none of them has kept, or ever intended to.

It grieved Kay, though, that her mother should die with her heart hardened and set. She seemed to have forgotten all the good times, how the two sisters, she and Auntie Ruth, would move the sewing machine out on the porch and, in the space of an afternoon, re-cover a chair or make a new set of kitchen curtains. They made these things for almost nothing, cutting them out of remnants they scrambled for in back-street fabric outlets.

Kay's mother sewed beautifully, but considered herself a novice beside her younger sister. 'Anyone can do plain sewing,' she would say, 'but your Auntie Ruth is a genius with the needle.' Then she went misty-eyed with recollection. 'Remember the year she came early to help with the ballet costumes? For the recital? They were tricky as can be, those little satin insets and the netting on the hats and at the wrists. Itchy to work with too, especially in hot weather. We worked right down to the wire. But we got them done.'

'I don't remember,' Kay said.

This was not true – she did remember, but saying she didn't was a way to strike out at her mother, letting her know she distrusted the touched-up trivia that formed the bulk of her remembrances and the treacly voice she used when invoking them. 'I don't remember.' She said it harshly, tossing it off.

'Well,' her mother said, wistful, 'you were very young. Just a baby. Probably too young to get anything much out of ballet lessons.'

There was a coolness between them at this time because of Philip. Her mother had taken Kay aside. She had things to say to her. Handsome men, she said, can bring about problems in a marriage. They think they can go their own way. They get spoiled by flattery, by women falling about them. This leads to a lack of responsibility on their part. You can't count on them, and that's what marriage is in the long run, two people counting on each other, in good times and bad as it says in the wedding service, always having, no matter what, that one person in the world you can turn to.

The trouble was, this wasn't advice she was giving. It was prophecy. And already too late.

Kay has always believed herself fortunate in having sisters. Her sister, Joan, white-haired, heavy in the hips, already several times a grandmother, lets her talk on and on. She thinks it does her good, and it does. Kay's other sister Dorrie is equally sympathetic, but has a different style. She prods and interrupts and brings up tricky points. 'What do you mean he forgets you?' she asked once. 'Do you mean just birthdays and anniversaries and so on?'

That too, but much, much more. Once he met an old friend in a restaurant and they decided to fly to Whitehorse just like that. He phoned her the next day to let her know.

'Once,' Dorrie pronounced, shrugging. 'A lapse.' Then asked, 'And other women?'

Of course there were other women, almost from the start, but that wasn't really the problem. 'He forgets I exist. Who I am. He looks at me but sees the wallpaper. He's courtly in the wrong way, like a man on automatic pilot. Even in bed –'

'Yes?'

Kay hadn't meant to get into this. 'Even then I feel him slipping away. His arms are around me, yes, but his head's somewhere else. We might as well be in different rooms.'

Kay also has long, frequent talks with her good friend Nils Almquist. Two or three times a month they have a drink together after work, around the corner at a place called The Laughing Moose. They favour a special table near a bank of potted begonias. Nils is every bit as good looking as Philip, but built along different lines, and Kay is about ninety-five per cent sure he's gay. She can tell him almost anything. He's one of those unusual people without twitches, able to sit for long periods of time with his body still and solid. It's this, she thinks, that encourages her confidences. One night not long ago she told him about Philip's final leaving, how he slipped off without a word, as though he'd suddenly remembered he had another existence elsewhere. How had she known it was the last time? Because of a sense of lightness that stole over her. To herself she said, almost laughing, 'Well, that's that.' She felt like someone getting up out of a sick bed, all her bones stiff but still in working order.

Besides her sisters and Nils and other assorted friends, she belongs to a weekly conversation group. A talk circle is the official term. This group meets at Trinity Church Hall on Monday nights in a room furnished with easy chairs and soft lights.

Some years earlier, when things were going badly, she had come across a little printed notice that said: 'Feeling alone and alienated? Coffee and conversation may be the answer.'

She feared the usual unctuous welcoming remarks, braced herself for forced joviality and whining accord. Normally she was scornful of such endeavours, preferring to believe that liberal, educated people, nurtured from the cradle on communication skills, had no need for such organised embarrassment.

At the first meeting the discussion centred on the subject of favourite smells. One woman said moth balls. Another said coffee just after you grind the beans. A man said old ice skates when you bring them up from the basement. Kay said the smell of new cloth spread on a table, before you pin a pattern to it. The moth ball woman said yes, that was hers too, only she hadn't thought to mention it. She and Kay became close friends. It's she who has 'Happiness is capability' on her refrigerator door.

Ecology is a frequent topic of discussion on these Monday nights, how to live more naturally and harmoniously in the world. Also the problem of public responsibility and private yearnings, the question of tolerance and instinct, or the spiritual self versus the material world.

But when things get too serious someone in the group will say, 'Aren't we getting a bit heavy here?' and for a while they'll retreat to the primary edge and talk about such things as My Most Trying Moment or The Book That Has Meant the Most to Me or My Favourite Colour and Why. Last week they talked about My Earliest Memory.

Kay described the dance recital. By some trick of inversion this memory precedes the rehearsals themselves.

The recital was held in a new, strange place, not the big mirrored room with the dusty floor. Kay was told to wait in a dark place behind heavy curtains. She was shushed by one of the bigger girls, told to stand still or she'd rip her costume, and someone else handed her a large golden basket. Not real gold, but a graceful willow basket, probably spray painted; the handle was twisted and elegant and fit smoothly over the crook of Kay's arm. A whisper welled up: 'Isn't she darling!' 'Yes.'

Then somebody, her sister Joan probably, gave her a push forward, whispering, 'One-two-three-jump,' and the next minute they were filing onto a small stage beyond which was nothing but a row of blinding lights and a wall of darkness. The darkness was false, full of held breath and heated expectations, that much Kay could understand.

A number of things seemed wrong. Her dance shoes made a different wash-wash sound on the slippery floor. There was a worrying sense of crowding and falling, and dazzle from the lights. Nevertheless she kept her eyes on the others, tried to do what they did, and reached, when the time came, into her basket. But what was this? This fragrant silky handful? Whatever it was fluttered upward into the air, a rounded spray of particles that drifted soundlessly to the floor. Again and then again.

There was too much surprise in this, too much of shock and disorder. She observed the cascade of waxy pink and white flakes as they slipped from the angle of her hand, falling on the floor and on the toes of her shoes, and at last identified what they were.

The flower petals, the enchanting basket, her own exalted role, so unexpected – none of these things diminished in any way the humiliation she felt. She had been tricked, caught in a loop of incomprehension, given the hard slap of adult licence. Adults were allowed to fool children, to withhold vital information, and this insult was sealed by the banked thunder of anonymous applause, as dense, unstartled and indiscriminate as the applause that comes out of a radio. Still she curtsied and smiled, feeling sick with shame.

Sick, Kay tells the Monday night group, and when she says sick, she means sick. She means weakness, fever, dizziness, shock, shortness of breath, all the fearful symptoms, but she had curtsied and smiled nevertheless.

Consciousness narrowed down to the width of her small hand in front of her face and the little dot of false light floating over the audience that she was unable to blink away.

But she stared straight ahead and willed herself to hold steady for a few seconds longer. Already she knew she would recover.

Dolls, Dolls, Dolls, Dolls

DOLLS. ROBERTA HAS written me a long letter about dolls, or more specifically about a doll factory she visited when she and Tom were in Japan.

'Ha,' my husband says, reading her letter and pulling a face, 'another pilgrimage to the heart's interior.' He can hardly bring himself to read Roberta's letters any more, though they come addressed to the two of us; there is a breathlessness about them that makes him squirm, a seeking, suffering openness which I suspect he finds grotesque in a woman of Roberta's age. Forty-eight, an uneasy age. And Roberta has never been what the world calls an easy woman. She is one of my oldest friends, and the heart of her problem, as I see it, is that she is incredulous, still, that the colour and imagination of our childhood should have come to rest in nothing at all but these lengthy monochrome business trips with her husband, a man called Tom O'Brien; but that is neither here nor there.

In this letter from Japan, she describes a curious mystical experience that caused her not exactly panic and not precisely pleasure, but that connected her for an instant with an area of original sensation, a rare enough event at our age. She also unwittingly stepped into one of my previously undeclared beliefs. Which is that dolls, dolls of all kinds – those strung-together parcels of wood or plastic or cloth or whatever – possess a measure of energy beyond their simple substance, something half-willed and half-alive.

Roberta writes that Tokyo was packed with tourists; the weather was hot and humid, and she decided to join a touring party on a day's outing in the countryside – Tom was tied up in meetings, as per usual.

They were taken by air-conditioned bus to a village where ninety per cent – the guide vigorously repeated this statistic – where ninety per cent of all the dolls in Japan were made. 'It's a major industry here,' Roberta writes, and some of the dolls still were manufactured almost entirely by hand in a kind of cottage-industry system. One house in the village, for example, made nothing but arms and legs, another the bodies; another dressed the naked doll bodies in stiff kimonos of real silk and attached such objects as fans and birds to the tiny lacquered female fingers.

Roberta's party was brought to a small house in the middle of the village where the heads of geisha dolls were made. Just the heads and nothing else. After leaving their shoes in a small darkened foyer, they were led into a surprisingly wide, matted workroom which was cooled by slow-moving overhead fans. The air was musty from the mingled straw and dust, but the light from a row of latticed windows was softly opalescent, a distinctly mild, non-industrial quality of light, clean-focused and just touched with the egg-yellow of sunlight.

Here in the workroom nine or ten Japanese women knelt in a circle on the floor. They nodded quickly and repeatedly in the direction of the tourists, and smiled in a half-shy, half-neighbourly manner; they never stopped working for a second.

The head-making operation was explained by the guide, who was a short and peppy Japanese with soft cheeks and a sharp 'arfing' way of speaking English. First, he informed them, the very finest sawdust of a rare Japanese tree was taken and mixed with an equal solution of the purest rice paste. (Roberta writes that he rose up on his toes when he reached the words *finest* and *purest* as though paying tribute to the god of superlatives.) This dough-like material then was pressed into wooden moulds of great antiquity (another toe-rising here) and allowed to dry very slowly over a period of days. Then it was removed and painted; ten separate and exquisitely thin coats of enamel were applied, so that the resulting form, with only an elegant nose breaking the white egg surface, arrived at the weight and feel and coolness of porcelain.

The tourists – hulking, Western, flat-footed in their bare feet – watched as the tiny white doll heads were passed around the circle of workers. The first woman, working with tweezers and glue, applied the eyes, pressing them into place with a small wooden stick. A second woman painted in the fine red shape of a mouth, and handed on the head to a woman who applied to the centre of the mouth a set of chaste and tiny teeth. Other women touched the eyes with shadow, the cheeks with bloom, the bones with highlight, so that the flattened oval took on the relief and contours of sculptured form. 'Lovely,' Roberta writes in her letter, 'a miracle of delicacy.'

And finally, the hair. Before the war, the guide told them, real hair had been used, human hair. Nowadays a very fine quality of blue-black nylon was employed. The doll's skull was cunningly separated into two sections so that the hair could be firmly, permanently rooted from the inside. Then the head was sealed again, and the hair arranging began. The two women who performed this final step used real combs and brushes, pulling the hair smoothly over their hands so that every strand was in alignment, and then they shaped it, tenderly, deftly, with quick little strokes, into the intricate knots and coils of traditional geisha hair dressing.

Finally, at the end of this circular production line, the guide held up a finished head and briefly propagandised in his sharp, gingery, lordly little voice about the amount of time that went into making a head, the degree of skill, the years of apprenticeship. Notice the perfection of the finished product, he instructed. Observe the delicacy, mark the detailing. And then, because Roberta was standing closest to him, he placed the head in her hands for a final inspection.

And that was the moment Roberta was really writing me about. The finished head in her hands, with its staring eyes and its painted veil of composure and its feminine, almost erotic crown of hair, had more than the weight of artefact about it. Instinctively Roberta's hands had cupped the head into a laced cradle, protective and cherishing. There was something *alive* about the head.

An instant later she knew she had overreacted. 'Tom always says I make too much of nothing,' she apologises. The head hadn't moved in her hands; there had been no sensation of pulse or breath, no shimmer of aura, no electrical charge, nothing. Her eyes went to the women who had created this little head. They smiled, bowed, whispered, miming a busy humility, but their cool waiting eyes informed her that they knew exactly what she was feeling.

What she *had* felt was a stirring apprehension of possibility. It was more than mere animism; the life, or whatever it was that had been brought into being by those industriously toiling women, seemed to Roberta to be deliberate and to fulfil some unstated law of necessity.

She ended her letter more or less the way she ends all her letters these days: with a statement that is really a question. 'I don't suppose,' she says, 'that you'll understand any of this.'

Dolls, dolls, dolls, dolls. Once – I forget why – I wrote those words on a piece of paper, and instantly they swam into incomprehension, becoming meaningless ruffles of ink, squiggles from a comic strip. Was it a Christmas wish list I was making? I doubt it. As a child I would have been shocked had I received more than one doll in a single year; the idea was unworthy, it was *unnatural*. I could not even imagine it.

Every year from the time I was born until the year I was ten I was given a doll. It was one of the certainties of life, a portion of a larger, enclosing certainty in which all the jumble of childhood lay. It now seems a long way back to those particular inalterable surfaces: the vast and incomprehensible war; Miss Newbury, with her ivory-coloured teeth, who was principal of Lord Durham Public School; Euclid Avenue where we lived in a brown house with a glassed-in front porch; the seasons with their splendours and terrors curving endlessly around the middle eye of the world which I shared with my sister and my mother and father.

Almost Christmas: there they would be, my mother and father at the kitchen table on a Saturday morning in early December, drinking drip coffee and making lists. There would come a succession of dark, chilly pre-Christmas afternoons in which the air would grow rich with frost and longing, and on one of those afternoons our mother would take the bus downtown to buy the Christmas dolls for my sister and me.

She loved buying the Christmas dolls, the annual rite of choosing. It's the faces, she used to say, that matter, those dear moulded faces. She would be swept away by a pitch of sweetness in the pouting lips, liveliness and colour in the lashed eyes, or a line of tenderness in the tinted cheeks – 'The minute I laid eyes on that face,' she would say, helplessly shaking her head in a way she had, 'I just went and fell head over heels.'

We never, of course, went with her on these shopping trips, but I can see how it must have been: Mother, in her claret-wine coat with the black squirrel collar, bending over, peering into glass cases in the red-carpeted toy department and searching in the hundreds of stiff smiling faces for a flicker of response, an indication of some kind that this doll, this particular doll, was destined for us. Then the pondering over price and value – she always spent more than she intended – having just one last look around, and finally, yes, she would make up her mind.

She also must have bought on these late afternoon shopping excursions Monopoly sets and dominoes and sewing cards, but these things would have been carried home in a different spirit, for it seems inconceivable for the dolls, our Christmas dolls, to be boxed and jammed into shopping bags with ordinary toys; they must have been carefully wrapped – she would have insisted on double layers of tissue paper – and she would have held them in her arms, crackling in their wrappings, all the way home, persuaded already, as we would later be persuaded, by the reality of their small beating hearts. What kind of mother was this with her easy belief, her adherence to seasonal ritual? (She also canned peaches the last week in August, fifty quarts, each peach half turned with a fork so that the curve, round as a baby's cheek, gleamed lustrous through the blue glass. Why did she do that – go to all that trouble? I have no idea, not even the seed of an idea.)

The people in our neighbourhood on Euclid Avenue, the real and continuing people, the Browns, the McArthurs, the Sheas, the Callahans, lived as we did, in houses, but at the end of our block was a large yellow brick building, always referred to by us as The Apartments. The Apartments, frilled at the back with iron fire escapes, and the front of the building solid with its waxed brown foyer, its brass mailboxes and nameplates, its important but temporary air. (These people only rent, our father had told us.) The children who lived in The Apartments were always a little alien; it was hard for us to believe in the real existence of children who lacked backyards of their own, children who had no fruit cellars filled with pickles and peaches. Furthermore, these families always seemed to be moving on after a year or so, so that we never got to know them well. But on at least one occasion I remember we were invited there to a birthday party given by a little round-faced girl, an only child named Nanette.

It was a party flowing with new pleasures. Frilled nutcups at each place. A square bakery cake with shells chasing each other around the edges. But the prizes for the games we played – Pin the Tail on the Donkey, Musical Chairs – were manipulated so that every child received one – was that fair? – and these prizes were too expensive, overwhelming completely the boxed handkerchiefs and hair ribbons we'd brought along as gifts. But most shocking of all was the present that Nanette received from her beaming parents.

We sat in the apartment under the light of a bridge lamp, a circle of little girls on the living-room rug, watching while the enormous box was untied. Inside was a doll.

What kind of doll it was I don't recall except that her bronzed hair gleamed with a richness that was more than visual; what I do remember was the affection with which she was lifted from her wrappings of paper and pressed to Nanette's smocked bodice, how she was tipped reverently backward so that her eyes clicked shut, how she was rocked to and fro, murmured over, greeted, kissed, christened. It was as though Nanette had no idea of the inappropriateness of this gift. A doll could only begin her life at Christmas. Was it the rigidities of my family that dictated this belief, or some obscure and unconscious approximation to the facts of gestation? A birthday doll, it seemed to me then, constituted a violation of the order of things, and it went without saying that the worth of all dolls was diminished as a result.

Still, there sat Nanette, rocking back and forth in her spun rayon dress, stroking the doll's stiff wartime curls and never dreaming that she had been swindled. Poor Nanette, there could be no heartbeat in that doll's misplaced body; it was not possible. I felt a twist of pity, probably my first, a novel emotion, a bony hand yanking at my heart, an emotion oddly akin – I see it clearly enough now – to envy,

In the suburbs of Paris is one of the finest archaeological museums in Europe – my husband had talked, ever since I'd known, about going there. The French, a frugal people, like to make use of their ancient structures, and this particular museum is housed inside a thirteenth-century castle. The castle, if you block out the hundreds of surrounding villas and acacia-lined streets, looks much as it always must have looked, a bulky structure of golden stone with blank, primitive, upswept walls and three round brutish towers whose massiveness might be a metaphor for that rough age which equated masonry with power.

The interior of this crude stone shell has been transformed by the Ministry of Culture into a purring, beige-toned shrine to modernism, hived with climate-controlled rooms and corridors, costly showcases and thousands of artefacts, subtly lit, lovingly identified. The *pièce de résistance* is the ancient banqueting hall where today can be seen a wax reconstruction of pre-Frankish family life. Here in this room a number of small, dark, hairy manikins squat naked around a cleverly simulated fire. The juxtaposition of time – ancient, medieval and modern – affected us powerfully; my husband and young daughter and I stared for some time at this strange tableau, trying to reconcile these ragged eaters of roots with the sleek, meaty, well-clothed Parisians we'd seen earlier that day shopping on the rue Victor Hugo.

We spent most of an afternoon in the museum looking at elegantly mounted pottery fragments and tiny vessels, clumsily formed from cloudy glass. There was something restorative about seeing French art at this untutored level, something innocent and humanising in the simple requirement for domestic craft. The Louvre had exhausted us to the glitter of high style and finish, and at the castle we felt as though the French had allowed a glimpse of their coarser, more likable selves.

'Look at that,' my husband said, pointing to a case that held a number of tiny clay figures, thousands of years old. We looked. Some of them were missing arms, and a few were missing their heads, but the bodily form was unmistakable.

'They're icons,' my husband said, translating the display card: 'From the pre-Christian era.'

'Icons?' our daughter asked, puzzled. She was seven that summer.

'Like little gods. People in those days worshipped gods made of clay or stone.'

'How do you know?' she asked him.

'Because it says so,' he told her. '*Icone*. That's the French word for icon. It's really the same as our word.'

'Maybe they're dolls,' she said.

'No. It says right here. Look. In those days people were all pagans and they worshipped idols. Little statues like these. They sort of held them in their hands or carried them with them when they went hunting or when they went to war.'

'They could be dolls,' she said slowly.

He began to explain again. 'All the early cultures – '

She was looking at the figures, her open hand resting lightly on the glass case. 'They look like dolls.'

For a minute I thought he was going to go on protesting. His lips moved, took the necessary shape. He lifted his hand to point once again at the case. I felt sick with sudden inexplicable anger.

Then he turned to our daughter, shrugged, smiled, put his hands in his pockets. He looked young, twenty-five, or even younger. 'Who knows,' he said to her. 'You might be right. Who knows.'

My sister lives 300 miles away in Ohio, and these days I see her only two or three times a year, usually for family gatherings on long weekends. These visits tend to be noisy and clamorous. Between us we have two husbands and six children, and then there is the flurry of cooking and cleaning up after enormous holiday meals. There is never enough time to do what she and I love to do most, which is to sit at the kitchen table – hers or mine, they are interchangeable – with mugs of tea before us and to reconstruct, frame by frame, the scenes of our childhood.

My memory is sharper than hers, so that in these discussions, though I'm two years younger, I tend to lead while she follows. (Sometimes I long for a share of her forgetfulness, her leisured shrugging acceptance of past events. My own recollections, not all happy, are relentlessly present, kept stashed away like ingots, testifying to a peculiar imprisoning, muscularity of recall.) The last time she came – early October – we talked about the dolls we had been given every Christmas. Our husbands and children listened, jealously it seemed to me, at the sidelines, the husbands bemused by this ordering of trivia, the children open-mouthed, disbelieving.

I asked my sister if she remembered how our dolls were presented to us, exactly the way real children are presented, the baby dolls asleep in stencilled cradles or wrapped in receiving blankets; and the schoolgirl dolls propped up by the Christmas tree, posed just so, smiling brilliantly and fingering the lower branches with their shapely curved hands. We always loved them on sight.

'Remember Nancy Lynn,' my sister said. She was taking the lead this time. Nancy Lynn had been one of mine, one of the early dolls, a large cheerful baby doll with a body of cloth, and arms and legs of painted plaster. Her swirled brown hair was painted on, and at one point in her long life she took a hard knock on the head, carrying forever after a square chip of white at the scalp. To spare her shame we kept her lacy bonnet tied on day and night. (Our children, listening, howled at this delicacy.)

One wartime Christmas we were given our twin dolls, Shirley and Helen. The twins were small and hollow and made of genuine rubber, difficult to come by in those years of shortages, and they actually could be fed water from a little bottle. They were also capable of wetting themselves through tiny holes punched in their rubber buttocks; the vulnerability of this bodily process enormously enlarged our love for them. There was also Barbara the Magic Skin Doll, wonderfully pliable at first, though later her flesh peeled away in strips. There was a Raggedy Ann, not to our minds a real doll, but a cloth-stuffed hybrid of good disposition. There was Brenda, named for her red hair, and Betty with jointed knees and a brave little tartan skirt. There was Susan – her full name was Brown-Eyed Susan – my last doll, only I didn't know it then.

My sister and I committed the usual sins, leaving our dolls in their pyjamas for days on end, and then, with a rush of shame and love, scooping them up and trying to make amends by telescoping weeks and even years into a Saturday afternoon. Our fiercely loved dolls were left out in the rain. We always lost their shoes after the first month; their toes broke off almost invariably. We sometimes picked them up by the arm or even the hair, but we never disowned them or gave them away or changed their names, and we never buried them in ghoulish backyard funerals as the children in our English stories seemed to do. We never completely forgot that we loved them.

Our mother loved them too. What was it that stirred her frantic devotion? – some failure of ours? – some insufficiency in our household? She spent hours making elaborate wardrobes for them; both my sister and I can remember the time she made Brenda a velvet cape trimmed with scraps of fur from her old squirrel collar. Sometimes she helped us give them names: Patsy, Gloria, Merry Lu, Olivia.

'And the drawer,' my sister said. 'Remember the drawer?'

'What drawer?' I asked.

'You remember the drawer. In our dresser. That little drawer on the left-hand side, the second one down.'

'What about it?' I asked slowly.

'Well, don't you remember? Sure you do. That's where our dolls used to sleep. Remember how Mother lined it with a doll blanket?'

'No,' I said.

'She thumbtacked it all around, so it was completely lined. That's where Shirley and Helen used to sleep.'

'Are you sure?'

'Absolutely.'

I remind her of the little maple doll cribs we had.

'That was later,' she said.

I find it hard to believe that I've forgotten about this, especially this. A drawer lined with a blanket; that was exactly the kind of thing I remembered.

But my sister still has the old dresser in the attic of her house. And she told me that the blanket is still tacked in place; she hasn't been able to bring herself to remove it. 'When you come at Christmas,' she said, 'I'll show it to you.'

'What colour is it?' I asked.

'Pink. Pink with white flowers. Of course it's filthy now and falling apart.'

I shook my head. A pink blanket with white flowers. I have no memory of such a blanket.

Perhaps at Christmas, when I actually look at the drawer, it will all come flooding back. The sight of it may unlock what I surely have stored away somewhere in my head, part of the collection of images which has always seemed so accessible and true. The fleecy pink drawer, the dark night, Shirley and Helen side by side, good night, good night as we shut them away. Don't let the bedbugs bite. Oh, oh.

It happened that in the city where I grew up a little girl was murdered. She was ten years old, my age.

It was a terrible murder. The killer had entered her bedroom window while she was sleeping. He had stabbed her through the heart; he cut off her head and her arms and her legs. Some of these pieces were never found.

It would have been impossible not to know about this murder; the name of the dead girl was known to everyone, and even today I have only to think the syllables of her name and the whole undertow of terror doubles back on me. This killer was a madman, a maniac who left notes in lipstick on city walls, begging the police to come and find him. He couldn't help himself. He was desperate. He threatened to strike again.

Roberta Callahan and JoAnn Brown and I, all of us ten years old, organised ourselves into a detective club and determined to catch the killer. We never played with dolls anymore. The Christmas before, for the first time, there had been no doll under the tree; instead, I have been given a wristwatch. My mother had sighed, first my sister, now me.

Dolls, which had once formed the centre of my imagination, now seemed part of an exceedingly soft and sissified past, something I used to do before I got big. I had wedged

Nancy Lynn and Brown-Eyed Susan and Brenda and Shirley and all the others onto a shelf at the back of my closet, and now my room was filled with pictures of horses and baseball stickers and collections of bird nests. Rough things, rugged things, tough things. For Roberta Callahan and JoAnn Brown and I desired, above all else, to be tough. I don't remember how it started, this longing for toughness. Perhaps it was our approaching but undreamed of puberty. Or the ebbing of parental supervision and certain possibilities of freedom that went with it.

Roberta was a dreamy girl who loved animals better than human beings; she had seen *Bambi* seven times and was always drawing pictures of spotted fawns. JoAnn Brown was short and wiry and wore glasses, and could stand any amount of pain; the winter before she had been hospitalised with double pneumonia. *Double pneumonia.* 'But I had the will to live,' she told us solemnly. The three of us were invited to play commandos with the boys on the block, and once the commando leader, Terry Shea, told another boy, in my hearing, that for a girl I was tough as nails. *Tough as nails.* It did not seem wildly improbable to JoAnn and Roberta and me that we should be the capturers of the crazed killer. Nancy Drew stalked criminals. Why not us?

In JoAnn Brown's house there was a spare room, and in the spare room there was a closet. That closet became the secret headquarters for the detective club. We had a desk which was a cardboard carton turned upside down, and there, sitting on the floor with Mr. Brown's flashlight and stacks of saltines, we studied all the newspaper clippings we could find. We discussed and theorised. Where did the killer hide out? When and where would he strike again? Always behind our plotting and planning lay certain thoughts of honour and reward, the astonishment of our parents when they discovered that we had been the ones who led the police to the killer's hideout, that we had supplied the missing clue; how amazed they would be, they who all summer supposed that their daughters were merely playing, believing that we were children, girls, that we were powerless.

We emerged from these dark closet meetings dazed with heat and determination, and then we would take to the streets. All that summer we followed suspicious-looking men. Short men. Swarthy men. Men with facial scars or crossed eyes. One day we sighted a small dark man, a dwarf, in fact, carrying over his shoulder a large cloth sack. A body? Perhaps the body of a child? We followed him for an hour, and when he disappeared into an electrical-supply shop, JoAnn made careful note of the address and the time of entry.

Back in the closet we discussed what we should do. Should we send a letter to the police? Or should we make our way back to the shop and keep watch?

Roberta said she would be too frightened to go back.

'Well, I'll go then,' I spoke bravely.

Bravely, yes, I spoke with thrilling courage. But the truth was this: I was for all of that summer desperately ill with fear. The instant I was put to bed at night my second-floor bedroom became a cave of pure sweating terror. Atoms of fear conjoined in a solid wall of darkness, pinning me down as I lay paralysed in the middle of my bed; even to touch the edges of the mattress would be to invite unspeakable violence. The window, softly curtained with dotted swiss, became the focus of my desperate hour-by-hour attention. If I shut my eyes, even for an instant, he, the killer, the maniac, would seize that moment to enter and stab me through the heart. I could hear the sound of the knife entering my chest, a wet, injurious, cataclysmic plunge.

It was the same every night; leaves playing on the window pane, adumbration, darkness, the swift transition from neighbourhood heroine, the girl known to be tough as nails, the girl who was on the trail of a murderer, to this, this shallow-breathing, rigidly sleepless coward.

Every night my mother, cheerful, baffled, innocent as she said good night, would remark, 'Beats me how you can sleep in a room with the window closed.' Proving how removed she was from my state of suffering, how little she perceived my nightly ordeal.

I so easily could have told her that I was afraid. She would have understood; she would have rocked me in her arms, bought me a night light at Woolworth's, explained how groundless my fears really were; she would have poured assurance and comfort on me and, ironically, I knew her comfort would have brought release.

But it was comfort I couldn't afford. At the risk of my life I had to go on as I was; to confess fear to anyone at all would have been to surrender the tough new self that had begun to grow inside me, the self I had created and now couldn't do without.

Then, almost accidentally, I was rescued. It was not my mother who rescued me, but my old doll, Nancy Lynn. I had a glimpse of her one morning in my closet, a plaster arm poking out at me. I pulled her down. She still wore the lacy bonnet on her chipped head, grey with dirt, the ribbons shredded. She had no clothes, only her soft, soiled, mattressy body and the flattened joints where the arms and legs were attached. After all these years her eyes still opened and shut, and her eyelids were a bright youthful pink in contrast to the darkened skin tone of her face.

That night she slept with me under the sheet, and malevolence drained like magic from the darkened room; the night pressed friendly and familiar through the dotted swiss curtains; the Callahans' fox terrier yapped at the streaky moon. I opened the window and could hear a breeze loosened in the elms. In bed, Nancy Lynn's cold plaster toe poked reassuringly at my side. Her cloth body, with its soiled cottony fragrance, lay against my bare arm. The powerful pink eyelids were inexpressibly at rest. All night, while I slept, she kept me alive.

For as long as I needed her – I don't remember whether it was weeks or months before the killer was caught – she guarded me at night. The detective club became over a period of time a Gene Autry Fan Club, then a Perry Como Record Club, and there must have been a day when Nancy Lynn went back to her closet. And probably, though I don't like to think of it, a day when she and the others fell victim to a particularly heavy spree of spring cleaning.

There seems no sense to it. Even on the night I first put her on the pillow beside me, I knew she was lifeless, knew there was no heart fluttering in her soft chest and no bravery in her hollow head. None of it was real, none of it.

Only her power to protect me. Human love, I saw, could not always be relied upon. There would be times when I would have to settle for a kind of parallel love, an extension of my hidden self, hidden even from me. It would have to do, it would be a great deal better than nothing, I saw. It was something to be thankful for.

Poaching

ON OUR WAY to catch the Portsmouth ferry, Dobey and I stayed overnight at a country hotel in the village of Kingsclere. The floors sloped, the walls tipped, the tap leaked rusty water and the bedclothes gave out an old, bitter odour.

At breakfast we were told by the innkeeper that King John had once stayed in this hotel and, moreover, had slept in the very room where we had spent the night.

'Wasn't he the Magna Carta king?' Dobey said, showing off. 'That would make it early thirteenth century.'

'Incredible,' I said, worrying whether I should conceal my fried bread beneath the underdone bacon or the bacon beneath the bread. 'Extraordinary.'

The innkeeper had more to tell us. 'And when His Royal Highness stopped here he was bit by a bedbug. Of course there's none of that nowadays.' Here he chuckled a hearty chuckle and sucked in his red cheeks.

I crushed my napkin – Dobey would call it a serviette – on top of my bacon and fried bread and egg yolk and said to myself: next he'll be rattling on about a ghost.

'And I didn't like to tell you people last night when you arrived,' the innkeeper continued, 'but the room where the two of you was – it's haunted.'

'King John?' I asked.

'One of the guards, it's thought. My wife's seen 'im many the time. And our Barbara. And I've heard 'im clomping about in his great boots in the dark of the night and making a right awful noise.'

Dobey and I went back to our room to brush our teeth and close our haversacks, and then we lay flat on our backs for a minute on the musty bed and stared at the crooked beams.

'Are you thinking kingly thoughts?' I said after a while.

'I'm thinking about those poor bloody Aussies,' said Dobey.

'Oh, them,' I said. 'They'll make out all right.'

Only the day before we'd picked up the two Australians on the road. Not that they were by any stretch your average hitchhikers – two women, a mother, middle-aged, and a grown daughter, both smartly dressed. Their rented Morris Minor had started to smoke between Farrington and Kingsclere, and we gave them a lift into the village.

They'd looked us over carefully, especially the mother, before climbing into the backseat. We try to keep the backseat clean and free of luggage for our hitchhikers. The trick is to put them at their ease so they'll talk. Some we wring dry just by keeping quiet. For others we have to prime the pump. It's like stealing, Dobey says, only no one's thought to make a law against it.

Within minutes we knew all about the Australians. They were from Melbourne. The mother had recently been widowed, and her deceased husband, before the onset of Addison's disease, had worked as an investment analyst.

Something coppery about the way she said 'my late husband' suggested marital dullness, but Dobey and I never venture into interpretation. The daughter taught in a junior school. She was engaged to be married, a chap in the military. The wedding was six months away, and the two of them, mother and daughter, were shoring themselves up by spending eight weeks touring Britain, a last fling before buckling down to wedding arrangements. It was to be a church ceremony followed by a lobster lunch in the ballroom of a large hotel.

The two of them made the wedding plans sound grudging and complex and tiresome, like putting on a war. The daughter emitted a sigh; nothing ever went right. And now they'd only been in England a week, had hardly made a dent, and already the hired car had let them down. It looked serious, too, maybe the clutch.

Everything the mother said seemed electrically amplified by her bright, forthcoming Australia-lacquered voice. She had an optimistic nature, quickly putting the car out of mind and chirping away from the back seat about the relations in Exeter they planned to visit, elderly aunts, crippled uncles, a nephew who'd joined a rock band and travelled to America, was signed up by a movie studio but never was paid a penny – all this we learned in the ten minutes it took us to drive them into Kingsclere and drop them at the phone box. The daughter, a pretty girl with straight blonde hair tied back in a ribbon, hardly said a word.

Nor did we. Dobey and I had made a pact at the start of the trip that we would conceal ourselves, our professions, our antecedents, where we lived, what we were to each other. We would dwindle, grow deliberately thin, almost invisible, and live like aerial plants off the packed fragments and fictions of the hitchhikers we picked up.

One day we travelled for two hours – this was between Conway and Manchester – with a lisping, blue-jeaned giant from Canada who'd come to England to write a doctoral thesis on the early language theories of Wittgenstein.

'We owe tho muth to Wittgenthtein,' he sputtered, sweeping a friendly red paw through the air and including Dobey and me in the circle of Wittgenstein appreciators. He had run out of money. First he sold his camera; then his Yamaha recorder; then, illegally, the British Rail Pass his parents had given him when he finished his master's degree. That was why he was hitchhiking. He said, 'I am going to Oxthford' as though he was saying, 'I am a man in love.'

He talked rapidly, not at all embarrassed by his lisp – Dobey and I liked him for that, though normally we refrain from forming personal judgements about our passengers. He spoke as though compelled to explain to us his exact reason for being where he was at that moment.

They all do. It is a depressing hypothesis, but probably, as Dobey says, true: people care only about themselves. They are frenzied and driven, but only by the machinery of their own adventuring. It has been several days now since anyone's asked us who we are and what we're doing driving around like this.

Usually Dobey drives, eyes on the road, listening with a supple, restless attention. I sit in the front passenger seat, my brain screwed up in a squint from looking sideways. At times I feel that giving lifts to strangers makes us into patronising benefactors. But Dobey says this is foolish; these strangers buy their rides with their stories.

Dobey prefers to pick up strangers who are slightly distraught, saying they 'unwind' more easily. Penury or a burned-out clutch – these work in our favour and save us from having to frame out careful questions. I am partial, though, to the calm, to those who stand by the roadside with their luggage in the dust, too composed or dignified to trouble the air with their thumbs. There was that remarkable Venezuelan woman who rode with us from Cardiff to Conway and spoke only intermittently and in sentences that seemed wrapped in their own cool vapours. Yes, she adored to travel alone. She liked the song of her own thoughts. She was made fat by the sight of mountains. The Welsh sky was blue like a cushion. She was eager to embrace rides from strangers. She liked to open wide windows so she could commune with the wind. She was a doctor, a specialist in bones, but alas, alas, she was not in love with her profession. She was in love with the English language because every word could be picked up and spun like a coin on the table top.

The shyest traveller can be kindled, Dobey maintains – often after just one or two strikes of the flint. That sullen Lancashire girl with the pink-striped hair and the colloid eyes – her dad was a coward, her mum shouted all the time, her boyfriend had broken her nose and got her pregnant. She was on her way, she told us, to a hostel in Bolton. Someone there would help her out. She had the address written on the inside of a cigarette packet. I looked aslant and could tell that Dobey wanted to offer her money, but part of our bargain was that we offer only rides.

Another thing we agreed on was that we would believe everything we were told. No matter how fantastic or eccentric or crazy the stories we heard, we'd pledged ourselves to respect their surfaces. Anyone who stepped into our backseat was trusted, even the bearded, evil-smelling curmudgeon we picked up in Sheffield who told us that the spirit of Ben Jonson had directed him to go to Westminster and stand at the abbey door preaching obedience to Mrs. Thatcher. We not only humoured the old boy – who gave us shaggy, hand-rolled cigarettes to smoke – but we delivered him at midnight that same day.

Nevertheless, I'm becoming disillusioned. (It was my idea to head for Portsmouth and cross the Channel.) I long, for instance, to let slip to one of our passengers that Dobey and I have slept in the bedchamber where King John was nipped by a bedbug. It's not attention I want and certainly not admiration. It's only that I'd like to float my own story on the air. I want to test its buoyancy, to see if it holds any substance, to see if it's true or the opposite of true.

And I ask myself about the stories we've been hearing lately: have they grown thinner? The Australian mother and daughter, for example – what had they offered? Relations in Exeter. A wedding in Melbourne. Is that enough? Dobey says to be patient, that everything is fragmentary, that it's up to us to supply the missing links. Behind each of the people we pick up, Dobey believes, there's a deep cave, and in the cave is a trap door and a set of stone steps which we may descend if we wish. I say to Dobey that there may be nothing at the bottom of the stairs, but Dobey says, how will we know if we don't look.

Scenes

IN 1974 FRANCES was asked to give a lecture in Edmonton, and on the way there her plane was forced to make an emergency landing in a barley field. The man sitting next to her – they had not spoken – turned and asked if he might put his arms around her. She assented. They clung together, her size 12 dress and his wool suit. Later, he gave her his business card.

She kept the card for several weeks poked in the edge of her bedroom mirror. It is a beautiful mirror, a graceful rectangle in a pine frame, and very, very old. Once it was attached to the back of a bureau belonging to Frances' grandmother. Leaves, vines, flowers and fruit are shallowly carved in the soft wood of the frame. The carving might be described as primitive – and this is exactly why Frances loves it, being drawn to those things that are incomplete or in some way flawed. Furthermore, the mirror is the first thing she remembers seeing, *really* seeing, as a child. Visiting her grandmother, she noticed the stiff waves of light and shadow on the frame, the way square pansies interlocked with rigid grapes, and she remembers creeping out of her grandmother's bed where she had been put for an afternoon nap and climbing on a chair so she could touch the worked surface with the flat of her hand.

Her grandmother died. It was discovered by the aunts and uncles that on the back of the mirror was stuck a piece of adhesive tape and on the tape was written: 'For my vain little granddaughter Frances.' Frances' mother was affronted, but put it down to hardening of the arteries. Frances, who was only seven, felt uniquely, mysteriously honoured.

She did not attend the funeral; it was thought she was too young, and so instead she was taken one evening to the funeral home to bid goodbye to her grandmother's body. The room where the old lady lay was large, quiet, and hung all around with swags of velvet. Frances' father lifted her up so she could see her grandmother, who was wearing a black dress with a white crêpe jabot, her powdered face pulled tight as though with a drawstring into a sort of grimace. A lovely blanket with satin edging covered her trunky legs and torso. Laid out, calm and silent as a boat, she looked almost generous.

For some reason Frances was left alone with the casket for a few minutes, and she took this chance – she had to pull herself up on tiptoe – to reach out and touch her grandmother's lips with the middle finger of her right hand. It was like pressing in the side of a rubber ball. The lips did not turn to dust – which did not surprise Frances at all, but rather confirmed what she had known all along. Later, she would look at her finger and say to herself, 'This finger has touched dead lips.' Then she would feel herself grow rich with disgust. The touch, she knew, had not been an act of love at all, but only a kind of test.

With the same middle finger she later touched the gelatinous top of a goldfish swimming in a little glass bowl at school. She touched the raised mole on the back of her father's white neck. Shuddering, she touched horse turds in the back lane, and she touched her own urine springing onto the grass as she squatted behind the snowball bush by the fence. When she looked into her grandmother's mirror, now mounted on her own bedroom wall, she could hardly believe that she, Frances, had contravened so many natural laws.

The glass itself was bevelled all the way around, and she can remember that she took pleasure in lining up her round face so that the bevelled edge split it precisely in two. When she was fourteen she wrote in her diary, 'Life is like looking into a bevelled mirror.' The next day she crossed it out and, peering into the mirror, stuck out her tongue and made a face. All her life she'd had this weakness for preciosity, but mainly she'd managed to keep it in check.

She is a lithe and toothy woman with strong, thick, dark-brown hair, now starting to grey. She can be charming. 'Frances can charm the bees out of the hive,' said a friend of hers, a man she briefly thought she loved. Next year she'll be forty-five – terrible! – but at least she's kept her figure. A western sway to her voice is what people chiefly remember about her, just as they remember other people for their chins or noses. This voice sometimes makes her appear inquisitive, but, in fact, she generally hangs back and leaves it to others to begin a conversation.

Once, a woman got into an elevator with her and said, 'Will you forgive me if I speak my mind? This morning I came within an inch of taking my life. There was no real reason, only everything had got suddenly so dull. But I'm all right now. In fact, I'm going straight to a restaurant and treat myself to a plate of french fries. Just fries, not even a sandwich to go with them. I was never allowed to have french fries when I was a little girl, but the time comes when a person should do what she wants to do.'

The subject of childhood interests Frances, especially its prohibitions, so illogical and various, and its random doors and windows which appear solidly shut, but can, in fact, be opened easily with a touch or a password or a minute of devout resolution. It helps to be sly, also to be quick. There was a time when she worried that fate had pencilled her in as 'debilitated by guilt', but mostly she takes guilt for what it is, a kind of lover who can be shrugged off or greeted at the gate. She looks at her two daughters and wonders if they'll look back resentfully, recalling only easy freedoms and an absence of terror – in other words, meagreness – and envy her for her own stern beginnings. It turned out to have been money in the bank, all the various shames and sweats of growing up. It was instructive; it kept things interesting; she still shivers, remembering how exquisitely sad she was as a child.

'It's only natural for children to be sad,' says her husband, Theo, who, if he has a fault, is given to reductive statements. 'Children are unhappy because they are inarticulate and hence lonely.'

Frances can't remember being lonely, but telling this to Theo is like blowing into a hurricane. She was spoiled – a lovely word, she thinks – and adored by her parents, her plump, white-faced father and her skinny, sweet-tempered mother. Their love was immense and enveloping like a fall of snow. In the evenings, winter evenings, she sat between the two of them on a blue nubby sofa, listening to the varnished radio and taking sips from their cups of tea from time to time or sucking on a spoonful of sugar. The three of them sat enthralled through 'Henry Aldrich' and 'Fibber Magee and Molly', and when Frances laughed they looked at her and laughed too. Frances has no doubt that those spoonfuls of sugar and the roar of Fibber Magee's closet and her parents' soft looks were taken in and preserved so that she, years later, boiling an egg or making love or digging in the garden, is sometimes struck by a blow of sweetness that seems to come out of nowhere.

The little brown house where she grew up sat in the middle of a block crowded with other such houses. In front of each lay a tiny lawn and a flower bed edged with stones. Rows of civic trees failed to flourish, but did not die either. True, there was terror in the back lane where the big boys played with sticks and jackknives, but the street was occupied mainly by quiet, hard-working families, and in the summertime hopscotch could be played in the street, there was so little traffic.

Frances' father spent his days 'at the office'. Her mother stayed at home, wore bib aprons, made jam and pickles and baked custard, and every morning before school brushed and braided Frances' hair. Frances can remember, or thinks she can remember, that one morning her mother walked as far as the corner with her and said, 'I don't know why, but I'm so full of happiness today I can hardly bear it.' The sun came fretting through the branches of a scrubby elm at that minute and splashed across her mother's face, making her look like someone in a painting or like one of the mothers in her school reader.

Learning to read was like falling into a mystery deeper than the mystery of airwaves or the halo around the head of the baby Jesus. Deliberately she made herself stumble and falter over the words in her first books, trying to hold back the rush of revelation. She saw other children being matter-of-fact and methodical, puzzling over vowels and consonants and sounding out words as though they were dimes and nickels that had to be extracted from the slot of a bank. She felt suffused with light and often skipped or hopped or ran wildly to keep herself from flying apart.

Her delirium, her failure to ingest books calmly, made her suspect there was something wrong with her or else with the world, yet she deeply distrusted the school librarian who insisted that a book could be a person's best friend. (Those subject to preciosity instantly spot others with the same affliction.) This librarian, Miss Mayes, visited all the classes. She was tall and soldierly with a high, light voice. 'Boys and girls,' she cried, bringing large red hands together, 'a good book will never let you down.' She went on; books could take you on magic journeys; books could teach you where the rain came from or how things used to be in the olden days. A person who truly loved books need never feel alone.

But, she continued, holding up a finger, there are people who do shameful things to books. They pull them from the shelves by their spines. They turn down the corners of pages; they leave them on screened porches where the rain and other elements can warp their covers; and they use curious and inappropriate objects as bookmarks.

From a petit-point bag she drew a list of objects that had been wrongly, criminally inserted between fresh clean pages: a blue-jay feather, an oak leaf, a matchbook cover, a piece of coloured chalk and, on one occasion – 'on one occasion, boys and girls' – *a strip of bacon*.

A strip of bacon. In Frances' mind the strip of bacon was uncooked, cold and fatty with a pathetic streaking of lean. Its oil would press into the paper, a porky abomination, and its ends would flop out obscenely. The thought was thrilling: someone, someone who lived in the same school district, had had the audacity, the imagination, to mark the pages of a book with a strip of bacon. The existence of this person and his outrageous act penetrated the fever that had come over her since she'd learned to read, and she began to look around again and see what the world had to offer.

Next door lived Mr. and Mrs. Shaw, and upstairs, fast asleep, lived Louise Shaw, aged eighteen. She had been asleep for ten years. A boy across the street named Jackie McConnell told Frances that it was the sleeping sickness, that Louise Shaw had been bitten by the sleeping sickness bug, but Frances' mother said no, it was the coma. One day Mrs. Shaw, smelling of chlorine bleach and wearing a flower-strewn housedress, stopped Frances on the sidewalk, held the back of her hand to the side of Frances' face and said, 'Louise was just your age when we lost her. She was forever running or skipping rope or throwing a ball up against the side of the garage. I used to say to her, don't make such a ruckus, you'll drive me crazy. I used to yell all the time at her, she was so full of beans and such a chatterbox.' After that Frances felt herself under an obligation to Mrs. Shaw, and whenever she saw her she made her body speed up and whirl on the grass or do cartwheels.

A little later she learned to negotiate the back lane. There, between board fences, garbage cans, garage doors and stands of tough weeds, she became newly nimble and strong. She learned to swear – damn, hell and dirty bastard – and played piggy-move-up and spud and got herself roughly kissed a number of times, and then something else happened: one of the neighbours put up a basketball hoop.

For a year, maybe two – Frances doesn't trust her memory when it comes to time – she was obsessed with doing free throws. She became known as the queen of free throws; she acquired status, even with the big boys, able to sink ten out of ten baskets, but never, to her sorrow, twenty out of twenty. She threw free throws in the morning before school, at lunchtime, and in the evening until it got dark. Nothing made her happier than when the ball dropped silently through the ring without touching it or banking on the board. At night she dreamed of these silky baskets, the rush of air and the sinuous movement of the net, then the ball striking the pavement and returning to her hands. ('Sounds a bit Freudian to me,' her husband, Theo, said when she tried to describe for him her time of free-throw madness, proving once again how far apart the two of them were in some things.) One morning she was up especially early. There was no one about. The milkman hadn't yet come, and there was dew shining on the tarry joints of the pavement. Holding the ball in her hands was like holding onto a face, it was so dearly familiar with its smell of leather and its seams and laces. That morning she threw twenty-seven perfect free throws before missing. Each time the ball went through the hoop she felt an additional oval of surprise grow round her body. She had springs inside her, in her arms and in the insteps of her feet. What stopped her finally was her mother calling her name, demanding to know what she was doing outside so early. 'Nothing,' Frances said, and knew for the first time the incalculable reward of self-possession.

There was a girl in her sewing class named Pat Leonard. She was older than the other girls, had a rough pitted face and a brain pocked with grotesqueries. 'Imagine,' she said to Frances, 'sliding down a banister and suddenly it turns into a razor blade.' When she trimmed the seams of the skirt she was making and accidentally cut through the fabric, she laughed out loud. To amuse the other girls she sewed the skin of her fingers together. She told a joke, a long story about a pickle factory that was really about eating excrement. In her purse was a packet of cigarettes. She had a boyfriend who went to the technical school, and several times she'd reached inside his pants and squeezed his thing until it went off like a squirt gun. She'd flunked maths twice. She could hardly read. One day she wasn't there, and the sewing teacher said she'd been expelled. Frances felt as though she'd lost her best friend, even though she wouldn't have been seen dead walking down the hall with Pat Leonard. Melodramatic tears swam into her eyes, and then real tears that wouldn't stop until the teacher brought her a glass of water and offered to phone her mother.

Another time, she was walking home from a friend's in the early evening. She passed by a little house not far from her own. The windows were open and, floating on the summer air, came the sound of people speaking in a foreign language. There seemed to be a great number of them, and the conversation was very rapid and excited. They might have been quarrelling or telling old stories; Frances had no idea which. It could have been French or Russian or Portuguese they spoke. The words ran together and made queer little dashes and runs and choking sounds. Frances imagined immense, wide-branching grammars and steep, stone streets rising out of other centuries. She felt as though she'd been struck by a bolt of good fortune, and all because the world was bigger than she'd been led to believe.

At university, where she studied languages, she earned pocket money by working in the library. She and a girl named Ursula were entrusted with the key, and it was their job to open the library on Saturday mornings. During the minute or two before anyone else came, the two of them galloped at top speed through the reference room, the periodical room, the reading room, up and down the rows of stacks, filling that stilled air with what could only be called primal screams. Why this should have given Frances such exquisite pleasure she couldn't have said, since she was in rebellion against nothing she knew of. By the time the first students arrived, she and Ursula would be standing behind the main desk, date stamp in hand, sweet as dimity.

One Saturday, the first person who came was a bushy-headed, serious-minded zoology student named Theodore, called Theo by his friends. He gave Frances a funny look, then in a cracked, raspy voice asked her to come with him later and have a cup of coffee. A year later he asked her to marry him. He had a mind unblown by self-regard and lived, it seemed to Frances, in a nursery world of goodness and badness with not much room to move in between.

It's been mainly a happy marriage. Between the two of them, they've invented hundreds of complex ways of enslaving each other, some of them amazingly tender. Like other married people, they've learned to read each other's minds. Once Theo said to Frances as they drove around and around, utterly lost in a vast treeless suburb, 'In every one of these houses there's been a declaration of love,' and this was exactly the thought Frances had been thinking.

To her surprise, to everyone's surprise, she turned out to have an aptitude for monogamy. Nevertheless, many of the scenes that have come into her life have involved men. Once she was walking down a very ordinary French street on a hot day. A man, bare-chested, drinking Perrier at a café table, sang out, '*Bonjour.*' Not '*bonjour, Madame*' or '*bonjour, Mademoiselle*', just '*bonjour*'. Cheeky. She was wearing white pants, a red blouse, a straw hat and sunglasses. '*Bonjour,*' she sang back and gave a sassy little kick, which became the start of a kind of dance. The man at the table clapped his hands over his head to keep time as she went dancing by.

Once she went to the British Museum to finish a piece of research. There was a bomb alert just as she entered, and everyone's shopping bags and briefcases were confiscated and searched. It happened that Frances had just bought a teddy bear for the child of a friend she was going to visit later in the day. The guard took it, shook it till its eyes rolled, and then carried it away to be X-rayed. Later he brought it to Frances, who was sitting at a table examining a beautiful old manuscript. As he handed her the bear, he kissed the air above its fuzzy head, and Frances felt her mouth go into the shape of a kiss, too, a kiss she intended to be an expression of her innocence, only that. He winked. She winked back. He leaned over and whispered into her ear a suggestion that was hideously, comically, obscene. She pretended not to hear, and a few minutes later she left, hurrying down the street full of cheerful shame, her work unfinished.

These are just some of the scenes in Frances' life. She thinks of them as scenes because they're much too fragmentary to be stories and far too immediate to be memories. They seem to bloom out of nothing, out of the thin, uncoloured air of defeats and pleasures. A curtain opens, a light appears, there are voices or music or sometimes a wide transparent stream of silence. Only rarely do they point to anything but themselves. They're difficult to talk about. They're useless, attached to nothing, can't be traded in or shaped into instruments or made to prise open the meaning of the universe.

There are people who think such scenes are ornaments suspended from lives that are otherwise busy and useful. Frances knows perfectly well that they are what a life is made of, one fitting against the next like English paving-stones.

Or sometimes she thinks of them as little keys on a chain, keys that open nothing, but simply exist for the beauty of their toothed edges and the way they chime in her pocket.

Other times she is reminded of the Easter eggs her mother used to bring out every year. These were real hens' eggs with a hole poked in the top and bottom and the contents blown out. The day before Easter, Frances and her mother always sat down at the kitchen table with paint brushes, a glass of water and a box of watercolours. They would decorate half-a-dozen eggs, maybe more, but only the best were saved from year to year. These were taken from a cupboard just before Easter, removed from their shoebox, and carefully arranged, always on the same little pewter cake stand. The eggs had to be handled gently, especially the older ones.

Frances, when she was young, liked to pick up each one in turn and examine it minutely. She had a way of concentrating her thoughts and shutting everything else out, thinking only of this one little thing, this little egg that was round like the world, beautiful in colour and satin to the touch, and that fit into the hollow of her hand as though it were made for that very purpose.

Hinterland

EVERYONE SEEMS TO have stayed put this year except Meg and Roy Sloan of Milwaukee, Wisconsin.

Although both Meg and Roy are patriotic in a vague and non-rhetorical way, and good mature citizens who pay their taxes and vote and hold opinions on gun legislation and abortion, they've chosen this year to ignore the exhortation of their president to stay home and see America first. The Grand Canyon can wait, Roy says in the sociable weekend voice he more and more distrusts. The Black Hills can wait. And the Everglades. And Chesapeake Bay.

And they can wait forever, he privately thinks – with their slopes and depressions and fissured rock and silence and stubborn glare. He and Meg have come this fine golden September, now turned grey, but an endurable grey, to the city of Paris, and have settled down for three weeks in a small hotel near the Place Ferdinand, determined for once to do the thing right.

For the first ten days the sun gives out a soft powdery haze. Then it starts raining, little whips of water dashing down. Beneath their hotel window the streets are stripped of their elongated shadows and stippled light; this is suddenly a differently ordered reality, foreign and purposeful, with a harsh workaday existence and citizens so bound to their routines that they scarcely notice the serious, slightly older, end-of-season tourists, like the Sloans, who are taking in the sights.

Over the years, in the seasonal rounds of business and pleasure and special anniversaries, Meg and Roy Sloan have set foot on most of the continents of the world: Asia, Australia, South America – and of course Europe. They have, in fact, been to Paris on two previous occasions: for a single night in 1956, early April, their honeymoon, passing through on their way to Rome; and three days in 1967, an exhausting, hedonistic, aggressive survey that embraced the Moulin Rouge and the Jeu de Paume, Montmartre and Notre Dame, the Comédie Française and Malmaison, and that terminated with the rich, suppressed shame of a dinner in the rue Royale where they suffered a contemptuous waiter, a wobbly table, scanty servings and a yellow-eyed madam guarding the *toilette* and demanding payment of Meg – who pretended not to understand – and who muttered fiercely into her saucer of coins, *ça commence, ça commence*, meaning Meg Sloan of Milwaukee and the tidal wave of penny-pinching tourists who would follow, the affluent poor, the educationally driven, budget-bound North Americans whom Europeans so resemble but refuse to acknowledge.

And now, in the autumn of 1986, an uneasy, untrustful time in the world's history, the Sloans have returned.

'But why?' quite a number of their friends said. 'Why Paris of all places!'

Meg Sloan is a small, dark, intense woman who, though not Jewish, might easily be thought to be. In any case, it seemed that Americans were singled out by terrorists, regardless of their background: bearded soft-spoken journalists taken hostage, nuns beaten and raped, a harmless old man pushed about and then shot, innocent children propelled through the suddenly gaping side of an aircraft. Why take needless risks, the Sloans' friends said. Why go out of your way to invite disaster? Furthermore the dollar had taken a rough punch, and you could get better nouvelle cuisine anyway right in Milwaukee, or at least Chicago, and not have to put up with people who were rude and unprincipled – remember that Greenpeace business last summer, still unresolved – besides which, three weeks devoted just to Paris seemed a lot when there was all of Europe to get a feel for.

'We're fatalists,' Meg had countered, 'and besides, we don't want to live out of a suitcase. Roy and I want to unpack for a change. You know, put our underwear in those big deep dresser drawers they have over there and actually hang up our clothes in one of those gorgeous armoire affairs and come back after a day of sightseeing and get into a bed we can depend on.'

'What we'd really like,' Roy said, 'is to see how the true Parisians live.'

In fact, he holds out little hope of this happening. At age fifty-five, the ability to penetrate and explore has left him, perhaps only temporarily – he hopes so. Mainly, as he sees it, he's forgotten how to pay attention, grown somehow incapacitated and lazy. At time he can't believe his own laziness. He chides himself, his sins of omission. He is a man so lazy, so remiss, he couldn't be bothered last spring to step into his own backyard for a glimpse of Halley's Comet. Halley's Comet won't come again, not in his lifetime – he knows this perfectly well. Unforgivable. Incomprehensible. What is the matter with him?

Both he and Meg were in need of a vacation. The long hot summer of patriotic excess at home had left him with what seemed like a bad case of flu, with aching muscles and slow settling fevers. His head felt stuffed with mineral whiteness: too many fireworks, too many hours before a TV set regarding the costly clamour over 'Lady Liberty' – the epithet drummed hard on the lining of his skull. Who are these buoyant children anyway, he asked himself, addressing the black windows of his living room, and by what power had they turned him peevish and dull and out of tune with his own instincts?

There were other problems too. The Sloans' daughter Jenny had separated from her husband Kenneth for reasons not yet fully explained, and returned to the family home, bringing with her from Green Bay her two small children whose presence had unbalanced the house. Meg's nerves flared up overnight, her old insomnia came back, her eyes grew dry and jittery. Mother and daughter under one roof – the old, old story, which neither of them would have credited, and each too tactful to overstep the other, each so protective of him, Roy (father, husband) that he was continually off-balance and awaiting an explosion that he doubted would ever come.

Then the idea of a vacation presented itself, getting away, the travel agent's mystic croon – a brief respite. A trip, a holiday. Escape. And it seemed, after some initial dithering, the thing to do. September was the worst possible time of the year for Roy to get away, but arrangements could always be –

and were – worked out, and he and Meg were free to go anywhere within reason; for some time now money has not really been a hindrance.

They know, though, how to travel thriftily, how to save their receipts and write off what they can as professional expenses. Meg Sloan, for the last ten years or so, has made hand-painted, one-of-a-kind greeting cards, whimsical lines and squiggles on squares of rag paper that retail for five dollars apiece, and she has come to see her trips as opportunities to scout out new ideas. Roy Sloan, who heads a technical college in downtown Milwaukee, makes solemn, uncomfortable forays to similar institutions when travelling abroad, keeping notes on curriculum and entrance requirements and capital costs. These tax write-offs serve as an enabling tactic since both Roy and Meg grew up in frugal midwestern families and require the assurance that things are not as costly as they appear.

Certainly Paris is far from cheap. Their hotel is small, twenty rooms in all, and inconspicuous, but charges five hundred francs a night, which is one hundred dollars at the current rate. Thirty years ago the young, honeymooning Sloans stayed in this same hotel and paid the grand sum of twelve dollars. 'Which included breakfast,' says Meg, who, with her merciless memory for the cost of things, equivocates and subtracts and mildly despairs. Admittedly, though, there have been a number of improvements since that time: chiefly, tiny module bathrooms fitted into the corners of each room, and orange juice of an oddly dark hue served along with the croissants and coffee.

For ten days now they've sat at the same little table in the hotel breakfast room and buttered their already buttery croissants and helped themselves to apricot jam. Away from home, Meg abandons her dieting and exercise programme. She grows careless and easy about her body which, in a matter of days, takes on a sleek, milky look. She has a different fragrance about her; her hands wander more rhythmically, almost musically.

Under Roy's knife the croissant shatters, leaving rings of tender flakes on the tablecloth, and one of these she picks up with the moistened tip of her finger and transfers to her tongue. Fresh flowers with tiny blue heads lean out of a glass bottle, an ordinary glass bottle, a vinegar bottle probably. Their waiter is young, square-jawed, from Holland. He's come to Paris to learn the business, he says, and also the French language, but to the Sloans he speaks a colloquial English, showing off. Clumsy but attentive, he brings a second jug of coffee without being asked, and more hot milk. Meg observes all this with a look of deep satisfaction; she tells Roy how rested and healthy she feels; already it seems she's forgotten she is the mother of a troubled daughter and the grandmother of two wearingly energetic children. Daylight enters the room in blocks and composes tall trembly shapes on the wallpaper behind her head. She is still a pretty woman. Roy wonders how long such prettiness lasts; his feeling is that any day now there will be an abrupt diminishment, and already he has begun to prepare himself for the tasks of pity and persuasion.

Before them, opened up on the table, is the map of Paris. They push the flowers to one side in order to make room, and Meg, with her reading glasses worn low on her nose, is pointing to the little red dot that is the Cluny Museum. Roy nods, takes a pen from his breast pocket and circles the dot. After a while they rise, sigh with contentment, and go into the street, stepping carefully around fresh dog turds, plentiful and perfectly formed, lying everywhere on the roughened oily pavement. They head for the Métro which is just around the corner.

Arm in arm they swing along. They feel younger in this foreign city, years younger than they do at home. The first few days in Paris were hectic and wasteful, but now everything has settled into a routine, and the two of them descend into the Métro with springy nonchalance, and blithely negotiate the turnstiles. After their first day they'd decided to buy a monthly pass, a *carte orange*, that bears their signature and photograph, and this document, more than anything else, carries them over an invisible frontier and makes them part of the wave of frowning commuters who flow through the gates and take possession of the platform. The Sloans have even acquired something of the Paris look of indifference and suffering, elbows tucked close to the body, feet sturdily planted, eyes directed inward as though recalling past holidays or rehearsing those to come: Brittany, the Alps, the spicy smell of forests, distances and vistas, here and yet not here, the Gallic knack of being everywhere and nowhere, of possessing everything and nothing.

At the entrance to the museum Roy counts out the exact change, thirty-two francs, and Meg opens her handbag automatically for inspection. Today there is the additional precaution of a body search. Smiling, they hold their arms straight out. A young man, who might be a student, frisks Roy by running his hands up and down his sides and between his legs; a broad-faced woman, biting her lips, performs the same swift operation on Meg.

The Sloans have been told that the bombs currently detonated in Paris are the size of three cigarette packets, and they naturally wonder what possible good these cursory inspections can do. They've concluded that the searches are symbolic, evidence that strict security measures are being observed, even though the situation is clearly impossible. Every day for a week now a bombing has occurred in Paris; yesterday the Hôtel de Ville, the day before a suburban cafeteria. Armed soldiers, looking absurdly young and pitifully barbered, stand guard on street corners, but there *is* no cure, there *are* no effective measures. The attacks are too random and insidious. The city is too large.

And yet the Sloans show no signs of alarm. They look relaxed and happy and, like everyone else entering the Cluny Museum this morning, they comply willingly when searched, even smiling at their inquisitors, anxious to demonstrate their innocence, their gratitude for care taken, their concern about the mounting gravity of the crisis, their feeling that, all things considered, America could easily be in a similar plight.

Once inside, arriving at the first of a series of exhibition rooms, they go their separate ways. They do this wordlessly, out of long habit. On the whole they have avoided the dismal symmetry of so many married couples. They confess their differences; they are people who move at different speeds. Their senses are differently angled. Meg's response to works of art is visual or tactile, Roy's is literal. Compulsively he studies titles and dates – stooping, squinting at the tiny print, drawing on his shaky Berlitz French to translate the brief explanations. Meg, on the other hand, stands well back with one hand cupping her chin, looking intently, absorbing and stowing away in some back compartment of her brain various shapes and colours and evolving patterns. She loves texture; she loves curious hand-wrought things; it doesn't matter to her if a tapestry – and the Cluny Museum is filled with tapestries – is six hundred years old or two hundred years. She looks for emblems and symbols and whimsical objects concealed in the muted backgrounds or receding borders, a fish motif, for example, or a mermaid or a lacework construction holding fruit. Whenever some detail strikes her forcefully, she rummages in her handbag for her pen and makes a notation, usually in the form of a little sketch.

Coming together afterward and discussing what they've seen, it's as though the Sloans have attended two separate exhibitions. Today they sit at a small round table in a bistro recommended by one of their many guidebooks, eating a light lunch, a salad of potatoes, watercress and walnuts. The pleasure of travel, Roy thinks, concentrates at these small public tables, he and Meg across from each other, composed for talk as they seldom are at home.

She can be an exasperating companion, nervous in the manner of pretty women, hovering, going off on tangents, sometimes given to finding untruthful reasons for the things she does, but, for all this, he prizes their intimacies. Away from home the boundaries between them loosen. He feels he can say anything, no matter how rambling or speculative, and be understood. She listens and nods. The shine in her eyes flatters him, and he is not, as he sometimes feels at home, a marauder in her busy, bracingly cluttered life. Now, today, she lifts her hands expressively, reversing her wrists, making an airy accompaniment for herself or perhaps for Roy or for the waiter in his floor-length apron. She is describing a particular gilded Virgin she saw this morning at the Cluny Museum. 'At the Cluny,' she says, innocently breezy, and Roy hears a swarm of echoes: *on the Champs, at the Luxembourg*. How soon his wife is able to slide her tongue around novelty, adopting what comes her way, without hesitation.

'What Virgin?' he asks.

'In that room, you know, that little anteroom where all the coins were.'

'I didn't see any coins.'

'They were in the same room. At least, I think it was the same room.'

'I must have missed it completely.'

'It was near the end,' she tells him. 'You were probably getting saturated, going in circles. I certainly was.'

'I suppose I could go back this afternoon.' Roy says this doubtfully at first.

'I loved her,' says Meg, returning to the Virgin. 'I *loved* her. Not that she was beautiful, she was more odd than beautiful. Her face, I mean. It was sort of frozen and pious, and she had these young eyes.'

'How young?'

'Very. Like a teenager's eyes. They bulged. But the main thing was her stomach. Or her chest rather. It opened up, two little golden doors on hinges, beautiful, and inside was this tiny shelf. It was amazing, like a toy cupboard.'

'And?'

'Inside her body, on this shelf – now this is pretty strange – was a whole crucifixion scene, all carved with little figures, tiny little things like dolls. I'm not describing it very well, but –'

He waits. He can smell her perfume across the table and is reminded of the measure of passion still stored at the heart of his feeling for her. He has given her this particular perfume, the same bottle every birthday. The buying of it, standing at a counter in a department store in Milwaukee and counting out bills, never fails to fill him with the skewed pleasure of the provider. An unwholesome pleasure nowadays, he has no doubt; dishonourable, his daughter Jenny would say, and something he should long ago have renounced.

'That's all,' Meg says. 'There she was, this little golden teenager, and inside her she was carrying a scene from the future. Like a video or a time bomb or something. It's the one thing I'll remember out of all that stuff we saw this morning. Just her.' She presses a hand to her chest, her neat, buttoned suit jacket. 'Opening up like that. It was – what will you remember?'

The question takes him by surprise. She means to surprise him, he's sure of it.

'The tapestries,' he says finally.

'Which one?' She eyes him closely.

He is a little drunk; too little food with too much wine. Which one? He tries to focus, to think, then gives a helpless lopsided shrug. But Meg is poking in her bag for her address book, too preoccupied now to notice how aptly the gesture reflects his condition.

'Which one?'

'All of them,' he says.

After lunch Meg leaves Roy sitting in the bistro.

Her best and oldest friend, Karen Craddock, has given her the address of a warehouse in north Paris where wonderful clothes can be had for a fraction of their retail cost. They are samples, according to Karen, worn once or twice by models in fashion shows, most of them in an American size eight, which is Meg's size – how she cherishes her smallness! – and also her daughter Jenny's.

Roy, whose feet ache, sits for an hour at the little table and makes himself drink two cups of bitter coffee. He reads the *Herald Tribune* carefully, item by item, concentrating, hoping to dispel the chalky pressure behind his eyes. Then he pays, puts on his damp raincoat and retraces his steps, back to the courtyard of the Cluny Museum.

Again he counts out money for a ticket, sixteen francs, wondering if the woman selling tickets is surprised to see him back so soon, such a zealous muscum goer, so admirably greedy for an afternoon of art. She is as young as Jenny, with hair combed back roughly and a look on her face of scornful preoccupation. Stacking coins, arranging them in rows, she scarcely looks up. But the inspector, the amiable young guard who searched him earlier in the day, seems to remember him and, with a nod, waves him through.

Along with a light, early afternoon crowd, Roy enters the series of exhibition rooms. There are a great many of them, and they open logically, harmoniously, one into the next, but there are also odd turning points, raised or lowered levels and narrow staircases, a number of which are temporarily closed because of an ambitious archaeological excavation going on beneath the building.

He has never had a sense of direction; it is an old family joke, how quickly he becomes lost. Within minutes today he is disoriented, twice returning to an odd, airy room holding the puzzling stone torsos of old kings and saints. He wonders if he should ask for assistance and tries to assemble a reasonable sentence. *Je cherche une vierge avec des portes sur sa poitrine.* Or is it *son poitrine?* Either way it sounds like the request of a madman.

And then, turning a corner, he finds her. She is standing on a rough stone plinth in a corner of a little room behind a glass case of coins, somewhat smaller than he imagined from Meg's description, but yes, the eyes did bulge noticeably, looking heavenward, as though dully unaware of her bright golden belly, her unimaginable destiny. The two gilded doors stand open – Roy imagines they are perpetually open, locked at a forty-five degree angle, summoning the visitor's eye. And inside, like a scene from an old play, the tiny sorrow-bent figures enact their story.

He is not alone. An elderly man and woman, each with copious white hair and each leaning upon a wooden cane, pause, peer inside, and exchange creaky looks of amusement. Close behind them glowers a lean, unpretty woman in a leather coat that she has tried to brighten with a green scarf. She shakes her head and clicks her tongue sharply, perhaps with disapproval, perhaps with wonder – Roy is unable to tell. A moment later he hears the surprise of a deep American voice uttering the words '. . . distortion of time.' Someone else, another man, replies with the speed of a ping-pong player, and also the frivolity. 'Yes, of course, it does have a primitive feel, but it's actually quite a sophisticated rendering.'

Roy steps back so the two men can have a clear view. Both are young, a tall, bony, raincoated pair. One carries a museum guide and regards the Virgin with hard critical eyes; the other has a priestly face and an expression of reverence. They are brothers, Roy thinks (that bony replication) or else, more probably, lovers. He longs to join in their discussion, if only to claim a bond with them, his fellow-travellers. The feeling of belonging to a stalwart, foolhardy minority in an alien land gives Roy at times an unearned sense of the heroic which he recognises as absurd. 'What do you mean by "primitive feel"?' he would like to ask, exaggerating his own midwestern vowels, but the two men move off – they seem to glide – leaving him alone with the Virgin.

He sees that her skin beneath the gold is smoothed wood, and her general outlines are stylised and conventional. She is really an ingenious little casket for the improbable sacrifice she bears, but her upward stare now strikes Roy as being impassively self-aware; certain covert bargains made in the past must now be paid for, and this payment, luridly dramatic, is rehearsed behind the pair of peek-a-boo doors. The silliness of art. The crude approximations. But he is moved, nevertheless, at the way a human life drains toward one revealing scene.

The doors themselves tempt him, especially their neatly worked hinges – but to touch them, he reasons, would probably set off an alarm. The whole museum is sure to be electronically monitored; it would be madness not to, given the current situation. He wonders if Meg had been similarly tempted, and thinks how she is always stopping to shut a bureau drawer, straighten a picture, adjust a chair cushion. She is more than just nervously neat; for Meg the believable world consists of touchable objects, mainly texture and angle and curve, that tremble above and powerfully rule her place in it. Or so he thinks, never having been able, even after all these years, to uncover her separate design or the source of her will.

He looks about and sees no one, though the density of the room seems to have shifted. He senses some material displacement, and at a distance hears what he believes to be the patter of rain falling on the ancient roof, a small fretful slap-slapping against stone. Quickly he reaches out and pushes one of the little doors. The tremor in his hand conveys itself to the mechanism, and it moves obediently in a small silken arc that delights him. But as he pushes it back to its original position he glimpses, at the periphery of his vision, a uniformed guard approaching.

The guard is wrinkled and stout with a squashed plum for a nose. The way he tilts his stoutness at Roy gives the impression of a formal, respectful bow, but his face is crimson – with anger, Roy thinks at first – and he speaks in a loud, throaty incomprehensible French and gestures roughly toward the entrance of the room.

Roy, in turn, points to the Virgin. He smiles benignly; he wants to protest that he's done no damage, only indulged a whim. '*Elle est si belle*,' he tries, anxious to placate the reddened face and show himself properly appreciative.

'You must leave the museum,' the guard announces loudly.

Roy, amazed to hear a complete English sentence coming out of this cracked old face, defends himself. 'I only touched the door,' he protests. Then, 'I'm very sorry.'

'You must leave the museum.' Louder this time.

To himself Roy says: This is ridiculous. He can hardly suppress a laugh. Here he is being scolded, reproved, being thrown out of a venerable French museum as if he were a teenage hooligan. He feels his arm firmly taken at the elbow. The old man's English apparently consists of a single phrase: 'You must leave the museum.'

Bewildered, Roy looks about, and then suddenly understands. *Everyone* is being asked to leave the museum. The sound that a moment ago he had taken for rain was the sound of footsteps moving across the stone floors, of people rapidly leaving the exhibition rooms and heading for the main door. To the stout old guard who is already moving away from him, he mumbles a feeble chant – *merci, merci, merci.*

There are fifty, sixty people, maybe more, working their way to the entrance – where had they come from? Moments ago Roy had looked around and seen only a handful.

He is struck at first by how orderly the crowd is and how silently it moves along. Not one person is screaming or shouting – no one, in fact, is even talking – and how similar, too, they all seem in their breathy, melancholy, measured strides, hurrying through the calm rectangular rooms of crusted statuary and large loaf-shaped tombs; the tapestries, the porcelain, the examples of medieval glass, the paintings on wood. There is only a rattling, insectlike sound of clothing rubbing, swishing, long purposeful strides moving in waves, in a single direction.

And then something happens: for no discernible reason the gait changes. As though a signal has been given – but there has been no signal – everyone is running, and Roy too is running, squeezing through the narrow arches that divide the rooms, swerving, stumbling on his thick-soled shoes. Even the white-haired, cane-bearing couple seen earlier have somehow, by awkward shifts of weight and sideways lurching, contrived to run. A fat young woman with wild hair, a child under her arm, its head bobbing crazily, runs past Roy, and out of her frilled lips comes a wordless bleat of panic, an oink like a pig's squeal. And then the two bony American men brush past, one of them knocking against him and breathing a dutiful, constricted *pardon*.

The overhead lights blink several times. Coins jingle in Roy's pocket. As he runs towards the exit he is thinking of nothing. Or rather, he thinks about how he is thinking of nothing. The cemented accumulation, all he has banked away inside his head, seems suddenly vaporised and lifted; everything outside the minute, *this* minute, falls away, the idle stories that pass through his brain late at night, the alternative choices he might have made, his lazy indifference and absurd fumblings. Newspapers, books, shifts of allegiance. Minor cruelties, a teacher who once said of an essay he'd written, 'Where hath grammar flown?' Meg emerging from the house one winter day, fastening her coat. Inca sculpture and lost phone numbers; a brief flirtation with a very young woman, how it came to nothing; snowbanks; trees; Jenny returning early from camp with a rash on her back; Jenny bringing Kenneth home for the first time and saying with light irony, 'Meet Mr Perfect.' A platter holding an immense turkey, heartless strategies, unremitting dialogue, the names of certain wild flowers, even the minor present pain of arthritis in his left thumb, a thumb broken at the age of eight, bent backwards on the asphalt schoolyard by someone whose name has just this minute slipped away. It has all slipped away. Nothing, not even the smallest spindle of thought, impedes his progress as he runs through room after room toward the main door of the Cluny Museum.

He stumbles at last through the foyer and sees, dreamily, that the ticket booth has been abandoned, the insolent girl vanished. Then he is in the cobbled courtyard, and then the street beyond. There he sees a number of panelled trucks, their windows lowered, the dark squares starred with the faces of boylike soldiers, numbly staring back at him. A few solders stand on the pavement, clustered around the main door, and it maddens Roy to see how one of them lolls, *lolls*, against the wall. 'What happened?' he asks, but already he knows. Nothing has happened, only a false alarm.

One of the young American men is vomiting quietly into a tub of begonias, and the other, he of the sacerdotal face, is standing by and murmuring, *Jesus, Jesus*. The fat girl with wild hair comes over to Roy and tells him she is from New York, Long Island. Roy explains he is from Milwaukee. The stringent circumstances make their brief exchange feel dreamlike and discordant. The white-haired couple explain they are from California. Their serious leathery faces suggest the pathos of good intentions and an unslaked hunger for human contact. They have been coming to France for twenty years, they tell Roy, and have never seen anything like this.

He walks back to the hotel, telling himself that the fresh air will do him good and, in fact, the rhythm of his shoes on the cement does bring calm – a man in a boy's shoes – as does the sight, a mere two streets away, of people selling melons and entering cafés. A well-brushed dog dances on a leash; its owner dances along behind. Every face Roy sees is clothed with the dumb shine of ignorance. He wonders, already he wonders, how he will describe this scene to Meg; he remembers nothing but the old guard tipping his capacious belly toward him and saying, 'You must leave the museum.' And how he ran stumbling out of the museum door into the courtyard. He is emptied out, light-headed, agonisingly alert. He feels he's been as close to the edge of his life as he's ever likely to be.

Meg and Roy Sloan will not always be sitting here at a little square table in La Petite Fourchette dining on marinated crab, roasted lamb cutlets with green beans, followed by a selection of cheeses, followed by sorbet cassis, followed by coffee and by two glasses of brilliantly coloured cognac. The authentic world will sweep them away, attributing their brief incandescence to the lamplight or the shift of weather or the conjoined sense of having escaped what they didn't even know they dreaded.

'Of course you ran,' pretty Meg Sloan says to her husband. 'Anyone would run. There's nothing shameful about wanting to save your own life. I mean, there's nothing selfish about it or cowardly. If the house were on fire, you'd run out of it, wouldn't you? I know I would. I'd run like crazy.'

Her shopping expedition to north Paris has failed. The warehouse, when she finally found it, had been filled with tourists much like herself, women of about her own age and size and possessed of the same financial ease and concentrated fervour. These women carried, too, the accumulated heft of discouragement; the clothes offered for sale were ugly and soiled and brought to mind instances of similar discouragement. Meg tried on one two-hundred-dollar dress that transformed her into an aged dwarf and brought tears to her eyes.

Her diminutive size, her chief vanity, seemed all at once shameful, contrived and unwholesome. She fled to a nearby post office and placed a long-distance call to her daughter in Milwaukee. The call went through quickly, much to her surprise, and caught Jenny in the throes of packing – she had patched things up with Kenneth; an understanding had been reached, a compromise of sorts, and she and the children were about to return to Green Bay. The weather in Wisconsin was glorious, frost at night, but temperatures in the daytime that qualified as Indian summer. The shrubs in the front yard had just started to turn.

Hanging up the telephone, still thrumming with her daughter's voice, its dying vibrancy, Meg had felt divided and dizzy, as though she had stepped into a room where the air was thinned and, at the same time, more tremblingly present. She was afraid she might faint or else choke and, for that reason, took a taxi back to the hotel.

'It was total extravagance,' she tells Roy. 'When I had my *carte orange* right in my purse. And phoning in the middle of the afternoon like that, at the most expensive time. On an impulse. I just felt –'

'It was money well spent,' Roy assures her, knowing he will forever, in one way or another, be called upon for reassurance.

'We talked for ages,' Meg then confesses. 'I could have bought that hideous dress for the same price.'

'Years from now,' he tells her, 'you'll look back and you'll never count the cost. You won't even remember it.'

The Sloans recognise but resist the details of the future, just as Meg knows about but can't see the friable skin of her breasts beneath her white sweater, and Roy the bald, highly burnished spot on the back of his head. They will get older, of course. One of them will die first – the world will allow this to happen – and the other will live on for a time. Their robust North American belief that life consists of stages keeps them from sinking, though ahead of them, in a space the size of this small table, waits a series of intricate compromises: impotence, rusted garden furniture, disordered dreams, and the remembrance of specific events which have been worn smooth and treacherous as the stone steps of ancient buildings. A certain amount of shadowy pathos will accrue between what they remember and what they imagine, and eventually one of them, perhaps lying limply on a tautly made-up bed, will gruesomely sentimentalise this Paris night. The memory will divide and shrink like a bodily protein, and terror, with all its freshness and redemptive power, will give way, easily, easily, to the small rosy singularity of this shaded lamp, and the arc of light that cuts their faces precisely in half.

Accidents

AT HOME MY WIFE is modest. She dresses herself in the morning with amazing speed. There is a flashing of bath towel across the fast frame of her flesh, and then, *voilà*, she is standing there in her pressed suit, muttering to herself and rummaging in her bag for subway tokens. She never eats breakfast at home.

But the minute we hit the French coast – we stay in a vacation flat owned by my wife's brother-in-law – there she is, on the balcony with her bare breasts rising up to the sun. And she has breakfasted, and so have I, on three cups of coffee and a buttered croissant.

Her breasts have remained younger than the rest of her body. When I see her rub them with oil and point them toward the fierce sunlight, I think of the Zurbarán painting in the museum at Montpellier which shows a young and rather daft-looking St. Agatha cheerfully holding out a platter on which her two severed breasts are arranged, ordinary and bloodless as jam pastries.

One morning something odd happened to my wife. She was sitting on the balcony working on her new translation of

Valéry's early poems and she had a cup of coffee before her. I should explain that the dishes and cutlery and cooking things in the flat are supplied, and that this particular coffee cup was made of a sort of tinted glass in a pattern which can be found in any cheap chain store in France. Suddenly, or so she told me later, there was a cracking sound, and her cup lay in a thousand pieces in the saucer.

It had simply exploded. She wondered at first if she had been shot at with an air rifle. There was another apartment building opposite under construction, and at any time of the day workmen could be seen standing on the roof. But clearly it would have required an extraordinary marksman to pick off a cup of coffee like that from such a distance. And when she sifted through the slivers of glass, which she did with extreme care, she found no sign of a pellet.

The incident unnerved her. She put on her blouse when she went out on the balcony later in the day, but I noticed she kept a cup of coffee in the middle of the table as though daring a second explosion to occur.

I knew, though I'm not a scientist, that occasionally tempered glass fractures spontaneously. It's thought to come about by a combination of heat, light and pressure. It happens sometimes to the windshields of automobiles, though it is extremely rare and not entirely understood.

I told all this to my wife. 'I still don't understand how it could have happened,' she said. I explained again, knowing my explanation was vague and lacking in precision. I was anxious to reassure her. I reached down and put my arms around her, and that was how my accident occurred. She turned to look at me, and as she did so, the back of her earring tore the skin of my face.

It was surprising how long the tear was, about four inches in all, and it was deeper than just a scratch, although the blood oozed out slowly, as though with reluctance. We both realised I would require stitches.

The doctor in the Montpellier clinic spoke almost perfect English, but with a peculiar tonelessness, rather like one of those old-fashioned adding machines clicking away. 'You will require a general anaesthetic,' he told me. 'You will be required to remain in the hospital overnight.'

My wife was weeping. She kept saying, 'If only I hadn't turned my head just at that moment.'

The doctor explained that since the hospital was full, I would have to share a room. Always, he said, gesturing neatly with both hands, always at vacation time there were accidents. A special government committee, in fact, had been established to look into this phenomenon of *accidents des vacances*, and someone had suggested that perhaps it might be the simplest solution if vacations were eliminated entirely.

I speak French fluently, having grown up in Montreal, but I have difficulty judging the tone of certain speakers. I don't know when someone – the doctor, for example – is speaking ironically or sincerely; this has always seemed to me to be a serious handicap.

While still under the anaesthetic I was put into a room occupied by a young man who had been in a motorcycle accident. He had two broken legs and a shattered vertebra and was almost completely covered in white plaster. Only his face was uncovered, a young face with closed eyes and smooth skin. I put my hand on my own face which was numb beneath the dressing, and wondered for the first time if I would be left with a scar.

My wife came to sit by my bed for a while. She was no longer crying. She had, in fact, been shopping and had bought a new pale-yellow cardigan with white flowers around the neck, very fresh and springlike. I was touched to see that she had removed her earrings. On her ear lobes there was nothing but a faint dimple, the tiny holes made, she once told me, by her own mother when she was fourteen years old.

There seemed little to talk about, but she had bought a *Herald Tribune*, something she normally refuses to do. She scorns the *Herald Tribune*, its thinness and its effete news coverage. And it's her belief that when you are in another country you should make an attempt to speak and read the language of that country. The last time she allowed herself to buy a *Herald Tribune* was in 1968, the week of Trudeau's first election.

The young man with the broken legs was moaning in his sleep. 'I hope he doesn't go on like this all night,' she said. 'You won't get any sleep at this rate.'

'Don't worry about me,' I said. 'I'll be fine tomorrow.'

'Do you think we should still plan to go over to Aigues Mortes?' she asked, naming the place we try to visit every summer. Aigues Mortes is, as many people have discovered, an extraordinary medieval port with a twelfth-century wall in near-perfect condition. It has become a habit with my wife and me to go there each year and walk around this wall briskly, a distance of two kilometres. After that we take a tour through the Tower of Constance with an ancient and eccentric guide, and then we finish off the afternoon with a glass of white wine in the town square.

'It wouldn't feel like a holiday if we didn't do our usual run to Aigues Mortes,' my wife said in a rather loud cheerful voice, the sort of voice visitors often acquire when they come to cheer the sick.

The man with the broken legs began to moan loudly and, after a minute, to sob. My wife went over to him and asked if she could do anything for him. His eyes were still closed, and she leaned over and spoke into his ear.

'Am I dead?' he asked her in English. 'Did you say I was dead?'

'Of course you aren't dead,' she said, and smiled over her shoulder at me. 'You're just coming out of the anaesthetic and you're not dead at all.'

'You said I was dead,' he said to her in clear carrying British tones. 'In French.'

Then she understood. 'No, we were talking about Aigues Mortes. It's the name of a little town near here.'

He seemed to need a moment to think about this.

'It means *dead waters*,' my wife told him. 'Though it's far from dead.'

This seemed to satisfy him, and he drifted off to sleep again.

'Well,' my wife said, 'I'd better be off. You'll be wanting to get to sleep yourself.'

'Yes,' I said, 'that damned anaesthetic, it's really knocked me for a loop.'

'Shall I leave you the *Herald Tribune*?' she asked, 'or are you too tired to read tonight?'

'You take it,' I told her, 'unless there's any Canadian news in it.'

That's another thing we don't like about the *Herald Tribune*. There's hardly ever any news from home, or if there is, it's condensed and buried on a back page.

She sat down again on the visitor's chair and drew her cardigan close around her. In the last year she's aged, and I'm grieved that I'm unable to help her fight against the puckering of her mouth and the withering away of the skin on her upper arms. She went through the paper page by page, scanning the headlines with a brisk professional eye. 'Hmmm,' she said to herself in her scornful voice.

'Nothing?' I asked.

'Well, here's something.' She folded back the page and began to read. 'Gilles Villeneuve is dead.'

'Who?'

'Gilles Villeneuve. You know, the racing driver.'

'Oh?'

'Let's see. It says Canadian racing driver, killed in practice run. Et cetera. Always claimed racing was dangerous and so on, said a year ago that he'd die on the track.' She stopped. 'Do you want to hear all this?'

'No, that's enough.' I felt the news about Gilles Villeneuve calmly, but I hope not callously. I've never really approved of violent sports, and it seems to me that people foolish enough to enter boxing rings or car races are asking for their own deaths.

'It's sad to die so young,' my wife said as if required to fill the silence I'd left.

The young man in the next bed began to sputter and cough, and once again my wife went over to see if she could do anything.

'You mustn't cry,' she said to him. She reached in her bag for a clean tissue. 'Here, let me wipe those tears away.'

'I don't want to die.' He was blubbering quite noisily, and I think we both felt this might weaken the shell of plaster that enclosed him.

My wife – I forgot to mention that she is still a very beautiful woman – placed her hand on his forehead to comfort him. 'There, there, it's just your legs. You've been sleeping and you're only a little bit confused. Where do you come from?'

He murmured something.

'What did you say?'

'Sheffield. In England.'

'Maybe I can telephone someone for you. Has the hospital sent a message to your people?'

It was an odd expression for her to use – *your people*. I don't think I've ever heard her use that particular phrase before.

'It's all right,' he said. He had stopped crying, but my wife kept her hand on his forehead for another moment or two until he dropped off to sleep.

I must have dropped off to sleep as well because when I opened my eyes she had gone. And after that it was morning and a nurse was opening the shutters and twittering something at me in French. The bed next to mine was empty, and she began to strip off the sheets.

'Where is he?' I asked her in my old formal schoolboy French. 'Where's my comrade with the broken legs?'

'*Il est mort*,' she said in the same twittering singsong.

'But he can't be dead. His legs were broken, that's all.'

'The spinal cord was damaged. And there were other injuries. Inside.'

A minute later the doctor came in and had a look under my dressing. 'You perhaps will have a little scar,' he said. 'For a woman this is terrible, of course. But for a man . . . ' He smiled and revealed pink gums. 'For a man it is not so bad.'

'I understand that he's died,' I said, nodding at the stripped bed.

'Ah yes. Multiple injuries. There was no hope, from the moment he was brought in here yesterday.'

'Just a young man,' I said.

He was pressing the bandage back into place. '*Les accidents des vacances*. Every year the same. What can one do? One should stay home, sit in the garden, be tranquil.'

When my wife comes for me in half an hour or so, I will have prepared what I'll say to her. I know, of course, that the first thing she'll ask me is: how is the young man from Sheffield? She will ask this before she inquires about whether I've had a good night or whether I'm suffering pain. I plan my words with precision.

This, luckily, is my métier, the precise handling of words. Mine is a profession that is close to being unique; at least I know of no one else who does the same sort of work on a full-time basis.

I am an abridger. When I tell people, at a party for instance, that I am an abridger, their faces cloud with confusion and I always have to explain. What I do is take the written work of other people and compress it. For example, I am often hired by book clubs to condense or abridge the books they publish. I also abridge material that is broadcast over the radio.

It's a peculiar profession, I'm the first to admit, but it's one I fell into by accident and that I seem suited for. Abridging requires a kind of inverse creativity. One must have a sharp eye for turning points and a seismic sensitivity for the fragile, indeed invisible, tissue that links one event with another. I'm well paid for my work, but I sometimes think that the degree of delicacy is not appreciated. There are even times when it's necessary to interfere with the truth of a particular piece, and, for the sake of clarity and balance, exercise a small and inconspicuous act of creativity which is entirely my own. I've never thought of this as dishonesty and never felt that I had tampered with the integrity of a work.

My wife will be here soon. I'll watch her approach from the window of my hospital room. She still walks with a kind of boyish clip-clop, as though determined to possess the pavement with each step. This morning she'll be wearing her navy blazer; it's chilly, but probably it will warm up later in the day. Probably she'll have her new yellow cardigan on underneath, but I won't be able to tell from here if she's wearing earrings. My guess is that she won't be. In her hand she'll have a small cloth bag, and I can imagine that this contains the picnic we'll be taking with us to Aigues Mortes.

'And how is *he*?' she's going to ask me in a few minutes from now. 'How is our poor young friend with the broken legs?'

'He's been moved to a different place.' I'll say this with a small shrug, and then I'll say, quickly, before she has a chance to respond, 'Here, let me carry that bag. That's too heavy for you.'

Of course, it's not heavy at all. We both know that. How could a bag containing a little bread and cheese and perhaps two apples be heavy?

It doesn't matter. She'll hand me the bag without a word, and off we'll be.

Collision

TODAY THE SKY is solid blue. It smacks the eye. A powerful tempered ceiling stretched across mountain ranges and glittering river systems: the Saône, the Rhine, the Danube, the Drina. This unimpaired blueness sharpens the edges of the tile-roofed apartment block where Martä Gjatä lives and hardens the wing tips of the little Swiss plane that carries Malcolm Brownstone to her side. What a dense, dumb, depthless blue it is, this blue; but continually widening out and softening like a magically reversed lake without a top or bottom or a trace of habitation or a thought of what its blueness is made of or what it's *for*.

But take another look. The washed clarity is deceiving, the yawning transparency is fake. What we observe belies the real nature of the earth's atmosphere which is adrift, today as any day, with biographical debris. It's everywhere, a thick swimmy blizzard of it, more ubiquitous by far than earthly salt or sand or humming electrons. Radio waves are routinely pelted by biography's mad static, as Martä Gjatä, trying to tune into the Vienna Symphony, knows only too well. And small aircraft, such as the one carrying Malcolm

Brownstone eastward across Europe, occasionally fall into its sudden atmospheric pockets. The continents and oceans are engulfed. We are, to speak figuratively, as we more and more do, as we more and more *must* do, smothering in our own narrative litter-bag.

And it keeps piling up. Where else in this closed lonely system can our creaturely dust go but up there on top of the storeyed slag heap? The only law of biography is that everything, every particle, must be saved. The earth is alight with it, awash with it, scoured by it, made clumsy and burnished by its steady accretion. Biography is a thrifty housewife, it's an old miser. Martä Gjatä's first toddling steps are preserved and her first word – the word *sjaltë*, which means honey – and her dead father's coldly aimed praise – 'For a girl you have sharp ways about you.'

These are fragments, you say, cracker crumbs, lint in your shirt pocket, dizzy atoms. They're off the map, off the clock, floating free, spring pollen. That's the worst of it: there's nothing selective about biography's raw data, no sorting machine, no briny episodes underlined in yellow pencil or provided with bristling asterisks – it's all here, the sweepings and the leavings, the most trivial personal events encoded with history. Biography – it sniffs it out, snorts it up.

Here, to give an example, is Malcolm Brownstone's birth squawl from fifty-odd years ago, a triple-note *yawolll* of outrage bubbling up through the humid branches of his infant lungs, and again, *yawolll*. And the sleepless night he spent, aged twelve, in a rain-soaked tent in the Indian Hills, and also the intensity with which he reads newspapers and promptly forgets most of what he reads, and his dreamy neurotic trick of picking up a spoon and regarding his bent face in the long sad oval of its bowl.

In a future world, in a post-meltdown world, biography may get its hands on the kind of cunning conversion that couples mass and energy. We may learn, for instance, to heat our houses with it, build bigger lasers with its luminous run-off or more concentrated fictive devices.

But for the time being, every narrative scrap is equally honoured and dishonoured. Everything goes into the same democratic hopper, not excluding the privately performed acts of deceased spinners and weavers, or contemporary ashtray designers and manicurists, or former cubists and cabinet ministers, and young mothers pushing prams and poets who seek to disarm their critics – even these seemingly inconsequential acts enter the biographical aggregation and add to the weight of the universe.

It's crowded, *is it ever crowded*! Inside a single biographical unit, there are biographical clouds and biographical shadows, biographical pretexts and strategies and time-buying sophistries and hair-veined rootlets of frazzled memory. Long complex biographies, for example, have been registered and stored for all the ancestors, friends and acquaintances of the Japanese pop singer, who right this minute is strolling in the sunshine down the Champs-Elysées wearing a leopard (genuine) jacket and a pair of pale pressed jeans. There are detailed dossiers for each of the twelve girls and twenty-six boys who competed for the state whistling championship in Indianapolis in 1937. Every particular is recorded, and also every possibility and random trajectory, even those, to cite the case of Martä G. and Malcolm B., that have only a partial or wishful existence.

Written biography, that's another matter, *quite* another matter! Memoirs, journals, diaries. Works of the bio-imagination are as biodegradable as orange peels. Out they go. Psssst – they blast themselves to vapour, cleaner and blonder than the steam from a spotless kettle. Nothing sticks but the impulse to get it down. Consider Martä Gjatä's four great-grandfathers. Three of them were illiterate shepherds; the fourth was a famous autodidact, a traveller, a minor politician, a poet of promise and, in his old age, the writer of a thick book entitled *The Story of My Life* (Lexoni Bardhë Këtë). Copies of this book can still be found in rural libraries throughout the Balkans, but not a word of the text has entered the cosmology of biography, of which the four great-grandfathers, shepherds and sage alike, have a more or less equal share.

Martä herself does not keep a diary, living as she does in a part of the world where one's private thoughts are best kept private. She is a droll, intelligent woman of wide-ranging imagination, as anyone on the streets of her city will tell you, but the one thing she cannot imagine is her encounter, just a few hours away, with the large, clean-faced, bald-headed North American named Malcolm Brownstone. The meeting, if such a slight wordless collision can be called a meeting, will originate in the lace-curtained coffee salon of the Hotel Turista. She will arrive early, a few minutes before Malcolm Brownstone, and will wear a green checked linen dress and polished leather shoes with rather higher than usual heels.

She is a citizen, indeed a Party member, of a small ellipsoid state in eastern Europe resembling in its dimensions a heaped-up apple tart viewed in profile. The top crust presses northward toward a sparsely populated mountainous area that still erupts from time to time with primitive vendettas whose roots go back to the time of the Turkish occupation. This is harsh terrain for the most part, with scanty soil and rough roads, but the southern corner of the geo-pie plate tilts onto a green curve of the Adriatic, and this short, favoured stretch is about to be developed into a full-scale tourist facility. At present there is only a four-storey concrete hostel suitable for the busloads of students or workers who have lately been encouraged to come here for their twenty-four-day vacation period. But the time for expansion has arrived; even in this part of the world people are talking foreign currency; foreign currency's the key. The beaches here are broad and breezy, and despite an overrun of tufted sea grass, the potential's unlimited. A recreational consultant, Malcolm Brownstone, is being sent, today, by an international cooperative agency to advise on the initial stages of development.

A mere thirty miles from this future fantasyland is the capital city where Martä Gjatä lies. Hers is a country often confused with toy principalities like Andorra and Monaco, but in fact it is a complex ensemble of mountains and streambeds and rich deposits of iron and chromium and annual rainfall statistics going back to the year 1910. There are also some Roman ruins and a number of mosques, now turned into museums, and the busy capital city (pop. 200,000) where Martä and her mother and her mother's brother Miço live. (A fourth member of the household is old Zana, a family servant before Liberation, now lingering on as an honorary aunt and in winter sharing her bed with Uncle Miço, an *Ethnoggraphi Emerti* at the National University.) The apartment is small. The cooking facilities are rudimentary and the food somewhat monotonous, but Martä, aged forty-two, prides herself on creating a style to suit her confining circumstances. She makes a delicious *mjarzadjpër*, which is a mixture of cabbage, cheese and onions spiced with pepper.

And the green checked dress she wears today is one she made herself.

She is a worker in the state film industry which last year produced fourteen feature films and more than twenty documentaries. She is also one of the few women to have been promoted to *Direktor*. This was three years ago. Before that time she was a celebrated film actress. *The Scent of Flowers* and *Glorious Struggle* are her most beloved films and the ones that have made her famous in her country. In the first of these she played the daughter of a patriot. She wore a kerchief and an embroidered apron (borrowed from Zana, since there was no such thing as a wardrobe department in the early days) and served glasses of raki to filthy, wounded soldiers, falling passionately in love with one of them, a mere boy whose legs had been crudely amputated after battle. (In real life this young man, Dimitro Puro, had been run over by a tractor.) The film closes with a village wedding scene (Dimitro and Martä) that is exuberantly folkloric but sadly muted by the spotty black and white film then in use, colour film having been forbidden before the cultural revolution of 1979.

The cultural revolution lasted two days and consisted of a letter written by Martä Gjatä to the Minister of Kulture pleading for a change from black and white film to bourgeois colour. Martä delivered the request herself, placing it in the Minister's hand and giving his wide cheek a playful pat. That was the first day. The next day she had her answer, a typed directive delivered to her apartment saying: 'If you think the time has come, my darling Martä, then the time has come.' Both letters were immediately destroyed, though they continue to exist as part of the biographical patrimony, along with all other gestures, events, and texts of this curious period. Biography works both sides of the street. Iron curtain, velvet curtain, it's all the same to biography.

In her final film, *Glorious Struggle*, Martä played the perplexed middle-aged mother – though she was herself still in her thirties – of a brilliant eighteen-year-old daughter who elects a career in Civil Engineering. The film was immensely popular, but was later criticised for its too obvious didacticism, its repetitious and ultimately tiresome plea for gender equality. Still, Martä's performance, her face passing through wider and wider rings of comprehension, raised it to the level of near-art, and there was talk for a time of international distribution. 'No' came an order from higher – much higher – up. 'Not yet.'

A year ago the Minister of Kulture died. He and Martä had been lovers for some twenty years, but out of oversight or mutual evasion had not married. His death was caused by choking; a laurel leaf buried in a mutton stew caught in his throat. This was during a dinner at the Rumanian Embassy. He was not yet fifty, still a relatively young man with dark hair rising cleanly from a blank forehead. He might have grown beautiful with time; white hair might have given him distinction, putting edges on his large weak face and blunted features, connoting kindness or refinement. Maybe.

Martä was away at the time of his death, directing a documentary on the glass industry in the north of the country. This was not at all the kind of film she was used to working on, and the thought came to her that her lover had sent her away deliberately in order to get her out of the way. She has no proof of this, only a suspicion that confirms itself by a muttering inattention. She knows what she knows, just as her tongue apprehends the crenellations of her teeth but can't describe them. The love affair had grown desultory on both sides; occasionally she had felt herself straining to play refining fire to her lover's rather dainty brutality. 'Little Martä,' he often said, kissing her small breasts and giving a laugh that came out a snicker.

There is no laugh like a snicker. We want to cover our ears with shame and shut it out, but in biography the snicker lives on, a laugh trying to be a good laugh but not knowing how. Like radioactive ash or like the differentiated particles of luminescence that cling to the dark side of the globe, the chambered beginnings, middles and ends of human encounters persist, including aberrations, nervous tics and malfunctions of the spirit. A snicker cannot easily be disposed of, certainly not a habitual snicker, and, thinking about her lover after his death, Martä is unable to imagine him without the stale accompaniment of snorting air. It condenses on her neck and eyes. Her remembrances taste of yellow metal, not nostalgia, and her lover's glum, puffy face continues to retreat behind a series of small puckered explosions. She did not return to the capital for his official internment and memorial ceremony, claiming quite rightly that the documentary on the glass industry must come first.

Glass has been manufactured in Martä's country only since the 1950s, before which time it was imported from Yugoslavia. The quality of domestic glass is poor. (Tumblers and wine glasses possess an ineradicable greenish tinge, and it has proven difficult to achieve quality control; household glassware is either too thick or too thin and often breaks the first time it's put into hot water.) But there has been considerable success with industrial glass, perhaps because a higher priority has been assigned, with the result that there is now a surplus of such products, and it has been decided to seek foreign markets. Hence the making of the documentary film.

Martä has always loved glass, and her biography is punctuated with references to the colours of glass, the clarity, the fluid shapes and artful irregularities, to the opaque glass grotto of her earliest memory, the time as a young child when she scratched her name, Martä Gjatä, on a frost-coated window, putting the scrapings of shirred ice on her tongue where they deliciously melted. Around her neck, on a fine chain, she wears a pendant of seaglass, a gift from the legless actor/soldier, now a translator of textbooks, who played opposite her in *The Scent of Flowers*. A shelf in her apartment holds an antique goblet of lead crystal brought back from Venice by the Minister of Kulture shortly before his death. When Martä flicks at it, hard, with her duster (a pair of old underpants), she is forced to balance the slack fleshiness of his face against their many tender hours of love, sometimes in the woods outside the city, sometimes very quietly on the dusty linoleum floor of a storeroom in the basement of the Palace of Kulture. She has time while dusting for her memories to bloom into flower silhouettes and glide slowly past her, a shadow parade with a cracked element of confusion. She's glad at these times that she has her work to distract her and deaden her thoughts.

The creation of the documentary presented certain structural problems, and these Martä solved by dividing the glass-making process into a series of elegant steps, and running beneath them a counter-process of poetic permutation that sent transparency flowing backward into elemental sand. She spent several weeks editing the footage, insisting on doing it herself, working even on Sunday, which was the day she had once spent walking in the woods outside the city with her lover. The work took her mind off the unfilled space ahead of her which seemed now, with its blocky weekends and solid uncomplicated months, too large to contain her small patient undertakings and too indifferent to provide the sort of convulsion she is secretly hoping for.

For its kind, the glass documentary is a success – thirty minutes of witty, visual exposition in which even the machinery of the glass factory seems to be smiling. It has already been dubbed into four languages, French, Italian, German and English – not one of which Martä understands, languages being her single failing – and an illustrated catalogue has been prepared. Martä has brought the catalogues to the Hotel Turista today where she will shortly be meeting a two-man trade delegation from Austria.

She is early, seated at a low, rather battered table, drinking coffee. Her cardboard satchel of film catalogues is on the floor beside her. From time to time she peers out of the window through the lace curtains and sees that the blue sky is now blackened with cloud, what looks like forewarnings of rain. The Austrians apparently are still in the dining room, taking their time over lunch, and the coffee salon is empty except for Martä herself in her checked dress and, at the far end of the room, a bald-headed man bent heavily over a pile of papers. Martä glances in his direction and identifies him as a foreigner – there's a certain opacity about him, a largeness and lope to his shoulders and arms, and a visitor's face on his face – but she has no way of knowing who he is or why he's here.

The arrival of a Recreation and Resort Consultant (Malcolm Brownstone's official title) is a portent, a sign the country is opening up and welcoming the high-tech wizardry of the West. Even more remarkable is the notion of exploitable hedonism, a new idea in this country and one which Malcolm ironically represents (a biographical fault line here, since he is known to be a hard-working man of puritan tastes, but one whose last thirty years have been beamed in the direction of pleasure).

He is comfortable with the lace curtains in the Hotel Turista, more than comfortable; he loves them and is reminded of the small frame house where he grew up, a rented house with a curved brow of shingles and two upstairs windows like staring eyes. The house held many of the usual mid-continental variables: bibles, hairbrushes, folded blankets on shelves, an enamel breadbox with the word 'bread' stamped on its hinged lid, a modest lean-bodied father with a mild passion for horseshoe pitching and a mother with a tinkling laugh and reserves of good health. There were two sisters, both of them scholarly, both of them pretty. The sisters, and Malcolm too, made the most of their opportunities, never suspecting that their opportunities were limited. They married, bore children, were rewarded and punished, sought friends, took vacations, saved their money, also spent it, and grew older, making regular compulsory deposits as they went along to biography's vast holdings.

Out of all this planetary chaff it might be thought that a mathematical model could be fashioned, an orderly superbio whose laws and forms are predictable and reduced. But this is where anarchy enters in, or, depending on your perspective, systematic rebellion. At various times, for instance, it has been forbidden to eat tomatoes, to poach pheasants, to curse God, to strangle infants and to break promises. Still, people did these things and survived and contributed their chapters of anomaly and exception. The otherwise cases, the potent singularities – they also survive, along with precarious half-heard harmonies and the leaky disrepair of memory (Malcolm Brownstone's mystic experience on a Ferris wheel in 1947 when he observed curls of crisp gold ravelling off the sun; Martä Gjatä's love letter – to a paraplegic film actor – which she later tore into forty-three pieces and hurled into a weedy pond).

One of Malcolm Brownstone's first undertakings as a young architect was the development of a 'theme park' in a region of his own country that seemed to possess no outstanding characteristics (high unemployment figures notwithstanding), and very little in the way of historical resonance. There was nothing, *nothing*, he could draw on other than the longings of displaced agricultural workers to become once again solvent and respectable. These longings he translated into dreams, and thus Dreamland was born, a commercial wonder, then as now. It contains a Dream City, a Dream Palace, a Dream Mountain, a Dream-o-rama where Dreamobiles race along banked curves, and a Dream-Stream on which floats a Dreamboat commandeered by Dream Maids dispensing at reasonable prices such dream favours as Dreamy Candy Floss and Dreamy-Ice.

Wisely he bought shares and immediately incorporated himself, an act of biographical distortion in which a single life sometimes gives the impression of multiple tracks. He grew rich, which did not surprise him. What surprised him was his baldness at the age of thirty-five. His biography is starred with attempts to reconcile himself to his few last scurrying hairs and the melon of scalp rising above an eave of bone. He cannot pass a mirror, even today, without a stab of confusion – who is this person? Today at the airport he was met by an official car; the driver, he noticed, had a headful of thick, thrusting hair. The two of them drove silently past fields of cabbages and women with scarves wrapped around their heads leading donkeys down the road, but all he could see was the driver's strongly rooted hair and his own slicked skull bounding whitely off the rear-view mirror.

He is an earnest man, an Organisation man, but with the kind of dislocated piety that the Organisation finds awkward. His ordered, monotone missions to marginal-economy countries are undertaken with unfashionable fervour. He wants, he says aloud, to help people. His sense of vocation arrived suddenly during a trip he and his wife took to North Africa in 1976. Standing in a village souk, his eyes travelled accidentally past a wool dyer's stall to the dark room beyond where he beheld an earthen floor and children who were of an age to be in school. He seemed to hear the words: 'You are close to discovering a way to make life meaningful.' A month later, in a mood of panic and high drama, he disincorporated himself – another bio blip – and joined the Organisation as a dollar-a-year man.

His wife sniffled and wept. She hated to travel, to pack and unpack, to plug her hairdryer into complicated converters and risk danger. On one occasion she was startled by a large oily beetle that climbed out of a bath drain. She had frequent gastric upsets and skin rashes. Some of the countries where they were sent had unreliable water supplies and incomprehensible languages (neither she nor her husband had any aptitude for foreign languages) and systems of public morality that seemed whimsically derived from the demands of long-standing hunger.

Two years after Malcolm joined the Organisation, his wife died of a stroke. Her last words before slipping into the coma that ended her life were, 'You were always such a cold potato.'

That's what he lives with, this icy epitaph – not even, in fact, true – and his awareness, always with him, of his scraped head. The two images overlap cruelly – potato/head – and churn him to action. Spareness, openness, bareness – these he avoids for the organised compression of public gathering places, parks and fairs, playgrounds and carnivals, pleasure domes and civic squares, the whole burning convivial world where he feels the massed volume of other lives. The truth is, though he doesn't realise it, there is not one corner of our cold green rocky world that isn't silted down by biography's buzzing accumulation. It's a wonder we can still breathe, a miracle we can still move about and carry on with the muffled linearity that stretches between the A of birth and the B of death. Malcolm Brownstone imagines that he is two-thirds along that mortal line, an alarming thought but also a comforting one.

Today, in the coffee salon of the Hotel Turista, he is joined by three *functionari* from the Ministry of Interior Development. They are all of them men with short necks and copious hair – is there no end to this hair? – and dressed alike in suits so dark that the folds of cloth are without shadows. Against Malcolm's vast beige wall of tweed they seem to merge one into the other. An interpreter is necessarily present. A very young woman, still a student, she has made an attempt at fashion by pinning a crocheted collar to a plain brown sweater. This collar she touches now and then as she transforms Malcolm's preliminary recommendations into the furze and petals and throaty moss of the national language. Her biographical density is powerful, since very little as yet has been expended, and it hurts Malcolm's heart to look at her, the way she fingers her collar and twists an earring as she exchanges the sprawled flowers of her native tongue for the thudding bricks of his own English.

It puzzles him, but only a little, that official business in this part of the world should be conducted in the homey, lace-curtained public rooms of hotels rather than in offices or boardrooms. He is not at all sure that such offices and boardrooms exist. But what does it matter, he asks himself, as long as progress is made.

And in the next two hours, between three-thirty and five-thirty, two small international agreements are reached, one in each end of the coffee salon. The room darkens subtly as though in acknowledgement. Raki is ordered and cakes are brought around.

To her Austrian visitors Martä Gjatä delivers nothing, promises nothing, but through a burly boy of an interpreter persuades them that their opportunities will be diminished if they return home without her explanatory brochures and a copy of her film which has been given the engaging title *Jepnï Nje Lutëm (A Gift of Brightness)*.

Malcolm Brownstone has determinedly sold his vision to his hosts, assuring them that Pleasure with a capital P is the springboard not only of profit but of progress, that healthy relaxed bodies roasted by the sun and bathed in a benign sea are all the more ready to stand on guard for the State. Though he won't actually visit the site until the following morning, he has already studied the pertinent maps, charts, graphs, blueprints and photographs. He mentions matching funds, contract requirements, climate variables, the components of tide, wind, and hours of annual sunshine.

By chance or perhaps by some diminution of an electric charge running from one end of the room to the other, the two meetings break up at the same moment. The Austrian duo shakes hands with Martä and heads for the *boîte de nuit* in the basement of the hotel where they will while away a few hours with green beer and illicit dancers. They kindly suggest that Martä join them, but she declines. She is expected at home, she says; she must catch her bus at the People's Square.

The three dark-suited *functionari*, through the medium of their blushing translator, bid good evening to their distinguished guest, Malcolm Brownstone. They wish him a pleasing night. They are sorry, they say, that the rain has spoiled the evening, but the countryside has been needing such a wetting. His suggestions have greatly animated them and they look forward to travelling with him on the morrow to the coast. A car will call for him at eight-thirty and it is hoped that this very hour is agreeable.

Badly translated languages fill Malcolm with sentiment, touching his primal sense of what a language should be, every word snugged in a net of greeting. He is charmed by inversions. He welcomes the derangement of grammar and the matching derangement of his senses. Affection surges. He would like to embrace these three chunky men, as well as the earnest translator who is now giggling helplessly and struggling into a raincoat. Instead he bows elegantly, like an oversized actor, and shakes hands all round. A minute later he finds himself, too suddenly, alone.

A walk is what he needs. A stroll on the Boulevard Skopjerlë, at dusk, at twilight, a look at the famous People's Square in the centre of the city. Outside the rain is pouring down, but luckily in his briefcase he has a folding umbrella, a marvel of hinged ribs and compacted nylon. He never travels without it.

At the wide front door of the hotel – marble flooring stained and splitting – he collides with Martä Gjatä. She salutes him with her droll eyes and the smallest of shrugs. *Rain* is what her look says, *rain and me without an umbrella.* She bites her lower lip and smiles.

The smile might mean anything. Malcolm interprets it as the spasm of tension that often follows a moment of disconnection. He feels the same tension himself, and so returns the smile, but doubles the kilowatts. A real smile; no cold potato here, but a man of warmth and spontaneity; charming, helpful.

Not only does Martä not have her umbrella with her, she has no raincoat, not even a square of plastic to tie around her head. She doesn't mind about this. It's the cardboard briefcase she's worrying about; will it melt away in this deluge, and what about the rest of the brochures? They'll be ruined. She takes a tentative step forward, one high-heeled shoe advancing through the doorway and onto the flooded marble steps, then quickly retreats to the dry lobby.

Ssschwippp – the noise of an umbrella unfurling, Malcolm's made-in-Montreal umbrella; a cunning button pressed, and *voilà*! He gestures broadly at Martä and then at the umbrella. His forehead is working rhythmically, saying the unsayable in lines of brow.

In response Martä swings a dramatic arm in the direction of the open door, a perennial actress with unstartled eyes and a cheerful shrug of complicity. She points to the cardboard valise, *helpless, helpless*, and pulls a rueful face.

Time to take charge. Malcolm nods northward in the direction of the People's Square. A query, a proposition. He touches his tweed chest, a vigorous me-too sign and, with surprising delicacy for such a large person, mimes the classic gesture of invitation, a hand uncurled, beckoning, one finger leading and the others following quickly. Why not? his look says.

Why not? Martä mimes back. No coyness here, not at age forty-two, not from a woman whose biography drills straight through to struggle and achievement and recent pools of terrible loneliness. She ducks under the umbrella and together they set off, down the broad marble steps, a turn to the right smoothly performed, and then along the wide pavement skirting the boulevard.

'You a visitor here also?' asks Malcolm, shouting above the noise of the battering rain and reverting to the wooden English he uses when visiting foreign countries.

'*Ko yon skoni?*' Martä asks, waving a pretty arm, baring her teeth.

'A rainy night,' Malcolm says loudly.

'*Por farë feni* (with great pleasure),' Martä replies.

They both stop suddenly and smile. The futility of language. The impossibility.

Hundreds of people fill the street, some of them running, only a few equipped with umbrellas, most of them comically drenched. Who would have thought the weather would turn so suddenly! Men, women and children. The end of the working day. Everyone seems to be carrying a bundle of some sort, vegetables or kindling or books, and these they attempt to shield from the downpour. Under Malcolm's strong black umbrella Martä and her cardboard case stay dry. She has given up on conversation; so has Malcolm.

They step with care. Portions of the boulevard have been smoothed with concrete, but in other places the old cobbles poke through, making the surface tricky, especially for Martä in her high-heeled shoes. In order to keep her balance (and because it is difficult for a short woman to walk with a tall man under an umbrella) she takes Malcolm's arm. Not a bold gesture, not at all, but a forthcoming one, also intimate. It is likely that Malcolm extended his elbow slightly by way of entreaty – half a centimetre would have done it, would have given permission; an old-worldly habit to walk arm-in-arm, emphatically neutral but with a ripple of protective tribute.

The distance between the Hotel Turista and the People's Square is only a kilometre, a mere stroll, 0.6 of a mile. The rain grows more intense, but instead of hurrying them along, it slows them down. First Malcolm must adjust his long steps to match Martä's and, after a minute or two of faltering, of amused back and forth glances, they find their ideal stride, a strolling, rolling gait, right and left, right and left. Malcolm brings his elbow closer to his body so that the back of Martä's tucked hand is in contact with the large damp paleness of his jacket. There it stays, there it fuses.

Ahead of them the lights of the People's Square blink unsteadily. It is the slashing of the rain that gives this look of unsteadiness. Lights seen through a whorl of weather throb rather than shine, producing a rhythmic pulse that is always trying to mend itself but never catching up. Martä and Malcolm are locked together by this rhythm, left and right, left and right, one body instead of two. If only they could walk like this forever. Malcolm has spent his whole life arriving at this moment; this is the best bit of walking he's ever going to do, and it seems to last and last, one quarter-hour unfolding into a measureless present.

Martä, dazed by a distortion of time and light, thinks how this round black umbrella gives an unasked-for refuge, how the rain becomes a world in itself, how the kilometre of rutted city street has become a furrow of love. It will never end, she thinks, knowing it is about to.

Biography, that old buzzard, is having a field-day, running along behind them picking up all the bits and pieces. Biography is used to kinks and wherewithal, it expects to find people in odd pockets, it's used to surges of speechless passion that come out of nowhere and sink without a murmur. It doesn't care. It doesn't even have the decency to wait until Martä and Malcolm get to the People's Square, shake hands, go their separate ways and resume their different versions of time travel, not to collide again. This isn't one of Martä's movies, this is life. This is biography. Nothing matters except for the harvest, the gathering in, the adding up, the bringing together, the whole story, the way it happens and happens and goes on happening.

Others

FOR THEIR HONEYMOON, Robert and Lila went to France. Neither of them had been to Europe before, but Lila's mother had given them a surprisingly generous cheque, and they said to each other: why not?

They started out in Normandy, and their first night there, as they sat puzzling over the menu, a man approached them. He was an English civil servant on holiday. 'Excuse me,' he said, 'I overheard you and your wife speaking English, and I wonder if I might ask an enormous favour of you.'

The favour was to cash a personal cheque – the hotel in the village was being sticky for some reason. Robert agreed to cash it – it was only for fifty pounds – but with some concern. The world, after all, was full of con artists with trustworthy faces, and one couldn't be too careful.

The cheque went through, however, with no trouble, and the Englishman now sends Robert and Lila Christmas greetings every year. He signs them with a joint signature – Nigel and Jane – and adds a few words about the weather, the state of their health (both his and Jane's) and then thanks them yet again for coming to their rescue in Normandy. This has been going on now for twenty-five years.

Lila's grandfather was William White Westfield, the prosperous Toronto lawyer who, in the twenties, wrote a series of temperance novels that were printed by a church-owned press and distributed free to libraries across Ontario.

When Robert married Lila, her mother's wedding gift was a set of these books – this, of course, was in addition to the honeymoon cheque. 'Even if you never read them, Robert,' she said, 'I know you'll be amused by the titles.'

He was. *Journey to Sobriety. The Good Wife's Victory, A Farewell to Inner Cravings* and, his favourite, *Tom Taylor, Battles and Bottles*. Robert and Lila displayed the books in a little bookcase that Robert made out of bricks and plain pine boards. It gave their apartment a look of solidarity, a glow. They lived, when they were first married, in an old duplex just north of High Park that had three rooms, all painted in deep postwar colours – a purple kitchen, a Wedgwood-blue bedroom, and a Williamsburg-green living room. That winter they sanded the living room floor by hand. Later, this became their low-water mark: 'Remember when we were so broke we couldn't afford to rent a floor sander.' It took them a whole month, square foot by square foot, to sand their way through the sticky old varnish. Robert, who was preparing for exams, remembers how he would study for an hour – memorising the names of the cranial nerves or whatever – and then sand for an hour.

When they finished at last with the sanding and with the five coats of wax, and when Robert had passed his examinations, they bought a bottle of cheap wine, and sat in the middle of the shining floor drinking it. Lila lifted her glass toward the shelf of temperance books and said, 'Cheers.'

'Cheers' was what Nigel and Jane had written on their first Christmas card. Just a simple 'Cheers, and again our hearty thanks.'

The next winter they wrote, or rather Nigel wrote, 'A damp winter, but we've settled into our new house and find it comfortable.'

By coincidence, Robert and Lila had moved as well – to a new apartment that had an elevator and was closer to the hospital where Robert was interning. Thinking of Nigel and Jane and their many other friends, Lila arranged to have the mail forwarded to the new address. She missed the old duplex, especially the purple kitchen with its high curving cornices. She suspected Robert of having a cyst of ambition, hard as a nut. She was right. This made her feel lonely and gave her a primal sense of deprivation, but she heard in her head a voice saying that the deprivation was deserved.

It was only at night, when she and Robert lay in each other's arms, that everything slipped back into its proper place. Her skin became mysteriously feathered, like an owl's or some other fast-flying night bird. 'Open, open,' she begged the dark air of their little bedroom, and often it did.

It was different for Robert, who felt himself settling into marriage like a traveller without provisions. Sleeping with Lila in the first year of their marriage, he often thought: How can I use this moment? What can it teach me?

But finally he let himself be persuaded that he had come under the power of love, and that he was helpless.

*

Robert and Lila had a baby that was stillborn. It must not be thought of as a tragedy, friends told them; it was nature's way of weeding out the imperfect. They left soon afterward for three weeks in England because they were persuaded that a change of scene would do them good. The flight was very long, but smooth. Fresh Canadian blueberries were served on the plane, and all the passengers piled off, smiling at each other with blue teeth. 'We should get in touch with Nigel and Jane,' said Lila with her blue mouth.

But when they tried to find them in the telephone book, they discovered they weren't listed. There was nothing to be done. The Christmas cards had carried no return address, only a London postmark, and so Robert and Lila were forced to admit defeat. Both of them were more disappointed than they said.

The year before, Nigel had written: 'Our garden gives us great pleasure.' Lila had felt envious and wished she had a garden to give her pleasure.

Both Lila and Robert liked to stay in bed on Sunday morning and make love, but occasionally, four or five times a year, they went to church. There was pleasure to be had in passing through a set of wide oak doors into the calm carpeted Protestant sanctuary, and they enjoyed singing the familiar old hymns, Robert for their simple melodies and Lila for their shapely words which seemed to meet in the final verse like a circle completed. 'Reclothe me in my rightful mind,' was a phrase she loved, but was puzzled by. What was her rightful mind? All autumn she'd wondered.

At Christmas, the card from England came zipping through the mail slot with the message, 'An exceptional winter. Our pond has frozen over completely, and Jane has taken up ice skating, North-American style.'

Robert read the message over several times. Each inky letter was crisply formed and the Ts were crossed with merry little banners. 'How can they have a pond if they live in London?' he asked. He was thinking about Jane, imagining her whirling and dashing to and fro in a sky-blue skating costume and showing a pronounced roundness of thigh.

'Do you have any recollection at all of what Nigel looked like?' Lila asked Robert once, but Robert couldn't remember anything about him except that he had looked respectable and solid, and not much older than himself. Neither of them could remember Jane at all.

Lila took a job teaching in a French school, but quit six weeks later when she discovered she was pregnant. Twin boys were born. They were exquisite, lively and responsive, following with their quick little eyes the faces of their parents, the turning blades of a butterfly mobile and bright lights of all kinds. Robert and Lila carried them into the big chilly Protestant church one rainy Sunday and had them officially christened. The little house they rented filled up overnight with the smell of talcum powder and oats cooking; Robert became an improbable night visitor who smelled dark and cold in his overcoat. From across the ocean came the message: 'Summer found us back in Normandy, reliving old memories.'

'Where does the time go?' Robert said one morning in a voice that was less a lament than a cry of accomplishment. It seemed to him a good thing for time to pass quickly. He wondered sometimes, when he went off in the mornings, especially in the winter, if work wasn't just a way of coping with time. He also wondered, without jealousy or malice, what kind of salary Nigel pulled down.

They were surprised at how quickly routines and habits accrued. Patterns, rhythms, ways of doing things – they evolved without a need for conscious decision. The labour of the household split itself, not equitably, perhaps, but neatly. Robert ruled over the garage and the cement-lined kingdom of the basement, keeping an ear permanently cocked for the murmuring of machinery and for its occasional small failures. For Lila there was the house, the children, the bills and the correspondence. The task of writing Christmas cards fell mainly to her. One year she sat down at Grandfather Westfield's roll-top desk and wrote 175 cards. So many friends, so many acquaintances! Still she paused, lifted her head and melodramatically said to herself, 'I am a lonely woman.' She wished once again that she knew Nigel and Jane's address so she could send them a snap of the boys and ask them if they had any children – she suspected they didn't, in which case she would like to write them a few words of comfort, perhaps counsel patience.

Nigel had written that year about the coal strike, about a fortnight he and Jane had spent in Scotland, about the flooding of a river near their house.

Eight people were seated around a table. There were candles. Lila had made a salmon mousse and surrounded it with cucumber slices and, after that, there was a leg of lamb, wild rice and fresh asparagus. Robert walked around the table and poured wine. The conversation had taken a curious turn, with each couple recounting the story of their honeymoon. Some of the stories were touched-up sexual burlesques – the red wine brought a slice of the ribald to the table – and some were confused, unedited accounts of misunderstandings or revelations.

Robert and Lila described their month in France, and Robert, making a fine story of it, told the others about the cheque they had cashed for an English stranger who now sends them Christmas cards.

'And I've saved every single one of them,' Lila said.

This surprised Robert, who was proud to be married to a woman who was not a collector of trivia. Lila sent him a wide, apologetic smile across the roasted lamb and a shrug that said: Isn't it absurd, the things we do.

'You took a real chance,' someone at the table remarked. 'You could have lost the whole bundle.'

Robert nodded, agreeing. He thought again as he had thought before, how generous, open and trusting he and Lila must have been in those days. It was an image he cherished, the two of them, lost in their innocence and in each other.

Lila went to visit her mother one day and they had a quarrel. The argument was over something of no importance, a photograph Lila had misplaced. They both apologised afterward, but Lila cried on her way out to the parking lot, and a man stopped her and said, 'Pardon me. You seem to be in distress. May I help you?'

He had a kind, anonymous face. Lila told him she was upset because she had quarrelled with someone. The man understood her to mean she had quarrelled with a lover, and that was what Lila intended him to understand.

He walked her to her car, held her arm for a moment and said a few kind words. Things would look different in the morning. Things had a way of blowing over. Misunderstandings were inevitable, but sometimes they yielded a deeper sense of the other person.

Lila drove home in that state of benign suspension which can occur when a complete stranger surprises one by an act of intimacy. She felt not only rescued, but deserving of rescue.

Often, she thought how it would be possible to tell Nigel things she could never tell Robert. He would never drum his fingers on the table or interrupt or correct her. He would be patient, attentive and filled with a tender regard for women. She seldom thought about him concretely, but an impression of him beat at the back of her head, a pocket watch ticking against a silky lining. 'Jane has made a splendid recovery,' he wrote rather mysteriously at Christmas.

'A wonderful year,' Lila wrote to friends at Christmas. 'The children are growing so fast.'

When she wrote such things, she wondered what happened to all the other parts of her life that could not be satisfyingly annotated. She tried at first to rescue them with a series of graceful, old-fashioned observations, but she soon became tired and discouraged and suspected herself of telling lies.

Robert and Lila acquired a cat, which ran up a tree in a nearby park and refused to come down. 'He'll come down when he's good and hungry,' Lila assured her children, but several days passed and still the cat refused to descend. At length, Robert dipped a broomstick into a tin of tuna fish and, standing on a ladder, managed to coax the cat down by waving this fragrant wand before his stubborn nose.

A photographer for a Toronto newspaper happened to be standing not ten feet away, and he snapped a picture of Robert in the act of rescue. The picture and story were picked up by a wire service as a human-interest piece a few days later – this was during a quiet spell between elections and hijackings – and appeared on the inside pages of newspapers across the continent. Robert was amazed. He was, he realised, mildly famous, perhaps as famous as he would ever be again. It was not the kind of fame he had imagined for himself and, in fact, he was a little ashamed of the whole episode. Friends phoned from distant cities and congratulated him on his act of heroism. 'Yes,' Lila said with expansive good humour, 'I am indeed married to the illustrious cat rescuer.'

Robert couldn't help wondering if the picture had been published in the English dailies, and if Jane had seen it. It might have made her laugh. Jane, Jane. He imagined she was a woman who laughed easily. 'Jane and I are both in excellent spirits,' a recent Christmas greeting had reported.

Whenever Lila went into a café or restaurant, she slipped the little packets of sugar into her purse, even though she and Robert no longer used sugar. They had grown health-conscious. Robert swam laps twice a weeks at the sports club he joined, and he was making an effort to cut down on martinis. All this dieting and exercise had stripped away his flesh so that when they made love Lila felt his hip bones grinding on hers. She believed she should feel healthier than she did, what with all the expensive, fresh vegetables she carried home and cooked in the special little steamer Robert had brought back from San Francisco.

She wondered if Jane had to watch her figure as carefully as she herself did. She wondered if Jane were attractive. Sometimes, she saw women on the street, women who had a look of Englishness about them, someone wearing a simple linen dress or with straight greying hair. If these women wore perfume, it was something grassy. They were determinedly cheerful; they put a smiling face on everything, keeping life joyful, keeping it puffing along, keeping away from its dark edges. They swallowed their disappointments as though to do so was part of a primordial bargain.

'Jane and I are seriously considering a walking tour of the Hebrides next year,' Nigel had written.

Robert applied for a year off in order to do some research on the immune system, but almost from the start things went badly. The data he required accumulated slowly and yielded little that was specific. He learned too late that someone else, someone younger and with a larger grant, was on the same track at Stanford. He insisted on being given computer time in order to correlate his findings, and then discovered he was painfully, helplessly inept at using a computer. He began drifting to his club in the early afternoons to swim laps, or sometimes he drank in the bar and told Lila that he swam laps. His disappointment, his difficulty, his lies, his drunkenness, his life sliding away from him down a long blind chute, made him decide that the time had come to buy a house.

The house was expensive, ten rooms of glass and dark-stained wood cunningly perched on the side of a ravine, but it saved his life, or so he said at the time. He and Lila and the boys moved in at the end of November. As always, when they moved, Lila made careful, tactful, heroic efforts to have their mail forwarded. She looked forward to the barrage of Christmas greetings. Nigel and Jane's card came from the Hebrides that year, just a short note saying, 'We made it at last. The birds are magnificent.'

Lila had the use of her mother's summer cottage in Muskoka, and she and Robert and the children liked to spend four or five weeks there every summer. There was a particular nightgown she wore at the lake. It was altogether different from her city nightgowns, which were long, sliplike things in shiny materials and in colours such as ivory or melon or plum. The cottage nightgown was white cotton printed with quite large red poppies. There was a ruffle at the neck and another at the feet. On a bigger woman, it would have been comic; it was large, loose, a balloon of a garment.

Robert couldn't imagine where it had come from. It was difficult to think of someone as elegant as Lila actually going out to buy such a thing. She kept it in an old drawer at the cottage, and one summer they arrived and found that a family of mice had built a nest in its flower-strewn folds. The children ran screaming.

'Throw it away,' Robert told her.

But she had washed it in the lake with strong detergent and dried it in the sun. 'As good as new,' she said after she mended one small hole.

For a week the children called it her mouse gown and refused to touch it.

But Robert loved her in it. How he loved her! The wet, lakey smell was in her hair all summer long, and on her skin. She was his shining girl again, easy and ardent and restored to innocence.

*

Summer was one thing, but for most of the year Lila and Robert lived in a country too cold for park benches or *al fresco* dining or cuddling on yachts or unzipping the spirit. They suffered a climate more suitable for sobering insights, for guilt, for the entrenchment of broad streams of angst and darkness.

England, too, was a cold country, yet Nigel wrote: 'We've had a cheerless autumn and no summer to speak of, but as long as Jane and I have our books and a good fire, we can't complain.'

Just as heavy drinkers gather at parties to condemn others for overindulgence, so Lila lovingly gathered stories of wrecked marriages and nervous breakdowns – as though an accumulation of statistics might guard her sanity and her marriage, as if the sheer weight of disaster would prevent the daily erosion of what she had once called her happiness. She wailed, loudly and frequently, about the numbers of her friends who popped Valium or let their marriages slide into boredom. 'I'll go crazy if I hear about one more divorce.' She said this mournfully, but with a sly edge of triumph. Her friends' children were taking drugs or running away from home. She could weep, she told Robert, when she looked around and saw the wreckage of human lives.

But she didn't weep. She was, if anything, reaffirmed by disaster. 'I ran into Bess Carrier downtown,' she told Robert, 'and she looked about sixty, completely washed out, devastated. You wouldn't have known her. It was heartbreaking. I get so depressed sometimes. There must be something we can do for her.'

Robert knew it would come to nothing, Lila's plans to take Bess Carrier out for lunch or send her flowers or invite her around for a drink. Lila's charity seldom got past the point of corpse-counting these days; it seemed to take most of her time.

No one escaped her outraged pity – except perhaps Nigel and Jane. They were safe, across the ocean, locked into their seasonal rhythms, consumed by their various passions. They were taking Portuguese lessons, they had written. And growing orchids.

Lila loved parties, and she and Robert went to a great many. But when they drove home past lighted houses and streets full of parked cars, she was tormented by the parties she had missed, assuming, as a matter of course, that these briefly glimpsed gatherings glittered with a brighter and kinder light. She imagined rooms fragrant with woodsmoke and fine food – and talk that was both grave and charming. Who could guess what her imagination had cost her over the years?

The same plunging sense of loss struck her each year when she opened the Christmas greeting from Nigel and Jane. Elsewhere, these cards said to her, people were able to live lives of deep trust. How had it happened – that others were able to inhabit their lives with such grace and composure?

'He probably sends out thousands of these things,' Robert once said to Lila, who was deeply offended. 'He must be a bit off his rocker. He must be a real nut.'

It was the month of July. Robert bundled the boys into the station wagon and they drove across the country, camping, climbing in the mountains, cooking eggs and coffee over an open fire, breathing fresh air. Lila went to Rome on a tour with a group from the art gallery. While she was gone, her mother died of heart failure on the platform of the College Street subway station. The moment she collapsed, her straw hat flying into the air, was the same moment when Lila stood in the nave of St. Peter's, looked up into its magisterial vaulting and felt that she had asked too much of life. Like Nigel and Jane, she must try to find a simpler way of being: playing word games at the kitchen table, being attentive to changes in the weather, taking an interest in local history, or perhaps collecting seashells on a beach, taking each one into her hand and minutely examining its colour and pattern.

A snowy day. Lila was at home. There was a fire, a pot of Earl Grey and Beethoven being monumentally unpleasant on the record player. She turned the music off and was rewarded by a blow of silence. In the whole of the long afternoon there was not one interruption, not even a phone call. At seven, Robert arrived home and the peace was broken by this peaceful man.

A snowy day. Robert was up at seven. Granola in a bowl given to him by his wife. She was lost in a dream. He would like to have surprised her by saying something startling, but he was convinced, prematurely as it turned out, that certain rhythms of speech had left him forever. He knew this just as he knew that he was unlikely ever again to kiss the inner elbow of a woman and behave foolishly.

A snowy day. Nigel wrote: 'We are wrapped in a glorious blizzard, an extraordinary North Pole of a day. Jane and I send good wishes. May you have peace, joy and blessings of every kind.'

*

Loss of faith came at inappropriate times, settling on the brain like a coat of deadly lacquer. Lila thought of her dead baby. Robert thought of his abandoned research. But, luckily, seasonal tasks kept the demons down – the porch to open and clean, the storm windows to see to, the leaves. Robert and Lila always gave a party for the staff in the fall. After the fall party, there were the Christmas things to be done. The children were doing well in school. Soon it would be summer.

Occasionally, in a crowd, in an airport or a restaurant or in the street, Robert would see a woman's face so prepared in its openness for the appeal of passion, tenderness or love, so composed and ready, that he was moved to drop everything and take her in his arms. A thousand times he had been able to resist. Once he had not.

She was a woman not much younger than Lila and not as pretty. His feeling for her was intense and complicated. He was corrupted by the wish to make her happy, and the fact that it took little to make her happy touched him in the same way his children's simple wants had once aroused his extravagant generosity. He had no idea why he loved her. She rode a bicycle and pulled her hair back with a ribbon. Her hair ribbons, her candour, her books and records, and especially her strong rounded arms, put him in mind of Jane. When she closed a book she was reading, she marked her place with a little silk cord and folded her hands, one inside the other, in exactly the same way he imagined Jane would do.

Lila was stepping into a taxi on her way to see her lawyer. Nothing she could do, not even the bold, offhand way she swung her handbag on her shoulder, could hide the touching awkwardness and clumsy surprise of a woman who had been betrayed by someone she loves.

The taxi driver drove through the late-afternoon traffic. 'Would you object if I smoke?' he asked Lila, who was embarrassed by his courtesy. She wondered if he had a wife. His shoulder-length hair was clean and more than commonly fine, and on the fingers of his left hand there were three rings, so large and intricate and so brilliantly coloured that she was moved to comment on them.

'I go with a girl who did a jewellery course in New Brunswick,' he said. 'She keeps making me rings. I don't know what I'm going to do if she keeps making me rings.'

'Are you going to marry her?' Lila asked. Now that she was taking the first step to dissolve her marriage, she felt she had the right to ask all manner of outrageous questions.

'Marriage?' He paid grave attention to her question. 'I don't know about marriage. Marriage is a pretty long haul.'

'Yes, it is,' Lila said. She rolled down the window and looked at the heavy, late-afternoon sky which seemed now to form a part of her consciousness. Why wouldn't someone help her? She slumped, turned her face sideways and bit on the bitter vinyl of the upholstery. 'Nigel, Nigel,' her heart pleaded.

Robert missed his house, he missed his sons and often he missed Lila. Guilt might explain the trembling unease he felt when he stamped the snow off his shoes and rang the bell of what had been his front door. Inside he would find the smell of fresh coffee, that most forgiving of smells, and the spicy chalk smell of adolescent boys. And what else? – the teasing drift of Lila's perfume, a scent that reminded him of grass.

He arrived at 9:00 A.M. every Saturday, insisting, he said rather quaintly, on doing the household chores. More often than not these chores consisted of tapping on the furnace gauge or putting a listening ear under the hood of Lila's car or filling out some forms for the fire insurance. He did all these things with a good – some would say guilty – heart. He even offered to do the Christmas cards and advise their many, many friends that he and Lila were now separated.

Most of the friends replied with short notes of condolence. Several of them said, 'We know what you're going through.' Some said, 'Perhaps you'll find a way to work things out.' One of them, Bess Carrier, wrote, 'We've suspected for some time that things weren't right.'

Nigel wrote: 'We hope this Christmas finds you both joyous and eager for the new year. Time goes so quickly, but Jane and I often think of the two of you, so happy and young in Normandy, and how you found the goodness to come to our aid.'

Lila missed Robert, but she didn't miss him all the time. At first, she spent endless hours shopping; all around her, in the department stores, in the boutiques, people were grabbing for the things they wanted. What did she want, she asked herself, sitting before a small fire in the evening and fingering the corduroy of the slipcover. She didn't know.

She rearranged the house, put a chair at an angle, had the piano moved so that the sun struck its polished top. She carried her Grandfather Westfield's temperance novels out of the basement and arranged them on a pretty little table, using a piece of quartz for a book end. The stone scratched the finish, but she rubbed it with a bit of butter as her mother used to do, and forgot about it. Some days she woke up feeling as light as a girl, and as blameless. The lightness stayed with her all day, and she served her sons plates of soup and sandwiches for dinner. When summer came, she bought herself a pair of white cotton pants and a number of boyish T-shirts. One of them had a message across the front that said 'Birds are people too'.

She had a great many friends, most of them women, and sometimes it seemed to her that she spent all day talking to these women friends. She wondered now and then how Jane filled her days, if she knitted or visited the sick or what. She wished they could meet. She would tell Jane everything. She would trust her absolutely.

Certain kinds of magazines are filled with articles on how to catch a man and how, having caught him, to keep him happy, keep him faithful, keep him amorous. But Lila and her friends talked mainly about how few men were worth catching and how fewer still were worth keeping. Yet, when Robert asked if he might come back, she agreed.

She would have expected a woman in her situation to feel victorious, but she felt only a crush of exhaustion that had the weight and sound of continuous rain. Robert suggested they get away for a vacation, somewhere hot. Spain or Portugal. (Nigel and Jane had gone to Portugal where they had spent many hours walking on the beaches.)

Lila said: 'Maybe next year.' She was too tired to think about packing a suitcase, but next year she was bound to have more energy.

Robert gave Lila an opal ring. Lila gave Robert a set of scuba equipment. Robert gave Lila a book of French poems that he'd found at a garage sale. Lila gave Robert a soft scarf of

English wool and put it around his neck and patted it in place, saying, 'Merry Christmas.'

'Merry Christmas,' Robert said back, and to himself he said: There's no place in the world I would rather be at this minute.

The card from England was late, but the buff envelope was reassuringly familiar and so was the picture – a scenic view of Salisbury Plain under a wafery layer of snow. Inside, Nigel had written: 'Jane has been in a coma for some months now, but it is a comfort to me that she is not in pain and that she perhaps hears a little of what goes on about her.'

Lila read the words several times before they swam into comprehension. Then she phoned Robert at his office. Hearing the news he slumped forward, put a fist to his forehead and closed his eyes thinking: *Jane, Jane.*

'How can he bear this?' Lila said to herself. *Nigel.*

Later they sat together in a corner of the quiet living room. A clock ticked on the wall. This room, like the other rooms in the house, was filled with airy furniture and thick rugs. Fragile curtains framed a window that looked out onto a wooded ravine, and beyond the ravine could be seen the tops of apartment buildings. From the triple-paned windows of these apartments one could glimpse a pale sky scratched with weather whorls, and a broad lake that joined, eventually, a wide grey river whose water emptied into the Atlantic Ocean. As oceans go, this was a mild and knowable ocean, with friendly coasts rising smoothly out of the waves and leading directly to white roads, forests and the jointed streets of foreign towns and villages. Both Robert and Lila, each enclosed in a separate vision, could imagine houses filled with lighted rooms, and these rooms – like the one they were sitting in – were softened by the presence of furniture, curtains, carpets, men and women and children, and by that curious human contrivance that binds them together.

They know after all this time about love – that it's dim and unreliable and little more than a reflection on the wall. It is also capricious, idiotic, sentimental, imperfect and inconstant, and most often seems to be the exclusive preserve of others. Sitting in a room that was slowly growing dark, they found themselves wishing they could measure its pure anchoring force or account for its random visitations. Of course they could not – which was why, after a time, they began to talk about other things: the weather, would it snow, would the wind continue its bitter course, would the creek freeze over, would there be another power cut, what would happen during the night.

The Journal

WHEN HAROLD AND Sally travel, Sally keeps a journal, and in this journal Harold becomes H. She will write down such things as, 'H. exclaimed how the cathedral (Reims) is melting away on the outside and eroding into abstract lumps – while the interior is all fluidity and smoothness and grace, a seemingly endless series of rising and arching.'

Has Harold actually *exclaimed* any such thing? The phrase *seemingly endless* sounds out of character, a little spongy, in fact, but then people sometimes take on a different persona when they travel. The bundled luggage, the weight of the camera around the neck, the sheer cost of air fare make travellers eager to mill expansive commentary from minor observation. Sally, in her journal, employs a steady, marching syntax, but allows herself occasional forays into fancy.

Both Harold and Sally are forty years old, the parents of two young children, boys. Harold possesses a mild, knobby face – his father was Swedish, his mother Welsh – and the natural dignity of one who says less than he feels. After he and his wife, Sally, leave the cathedral, they walk back to the

Hôtel du Nord where they are staying, down one of those narrow, busy streets which the French like to describe as *bien animé*, and everywhere, despite a thick mist of rain, people are busy coming and going. Since it is close to five o'clock, they're beginning to gather in small cafés and bars and *salons de thé* in order to treat themselves to glasses of wine or beer or perhaps small cups of bitter espresso. A *quotidian quaff* is the tickling phrase that pops into Harold's head, and it seems to him there is not one person in all of Reims, in all of France for that matter, who is not now happily seated in some warm public corner and raising pleasing liquids to his lips. He experiences a nudge of grief because he does not happen to live in a country where people gather publicly at this hour to sip drinks and share anecdotes and debate ideas. He and Sally live on the fringe of Oshawa, Ontario where, at the end of the working day, people simply return to their homes and begin to prepare their evening meal as though lacking the imagination to think of more joyous activities. But here, at a little table in France, the two of them have already gone native – 'H. and I have gone native . . . ' – and sit sipping cups of tea and eating little pancakes sprinkled with sugar. Harold feels inexpressibly at peace – which makes him all the more resentful that he can't live the rest of his life in this manner, but he decides against mentioning his ambivalent feelings to Sally for fear she'll write them down in her journal. ('H. laments the sterility of North American life which insists on the isolation of the family rather than the daily ceremony of . . . ')

The Hôtel du Nord is much like other provincial hotels in its price bracket, possessing as it does a certain dimness of light bulbs, rosy wallpaper printed with medallions, endless creaking corridors lined with numbered doors and, especially, a proprietor's young brown-eyed son who sits in the foyer at a little table doing his homework, his *devoir* as he calls it. It's a lesson on the configuration of the Alps that occupies this young boy and keeps his smooth dark head bent low. The angle of the boy's bent neck sharpens Harold's sorrow, which has been building since he and Sally left the cathedral. ('H. was deeply moved by the sight of . . . ')

Their room is small, the bed high and narrow and the padded satin coverlet not quite clean. Between coarse white sheets they attempt to make love, and almost, but not quite, succeed. Neither blames the other. Sally curses the remnant of jet lag and Harold suspects the heaviness of the bedcovers; at home they've grown used to the lightness of a single electric blanket. But the tall shutters at the Hôtel du Nord keep the little room wonderfully, profoundly, dark, and the next morning Harold remarks that there's probably a market in Canada for movable shutters instead of the merely decorative Colonial type. ('H. has become an enthusiastic advocate of . . . ')

It seems that the hotel, despite its great number of rooms, is almost empty. At least there is only one other guest having breakfast with Sally and Harold the next morning, a young man sitting at the table next to theirs, drinking his coffee noisily and nibbling a bun. Out of pity – for the young, for the solitary – they engage him in conversation. He's an Australian, hungry for cricket scores, scornful of New Zealanders, and illiterate in French – altogether a dull young man; there's no other word for it. ('What a waste, H. says, to come so far and be so dull!!')

Rain, rain, rain. To cheer themselves up, Sally and Harold drive their rented Peugeot to Dijon and treat themselves to a grand lunch at an ancient *auberge*. ('Awnings, white tablecloths, the whole ball of wax.') Sally starts with a lovely and strange salad of warm bacon, chicken livers, tomatoes, lettuce and parsley. Then something called *Truite Caprice*. When she chews, an earnest net of wrinkles flies into her face, and Harold finds this so endearing that he reaches for her hand. ('H. had the alternate menu – herring – which may be the cause of his malaise!')

Sunshine, at last, after days of rain, and Sally and Harold arrive at the tall gates of a château called Rochepot which their *Guide Michelin* has not awarded the decency of a single star. Why not? they wonder aloud.

Because it is largely a restoration, their tour guide says. She's middle-aged, with a broad fused bosom, and wears an apron over her green wool suit. Stars, she says, are reserved for those things that are authentic. Nevertheless, the château is spectacular with its patterned roofs and pretty interior garden – and Sally and Harold, after the rain, after yet another night of sexual failure, are anxious to appreciate. The circular château bedchambers are filled with curious hangings, the wide flagged kitchen is a museum of polished vessels and amusing contrivances, but what captures Harold's imagination is a little plaque on the garden wall. It shows a picture of a giraffe, and with it goes a brief legend. It seems that the King of Egypt gave the giraffe to the King of France in the year 1827, and that this creature was led, wearing a cloak to keep it from the chill, through the village of Rochepot where it was regarded by all and sundry as a great spectacle. Harold loves the nineteenth century, which he sees as an exuberant epoch that produced and embraced the person he would like to have been: gentleman, generalist, amateur naturalist, calm but sceptical observer of kingships, comets and constellations, of flora and fauna and humanistic philosophy, and at times he can scarcely understand how he's come to be a supervisor in the public school system on the continent of North America. ('H. despairs because . . . ')

In Le Grand Hôtel in Beaune, in a second-floor room that faces onto the rue Principal and which is directly accessible all night long to the river of loud traffic destined for the south, Sally and Harold achieve one of those rare moments of sexual extravagance that arrives as a gift perhaps two or three times in one's life. Whether it was an enabling exhaustion – exhaustion can be cumulative, as all travellers know – or whether it was the bottle of soft, pale-red dinner wine – softer than rain, softer even than the sound of the word *rain* – or whether they felt themselves preciously and uniquely abandoned in the strange, many-veined hexagon of France where their children and their children's babysitter and their aged parents and even the Canadian embassy in Paris could not possibly track them down – whatever the reason, they've been led, extraordinarily, into the heaven of ecstasy and then into the cool, air-filled condition of deep rest. Harold sleeps, his eyelids unmoving, and Sally, entering a succession of linked dreams, transcends herself, becoming S., that brave pilgrim on a path of her own devising. The ubiquitous satin coverlet presses and the shutters preserve darkness – though they do next to nothing to keep out the sound of traffic – and the long night leans in on them, blessing the impulse that coaxed them away from Oshawa and from the North American shore into this alien wine-provisioned wilderness where they are minutely and ecstatically joined and where they exchange, as seldom before in their forty-year lives, those perfect notices of affection and trust and rhapsody. ('H. and I slept well and in the morning . . . ')

Fuel for the Fire

WHEN YOU THINK about holidays like Thanksgiving and Christmas and Easter, and those huge traditional dinners with roast meat and bowls of mashed potatoes and fruit pies laid out, you tend to imagine city families wrapping up in their warm coats and climbing into cars and driving out to the family farm. That's the way it was with us, but no longer. Now, since Mom died three years ago, my dad comes into Winnipeg for those special days. He drives the pick-up, not the Pontiac. He's used to it, he says. It hugs the road better, and it seems there's always something or other he needs to haul. As a matter of fact, he's here most Sundays too. It's only forty-five miles, and he's careful to pick a time when the highway's relatively quiet.

He's never been the world's best driver. Not that he's ever had a real accident, but traffic makes him nervous. He gets heart palpitations, so he says. He's okay on secondary roads, and around McLeod, but not in the city. When Mom was still in good health he always tried to wheedle her into taking the wheel when they went to Portage to shop. We used to kill ourselves laughing about that, the traffic in Portage la

Prairie. But now he sails into Winnipeg almost every week. He comes in on the Number 1 Highway, takes a left at Silversides Boulevard, another left at Union, and then a sharp right into our driveway.

I always give him a cup of coffee the minute he gets here. Or, if it's lunchtime, a bowl of soup. He can sink down a pan of soup just like that, cream of chicken or asparagus, if I've got it on hand. Campbell's asparagus, that's his idea of real gourmet. He doesn't mind trying new things, even lasagne or beef curry. I read an article not long ago about how old people's taste buds shrivel up with age so that they actually need more spice in their food, not less. When I told him we were having goose for New Year's Day dinner, he looked really interested. He's never had goose before. Neither have I for that matter. Neither has Dennis.

But we're all sick of turkey. We had turkey last week for Christmas, and a pork loin for Boxing Day, and I know Dad wouldn't touch lamb. So what's left? There aren't all that many edible animals when you think about it. Which is why I decided to try a goose this year, a ten-pounder. I ordered it special from DeLuca's downtown, and if Dad knew what I paid for this hunk of bird he'd have a conniption. If he asks me outright, as he's apt to do, I plan to start humming loudly or put the radio on.

It's early morning, only eight o'clock, when I get out of bed on New Year's Day. Dennis and I were out at our annual potluck last night, just four couples, the same bunch every year, and didn't get home till three-thirty – but I don't need all that much sleep. Today a dozen sirens kicked me awake. First, I forgot to take the goose out of the deep-freeze yesterday, and now I'm having to fast-thaw it in a sinkful of warm water, poking my arm way up into its icy ribcage. Its skin looks bluish-grey and very prickly around the thighs, not especially appealing. Then there's the stuffing to make. I'm trying out a new mushroom and cashew recipe, and I'm also going to serve a squash soufflé with green onions and chopped parsley for colour. I put chopped parsley on everything; it's got lots of iron. When Dennis and I were first married, he used to give me a hard time about my chopped parsley and said I'd probably sprinkle a handful on his dead corpse if he went first. Now he's used to it; he's actually got so he likes it.

He's still asleep, Dennis. I always get up first on holidays, there's so much to do. Besides the stuffing and the squash thing, I want to mop the kitchen floor and clean out the fireplace. I like to have things organised before the kids get too wound up and before Dennis starts thinking up projects. He'll want to take the tree down, I know that, but I want it up one more day. I'd just as soon take it down myself tomorrow when he's gone back to work and the kids are back at school.

There are going to be eight of us for dinner. Besides Dad and Dennis and the three kids and myself, I've invited Sally and Purse from next door. They're older than we are, just halfway in age between Dad's seventy-five and my thirty-four, and their two kids have grown up and moved east. Purse is a commodities dealer, oil seeds mainly, and Sally's been selling real estate for the last eight years. She's good at it. She's already made it into the Million Dollar Club. She had her membership key embedded in a silver disc and wears it like a brooch on the lapel of her coat. Dad gets a kick out of her. He really likes to get her going, and she eggs him on. He can't believe the prices of houses in Winnipeg, what people will pay for jerry-built construction and hanky-sized lots. Last week, never mind the slow December market,

Sally sold a house in Tuxedo for half a million dollars, and it didn't even have a full basement. The heating bills for this particular house are more than Dennis and I pay every month for our mortgage and taxes combined, but then our heating bills are pretty high too. Like everyone else around here, we switched from oil to gas a few years ago. This is a cold climate. You've got to put out a lot of your income on heat in this part of the country, but every night, from September to May, we have a fire in our fireplace, and I like to think that that takes some of the burden off the furnace.

Most of our friends who have fireplaces use them maybe three or four times a year. Cordwood's expensive, they say, but then they admit it's really the mess and bother of cleaning out the ashes. I do it fast first thing in the morning, a little whisk broom and dustpan and a metal pail for the ashes. I can clean our fireplace in three minutes flat, I've timed myself. The ashes I save to put on the garden in the springtime.

I love a fire. I'm addicted, we both are, but especially me. I get the kids to bed at night and, by the time I come downstairs, Dennis has a fair blaze going. We got into the fire habit when he was doing his graduate work in England (genetics, swine). We had a little rented house there, two rooms up, two rooms down. We didn't have a TV, we couldn't afford a babysitter, but we had this real fireplace. Of course, it wasn't a luxury there, it was how we heated the house more or less. But neither of us had grown up with a fireplace. It was something new. It was company, like a person, like our best friend. We made toast in it sometimes for a bedtime snack and, if I happened to have any orange peels left over, I'd throw them in and wait for the orange smell to fill up the room. We burned pine-cones too, if we found any, and once I remember we put in one of those padded book envelopes and watched the little plastic pillows of air explode in the heat. It was only a year and a half we were there, but it seemed to stretch out much longer, sitting in front of that fireplace with the radio on low and reading library books. We hadn't counted on this, it was a surprise. It was like living in a dark crack, just the two of us keeping warm in our own dust, and Danny sleeping in his crib upstairs.

Back home we borrowed money from my folks and started looking around for a house of our own. The one thing I wanted most was a fireplace. It was at the top of the list. I pretty well knew by then that being content had to do with crackling flames and baked shins. I didn't care about a garage or a family room or whether there was four inches of insulation in the roof, as long as we had something hot and alive to sit around at night, keeping *us* alive.

Our Winnipeg fireplace is painted-over brick, off-white to match the living-room walls, with a rounded opening like one of those old-fashioned bread ovens. It draws like a dream and it's got a damper we can open and close, which is very important in our climate. Next to it is a brass stand for the fireplace implements, and next to that is a woven brass basket holding birch logs. The birch logs are just for show; at the moment we're burning scrap lumber Dad hauled in from the farm.

He's crazy about our fireplace. He says he sees all kinds of pictures in the flames, a hundred times better than anything on TV. For a while he even tried to talk Mom into getting one installed at the farm. She wasn't too fussy about the idea, not after all those years she spent dealing with a cookstove, but she told him to go ahead if he had his mind made up. In the end he decided it was too much money. According to Sally, it costs about six thousand to install a fireplace after construction, but adds only fifteen hundred dollars to the value of a house.

In her old age my mother shrank down to nothing. Her feet ached all the time. She stopped driving the car, she stopped cooking. She got little fruity eyes and a dented chin. I hardly recognised her. She refused to go out of the house in wintertime, even to Portage. She didn't want to miss her shows, she said. She and the TV and the living-room rad were like a little unbreakable triangle. She wore a pair of wool and angora socks that came up over her knees, and a thick cardigan, and always had an afghan at hand. She hardly talked to us toward the end, she was so occupied with keeping warm and staying off her feet. It scared me seeing her like that, which is why, more or less, I signed up for the refresher course at the hospital this year with the idea of maybe going back to work part-time when Tom starts Grade One.

By midmorning I have the table set in the dining ell. I'm using Mom's old damask tablecloth today, which is murder to iron but shines flat like ice under my good tulip china. But not the damask napkins, not with three kids and a goose that looks like it's got a lot of bluish fat on it. I've splurged on big thick paper napkins in a soft shade of rose, also six pale pink candles for my crystal candlesticks. Knowing Sally and Purse, we'll have pink flowers on the table too, and Lara, our nine-year-old, will want to make place cards. I'll tell her to do them on white cardboard with a pink felt-tipped pen.

Dennis is a little crabby when he gets up. He watches me pile mushroom stuffing into the goose's insides and says, 'You sure that's going to be big enough to go around?'

'It's supposed to serve twelve,' I tell him, and I think again how much I paid for it. The thought just washes over me for a minute, all that money, what we used to spend on food in a whole week.

'Hmmmmm,' he says, his sceptical voice which I don't really appreciate. I ask him to carry some firewood up from the basement for tonight. Yes, yes, he says automatically, but he stands there drinking coffee and just looking at me.

Last summer my dad demolished an old shed in back of his barn. We don't know why he took it down. Dennis thinks he was just trying to keep himself busy. He doesn't actually farm anymore, but he lives in the old house and rents out the acreage. I've tried to talk him into moving to Winnipeg, and Sally even took him to view some basement suites not far from here. For a while he seemed interested. We tried to impress on him that he could walk over here and have dinner with us at night and see a lot more of the kids as they grew up. But I think he worried about what he'd do all day in a dinky basement suite. He's a very, very sociable man. Every morning, for as long as I can remember, he's driven the half-mile into McLeod for coffee and toast at the McLeod Luncheonette. He'll generally sit there for an hour, shooting the breeze. There are five or six of them, all farmers from around the area. He'd miss that. Sally finally took me aside and said she didn't think it was such a great idea, his moving to Winnipeg. She doesn't think he's ready. Maybe later on, she says, when he's less self-sufficient.

Besides being sociable, he's extremely active physically. Taking down that shed was hard work. You have to be methodical taking down a building, more so than putting one up, especially working on your own. You have to pay attention or the whole thing can come crashing down on your head. It took him about a week, and at the end of the week he drove into Winnipeg and delivered the first of several truckloads of two-by-fours and other assorted bits of wood. 'You might as well make use of this,' he said. 'In the fireplace.'

It wasn't that big a shed as I remember, but somehow we've ended up with this basement full of ugly lumber. Dennis says it's going to last us forever. The boards are full of nails and, when I clean out the ashes in the mornings, I have to gather up the blackened nails too. Some of them get stuck in the grate and it's a real job prying them out. But, on the other hand, there's not much point in buying firewood when we've got all this scrap wood to use up. It isn't as though we're heating the house with the fireplace, as Dad says. It's just for enjoyment. He can't believe that people actually go into supermarkets and buy Prestologs. Prestologs floor him completely, the whole idea of manufacturing something for the purpose of burning it up.

Around noon I give Dennis and the kids a pick-up lunch, and while we sit talking at the kitchen table I look up and see Dad passing by the window. We never even heard him drive up. He smiles at us through the frosted glass, and I can see how we must look to him with our grilled cheese and glasses of milk and talk. The shoulders of his big plaid jacket are stippled with snow and his eyes seem vague as though the pupils are only parked there temporarily. 'Is that goose I'm smelling?' he asks, coming in through the back way. I say yes, that I put it in the oven an hour ago. He looks happy, anticipatory.

In the afternoon, while the goose spits and crackles in the roasting pan, Dennis takes Dad to the New Year's Day Levee at the Legislative Building. This happens here every

New Year's Day. In the old days it was a military affair, a strictly male-only event, but now the general public is invited, even kids. For entertainment there's an RCMP band and a troop of Scotch pipers in full regalia. You line up and shake hands with the premier of Manitoba and his wife, the lieutenant governor and *his* wife, and then you have a glass of Gimli Goose, which is a kind of pinkish wine, and some fruitcake or shortbread.

Our two older kids look as though they wouldn't mind going along, but I like the idea of Dennis and Dad being off on their own for a change. Dennis's folks live down in Nova Scotia, and they're not the sort that gets together anyway. A few times Dennis has tried taking Dad to hockey games, but it's not easy for an older man sitting so long on those hard seats. He always looks forward to the New Year's Levee. Today he's brought along his suit on a hanger and his white shirt and tie. He changes just before they set off, and on the way they drop the kids off at the rink.

The afternoon is slow and dozy, and the sun pouring in through the front window makes me feel sleepy. I settle down on the chesterfield and read an article in the paper about the right kind of clothes to wear for job interviews. I've read this same kind of article a thousand times, but I still need to read it, something makes me. Not too much jewellery. No sandals. A well-made suit in a neutral tone is still the best bet, with a muted scarf for a feminine touch. That's as far as I get before dropping off to sleep.

I can't have slept for long, maybe three-quarters of an hour, but when I wake up I sniff the air for the smell of goose and don't smell anything. I head straight for the kitchen, and sure enough the oven's barely warm. So down I go to the basement to check the fuses, but they're all in order. Then I put on my oven mitts and jiggle the element at the bottom of the oven, in case it's worked its way loose. A corner of it looks black and slightly shrivelled. This happened once or twice before, a burnt-out element, but not on a holiday, and not when I was cooking an expensive goose.

My first idea is to carry the roasting pan over to Sally's and finish it off in her oven, but then I remember that she and Purse are out for the afternoon. And all the other people around here are using their ovens for *their* holiday dinners. I consider what would happen to the poor old thing if I tried cooking it very slowly on top of the stove, maybe pouring a little wine around to keep it from burning. It would probably get rubbery, or else stringy. Boiled goose doesn't sound like much of a dish. But at that moment, luckily, Dennis and Dad come through the back door.

They take off their coats and go straight to work. First Dennis takes the goose out and wraps it up with foil to try to preserve what little heat is left. Then he and Dad pull the stove away from the wall, disconnect it, and start examining the bolts that hold the element in place. Definitely burnt out, Dennis says, sounding not one bit dismayed, not an iota, just the opposite.

From the basement he carries up a set of screwdrivers and wrenches, as well as his soldering gear. Before buckling down to work, he pours Dad a tall rye and ginger ale, a heart-starter he calls it, and one for himself. He's humming away and concentrating hard as he slips his wrench around the first of the bolts.

I pull up the aluminium foil for a peek at my goose. It looks pale and glum with its dead meaty chest cooling down fast. I remember the time Dennis and I went to the British Museum to look at the mummies, how depressed I was to find just how dead you could actually get, but Dennis was all over the room, peering at everything and snapping photographs, though, strictly speaking, this wasn't allowed.

He'll have the stove working in less than an hour, he tells me. He doesn't even stop to think about what he's going to do. It's as though he's got a pocket of his brain filled with little mechanical puzzles that he can undo at will. He's going to remove the burnt-out unit and move the broiler element temporarily down to the bottom of the oven. An emergency tactic. He's whistling now. Unlike me, he appreciates the unexpected. Dad is handing him tools in a rhythmic nurse-to-surgeon manner and trying hard, I can tell, to bite his tongue and keep from giving Dennis advice. It's hard for him not being in full charge. He's a sweetheart, but pig-headed at times.

Right after Mom died – I'm talking about one month after she went – Dad cut down all the lilac bushes around their house. These lilacs were old, more like trees than bushes. They'd always been there, protecting the house from the wind and the open stare of the road. He claimed he and Mom had often talked about chopping them down so they could get more sunshine into the house. I have my doubts about this – my mother loved those lilacs – but we let the story stand.

He cut the twisted old lilac wood into short lengths and bundled them up for our fireplace. Good for kindling, he said. And he also hauled the roots, sixteen of them, into town. First he shook off as much dirt as he could. Lilac roots are dense, damp, shrubby things, irregular in shape and amazingly large. I think he was surprised himself at the size of them.

They burned very slowly. A single lilac root takes a whole evening to burn. You have to poke it continually to keep it going, and it smoulders rather than flames. Now and then it gives off a turquoise colour, just a flash. There's no smell of lilac at all, but from time to time the whole root takes on a sort of glow, shadowy and three-dimensional like a human face burning, eyes and mouth and wrinkled cheeks all lit up and keeping itself intact right to the point of disintegration. We still talk about it, Dad and his lilac roots. Even the children remember, or say they can.

By five o'clock the goose is back in the oven, sputtering fat and getting golden. And by seven o'clock the eight of us are seated at the table. Our faces look coral. Dennis carves, looking not quite at me, across the table. Dad carefully tastes a bit of goose, then says, as if he's looking a long way back into the past, 'It reminds me a bit of pheasant, only meatier.' Sally runs through her recent Tuxedo triumph and Purse shares his nice rambling educated laugh around the table. We go counter-clockwise, telling our New Year's resolutions. Dad says he's going to think seriously about a trip to Florida, which I'll believe when I see it. Sally's signed up for calligraphy. Purse is giving up white sugar. The kids look giggly and secretive and won't say, even when I prod them. Dennis announces his resolution to run the mini-marathon in April. He says this in a staunch, wilful, but kindly way. I'm going to master the art of crepe making, I say, but my real resolve, the one I don't mention, is to stop managing everyone's lives for them.

After dessert the three men insist on doing dishes. Sally and I sit in the living room waiting for them. The waiting seems like a treasure we've piled up, something we owe ourselves. We settle back into soft cushions and put up our feet in front of the fireplace. But then I remember I've forgotten to lay a fire. And what with the goose crisis, Dennis has forgotten to bring up any firewood. We look at each other, at the birch logs sitting there, and say, why not?

'Hold on a sec,' Dad says, coming in from the kitchen. 'I'll be right back.' He puts on his coat and boots and five minutes later he's back with a large carton of bowling pins.

The bowling alley in McLeod has been shut down for years, just like the old McLeod movie theatre and the old high school and just about everything else. A lot of the small central region towns are shrinking away to nothing, and McLeod suffers particularly by being just a little too close to Portage. The old buildings were boarded up ages ago, but somewhere Dad heard about the stockpile of bowling pins sitting there going to waste in the abandoned bowling alley.

A signal must have registered in his head, a dotted line stretching from the old bowling lanes direct to our fireplace. Other people might see something nostalgic or sad, but he took a look and saw fuel. Bowling pins are wood. They're burnable.

It never before occurred to me to wonder what a bowling pin might look like on the inside, but I would have guessed they were solid through and through, cut with a lathe out of chunks of tough dry hardwood. But they're not. They're glued together in two lengthwise sections, and there's a little hollow – oval shaped – in the middle.

They take a while to catch alight. You need lots of kindling, little chips of hardwood or balled-up newspaper. Then you see a flare of white light, which is the paint catching fire (the pins are painted an ivory colour with a red stripe around their middles), and before you know it the entire skin is flaky ash. Then the fire finds a way into the core.

The centre burns brightly, deeply red, so that the sides look transparent, more like glass than wood, more like bottles than bowling pins. The red heart keeps getting brighter and brighter and then, suddenly, with a snap it cracks open. 'Thar she blows,' Sally says, seconds before the third pin splits itself exactly in two.

Dennis leans over and gently places two more nose to nose on the grate. He's loving this. By now we've turned out the floor lamp and all the table lamps, leaving just the lit tree and the light from the fire.

It makes me dizzy looking at those pins burning. I think, now they're going, now they're gone. I remember the last time Dennis and I were on a plane, and the pilot, crossing a time zone, asked us to adjust our time pieces. Our time pieces. What a word. We twiddled a dial, and there was an hour erased.

Purse is talking about growing up in Swan River, how he used to set pins after school, earning thirty cents an hour and how he read *True Detective Magazine* between lanes. The kids stare at his face, which happens to be a rather large, quiet, undemanding face, and I can tell they're wondering how things get so displaced and changed like this.

I look over at Dad who's asleep in his chair. It's been a longer day than he's used to, and I'm glad he's decided to sleep over. There's pink light from the fire colouring up his forehead and cheeks. It's extravagant looking, rich, and I can't decide whether it makes him look very old or young like a boy.

Sally sits close to me. Earlier, while the men were doing the dishes and the kids were tearing around the house, I told her I was thinking of going back to work as soon as possible, not waiting till next fall after all. She listened hard. She has a lot of strong curiosity about her. 'Don't rush,' she said. 'Work is only work.'

'One more?' Dennis asks us, and balances another pin delicately on its side in the glowing ashes. It flares, catches, glows, splits open and dies. I pay attention to it. Usually I'm so preoccupied, so busy, I forget about this odd ability of time to overtake us. Then something reminds me. Cemeteries – they stop me short, do they *ever* stop me short – and old buildings and tree stumps, things like that. And the sight of burning fires, like tonight, like right now, this minute, how economical it is, how it eats up everything we give it, everything we have to offer.

Love So Fleeting, Love So Fine

WENDY IS BACK! the sign said. It caught his eye.

It was a handprinted sign and fairly crude – not that he was a man who objected to crudeness; crayon lettering on a piece of cardboard: WENDY IS BACK! it said.

The sign was in the window of an orthopaedic shoe store on a dim back street in downtown Winnipeg. He passed it one morning on his way to the office, and the image of the sign, and all the questions it raised, stayed with him, printed as it were on the back wall of his eye.

Who is Wendy?

Where has she been?

Why is she back?

And why is her return the cause of joy?

Joy, there was no other word for it. The sign taped flat against the plate-glass window was a joyful announcement, a public proclamation, reinforced, too, by its light, high floater of an exclamation point (that fond crayoned slash of exuberance), testifying to the fact that Wendy's return, whether from visiting her grandmother in Portage or from vacationing with a girlfriend in Hawaii, was an event worthy of celebration. The question was, why?

She would be about his own age, he reasoned – which was thirty. Nobody over thirty was named Wendy, at least nobody he'd ever met. But where had she been? Perhaps she'd been sick; flu was going the rounds, a persistent strain. (He himself had missed three days at work only the week before, and now his wife had come down with it.) Or an operation. Impossible.

It was more likely that she'd been sent away to Toronto or Montreal or St. Catharine's for a job-upgrading course at some obscure community college specialising in the modern fitting of difficult feet. He mused, as he walked along, on what a narrow speciality it must be, the fitting of orthopaedic footwear, but necessary, of course, and how, like chimney cleaning and piano tuning, it was a vocation whose appeal to youth might not be immediately apparent. Undoubtedly, she, Wendy, had come back from the east with a new sense of buoyancy, brimming with the latest theories and 'tips', which she now felt eager to pass on to her customers.

It was easy to see that her popularity with clients was established. The store manager – a fatherly type – might even refer to it as 'phenomenal'. (Else, why this sign in his window? And why the Christmas bonus already set aside for her?) Customers doubtless experienced an upsurge of optimism at the sight of her wide blue eyes or at hearing her cheery early morning 'Hello there!'. Her particular humour would be difficult to pin down, being neither dry nor wry nor witty, but consisting, rather, of a wink for the elderly gents and broad teasing compliments for the ladies – 'These shoes'll put you right back in the chorus line,

Mrs. Beamish.' They loved it; they lapped it up,; how could they help but adore Wendy.

'Our little Wendy's back,' he imagined these old ones cackling one to another as they came in for fittings, 'and about time too.'

From North Winnipeg they came, from East Kildonan and Fort Garry and Southwood and even Brandon so that their warped and crooked and cosmically disfavoured feet could be taken into Wendy's smooth young hands, examined minutely and murmured over – but in that merry little voice of hers that made people think of the daughters they'd never had. Into her care they could safely put the shame of their ancient bunions, their blue-black swollen ankles, their blistered heels. Her strong, unerring touch never shrank when it came to straightening out crippled toes or testing with her healthy thumbs that peculiar soft givingness that indicates a fallen arch. By sheer banter, by a kind of chiding playfulness, she absolved her clients of the rasp of old calluses, the yellowness of soles, the damp dishonour attached to foot odour, foot foulness, foot obloquy, foot ignominy.

All this and more Wendy was able to neutralise – with forehead prettily creased – by means of her steady, unflinching manner. These feet are only human, she would be ready to say if asked. Tarsus and metatarsus; corn, callus and nail; her touch is tender and without judgement. Willingly she rises from her little padded stool and fetches the catalogue sent from the supply house in Pittsburg, and happily she points to Figure 42. 'This little laced oxford doesn't look like much *off*,' she concedes to Mrs. Beamish or whomever happens to be in her charge, 'but it's really a very smart little shoe *on*.'

He imagines that her working uniform is some kind of smock in a pastel shade, the nature of her work being, after all, primarily medical. A caring profession. A caring person. A person one cared about. Wendy! She was back!

And he loved her.

He admitted it to himself. Oh yes, it was like light spilling through a doorway, his love for her. Arriving at work and travelling in the elevator to the eleventh floor, he kept his eyes lowered, searching the feet of his fellow workers, noting here and there sturdy, polished, snub-nosed models with thickish heels. Had these people felt his Wendy's warm ministrations? He might, if he were bolder, announce loudly, 'Wendy is back!' as if it were an oblation, and watch as smiles of recognition, then euphoria and a kind of relief, too, spread across their faces.

Later, alone, at the end of the work day, while his wife lay reading the newspaper in bed, he examined his own feet under a strong light. Would they soon require professional attention? Might they benefit from extra bracing or support, a foam lift at the heel, say, or – well, whatever Wendy would care to suggest now that she was up on the latest theories from the east. But what could he say to her that would not seem callow or self-serving or, worse, a plea for her attention. She might look at his two feet, stripped of their socks and laid bare and damp, and suspect he had come because of ulterior motives. Namely love. He is sure she is vigilant against those who would merely love her.

He is a man who has been in love many times. Before the transfer to the Winnipeg office, he spent two years in Vancouver, and once, standing in line at a bakery on 41st Avenue, he found himself behind two solemn young women who were ordering a farewell cake for a friend. 'What would you like written on top?' the woman behind the counter asked them. They paused, looked uncertain, regarded each other, and then one of them said decisively, 'So long, Louise'.

Louise. Gold hair set off by a blue cotton square. Louise was leaving. Instinctively, he felt she didn't really want to go. All her friends were here. This was a beautiful city. She had a decent job, a pleasant apartment full of thick-leaved plants and bamboo furniture; she had a modest view of the mountains and a membership in a health club, but nevertheless she was leaving. SO LONG, LOUISE the pink icing on her farewell cake spelled out.

Something had forced the move on her – a problem that might be professional or personal, and now she would have to deal – alone, for how could he help her? – with storing her furniture, cancelling her subscriptions, and giving away to friends the books and oddments she loved. Her medical insurance would have to be transferred, and there would be the last heartbreaking task of going down to the post office to arrange to have her mail forwarded. It seemed unpardonable to ask so much of a young woman who barely had had time to savour her independence and to study love's ingenious rarefaction. She would have to face the horror of apartment-hunting elsewhere; a whole new life to establish, in fact. If only he could put his arms around her, his poor Louise, whom he suddenly realised he cared deeply, deeply, deeply about.

His lost Louise. That is how he thinks of her, a woman standing in the airport – no, the bus station – in her dark cloth coat of good quality and her two pieces of soft-sided luggage in which lay folded a number of pale wool skirts and sweaters, and her little zippered bag of cosmetics, toiletries, talcum powder and emery boards which would be travelling, ineluctably, with her out to the edges of the city and over the mountain ranges and away from his yet-to-be declared love.

Still, he won't forget her, just as he has never forgotten his young and lovely Sherri, whom he first encountered thirty miles north of Kingston – where his first transfer took him. There he had seen, spray-painted in red on a broad exposed rock face, the message HANK LOVES SHERRI. It had been the coldest of March days; the countryside was an unrelenting grey, and he, driving along the highway, found himself longing for a sign of life, anything at all. A moment later he had swung around a curve and confronted HANK LOVES SHERRI in letters that were at least three feet high.

He knows, of course, what the Hanks of the world are like: loud-mouthed and jealous, with the beginnings of a beer belly, the kind of lout who believes the act of love was invented to cancel out the attachment of the spirit, the sort of person who might dare to fling a muscled, possessive arm across Sherri's shoulders while coming out of a coffee shop on Princess Street and later swear to her that she was different from the other girls he'd known. *His* Sherri, who, with her hyacinth cologne and bitten nails, was easily, fatally, impressed by male joviality and dark sprinklings of chest hairs. She would never stand a chance. For a while, a few months, she might be persuaded that Hank really did love her in his way, and that she, in return, loved him. But familiarity, intimacy – those enemies of love – would intervene, and one day she would wake up and find that something inside her had withered, that core of sweet vulnerability which was what *he* had loved in her from the first day when HANK LOVES SHERRI had stopped him cold on the highway.

And now it's Wendy who sets off wavelets of heat in his chest. WENDY IS BACK! He walks by the orthopaedic footwear store again the next day – but this time more slowly. The loose leather wrappings on his feet scrape the pavement absurdly. His breath comes with pleasure and difficulty as though the air has been unbearably sweetened by her name – Wendy, Wendy, Wendy. Of course, he is tempted to peer closely through the dark plate glass, but finds it to be full of reflections – his own mainly, his hungry face. He might go in – not today, but tomorrow – on the pretext of asking the time or begging change for the parking meter or telephone. He'll think of something. Love invents potent strategies, and people in love are resourceful as well as devious. Wendy, Wendy is back. But for how long?

The ends of his love affairs always bring a mixed nightmare of poignancy and the skirmishings of pain. He feels stranded, beached, with salt in his ears. What is over, is over; he is realist enough to recognise that. But his loves, Sherri, Louise, Wendy – and the others – never desert him entirely. He has committed to memory the minor physics of veneration and, on dark nights, after his wife has fallen asleep and lies snoring quietly beside him, he likes to hang on to consciousness for an extra minute or two and listen to the sound of the wind rocking the treetops and brushing silkily against the window. It's then he finds himself attended by a false flicker on the retina – some would say vision – in which long, brightly coloured ribbons dance and sway before him. Their suppleness, their undulations, cut deeply into his heart and widen for an instant the eye of the comprehended world. Often he can hear, as well, the muted sound of female voices and someone calling out to him by name.

Chemistry

IF YOU WERE to write me a letter out of the blue, typewritten, handwritten, whatever, and remind me that you were once in the same advanced recorder class with me at the YMCA on the south side of Montreal and that you were the girl given to head colds and black knitted tights and whose *Sprightly Music for the Recorder* had shed its binding, then I would, feigning a little diffidence, try to shore up a coarsened image of the winter of 1972. Or was it 1973? Unforgivable to forget, but at a certain distance the memory buckles; those are the words I'd use.

But you will remind me of the stifling pink heat of the room. The cusped radiators under the windows. How Madam Bessant was always there early, dipping her shoulders in a kind of greeting, arranging sheets of music and making those little throat-clearing chirps of hers, getting things organised – for us, everything for us, for no one else.

The light that leaked out of those winter evenings filled the skirted laps of Lonnie Henry and Cecile Landreau, and you, of course, as well as the hollows of your bent elbows and the seam of your upper lip brought down so intently on the little wooden mouthpiece and the bony intimacy of your instep circling in air. You kept time with that circling foot of yours, and also with the measured delay and snap of your chin. We sat in a circle – you will prod me into this remembrance. Our chairs drawn tight together. Those clumsy old-fashioned wooden folding chairs? Dusty slats pinned loosely with metal dowels? A cubist arrangement of stern angles and purposeful curves. Geometry and flesh. Eight of us, counting Madam Bessant.

At seven-thirty sharp we begin, mugs of coffee set to one side. The routines of those weekly lessons are so powerfully set after a few weeks that only the most exigent of emergencies can breach them. We play as one person, your flutey B minor is mine, my slim tonal accomplishment yours. Madam Bessant's blunt womanly elbows rise out sideways like a pair of duck wings and signal for attention. Her fretfulness gives way to authority. *Alors*, she announces, and we begin. Alpine reaches are what we try for. God marching in his ziggurat heaven. Oxygen mists that shiver the scalp. Music so cool and muffled it seems smoothed into place by a thumb. Between pieces we kid around, noodle for clarity, for what Madam Bessant calls roundness of tone, *rondure, rondure*. Music and hunger, accident and intention meet here as truly as they did in the ancient courts of Asia Minor. '*Pas mal*,' nods our dear Madam, taking in breath, not wanting to handicap us with praise; this is a world we're making, after all, not just a jumble of noise.

We don't know what to do with all the amorous steam in the room. We're frightened of it, but committed to making more. We start off each lesson with our elementary Mozart bits and pieces from the early weeks, then the more lugubrious Haydn, then Bach, all texture and caution – our small repertoire slowly expanding – and always we end the evening with an intricate new exercise, something tricky to bridge the week, so many flagged, stepped notes crowded together that the page in front of us is black. We hesitate. Falter. Apologise by means of our nervy young laughter. 'It will come,' encourages Madam Bessant with the unlicensed patience of her métier. We read her true meaning: the pledge that in seven days we'll be back here again, reassembled, another Wednesday night arrived at, our unbroken circle. Foul-mouthed Lonnie H. with her starved-looking fingers ascends a steep scale, and you respond, solidly, distinctively, your head arcing back and forth, back and forth, a neat two-inch slice. The contraction of your throat forms a lovely knot of deliberation. (I loved you more than the others, but, like a monk, allowed myself no distinctions.) On and on, the timid fingerings repeat and repeat, picking up the tempo or slowing it down, putting a sonorous umbrella over our heads, itself made of rain, a translucent roof, temporary, provisional – we never thought otherwise, we never thought at all. Madame Bessant regards her watch. How quickly the time . . .

In Montreal, in January, on a Wednesday evening. The linoleum-floored basement room is our salon, our conservatory. This is a space carved out of the nutty wood of foreverness. Windows, door, music stands and chairs, all of them battered, all of them worn slick and giving up a craved-for weight of classicism. The walls exude a secretive decaying scent, of human skin, of footwear, of dirty pink paint flaking from the pipes. Half the overhead lights are burned out, but it would shame us to complain. To notice. Madam Bessant – who tolerates the creaky chairs, the grudging spotted ceiling globes, our sprawling bodies, our patched jeans, our cigarette smoke, our outdoor boots leaking slush all over the floor, our long uncombed hair – insists that the door be kept shut during class, this despite the closeness of the overheated air, choking on its own interior odours of jointed ductwork and mice and dirt.

Her baton is a slim metal rod, like a knitting needle – perhaps it *is* a knitting needle – and with this she energetically beats and stirs and prods. At the start of the lessons there seems such an amplitude of time that we can afford to be careless, to chat away between pieces and make jokes about our blunders, always our own blunders, no one else's; our charity is perfect. The room, which by now seems a compaction of the whole grey, silent frozen city, fills up with the reticulation of musical notes, curved lines, spontaneous response, actions, and drawn breath. You have one of your head colds, and between pieces stop and shake cough drops, musically, out of a little blue tin.

Something else happens. It affects us all, even Mr. Mooney with his criminal lips and eyes, even Lonnie H. who boils and struts with dangerous female smells. We don't just play the music, we *find* it. What opens before us on our music stands, what we carry in with us on our snow-sodden parkas and fuzzed-up hair, we know for the first time, hearing the notes just as they came, unclothed out of another century when they were nothing but small ink splashes, as tentative and quick on their trim black shelves as the finger Madam Bessant raises to her lips – her signal that we are to begin again, at the beginning, again and again.

She is about forty. Old, in our eyes. Not a beauty, not at all, except when she smiles, which is hardly ever. Her face is a somatic oval with a look of having been handled, moulded; a high oily worried forehead, but unlined. A pair of eye glasses, plastic framed, and an ardour for clear appraisal that tells you she wore those same glasses, or similar ones, through a long comfortless girlhood, through a muzzy, joyless adolescence, forever breathing on their lenses and attempting to polish them beyond their optical powers, rubbing them on the hems of dragging skirts or the tails of unbecoming blouses. She has short, straight hair, almost black, and wears silvery ear clips, always the same pair, little curly snails of blackened silver, and loose cheap sweaters that sit rawly at the neck. Her neck, surprisingly, is a stem of sumptuous flesh, pink with health, as are her wrists and the backs of her busy, rhythmically rotating hands. On one wrist is a man's gold watch that she checks every few minutes, for she must be home by ten o'clock, as she frequently reminds us, to relieve the babysitter, a mere girl of fourteen. There are three children at home, all boys – that much we know. Her husband, *a* husband, is not in the picture. Not mentioned, not ever. We sense domestic peril, or even tragedy, the kind of tragedy that bears down without mercy.

Divorce, you think. (This is after class, across the street, drinking beer at Le Piston.) Or widowed. Too young to be a widow, Lonnie H. categorically says. Deserted maybe. Who says that? One of us – Rhonda? Deserted for a younger, more beautiful woman? This seems possible and fulfils an image of drama and pain we are prepared to embrace; we begin to believe it; soon we believe it unconditionally.

We never talk politics after class, not in this privileged love-drugged circle – we've had enough of politics, more than enough. Our talk is first about Madam Bessant, our tender concern for her circumstances, her children, her babysitter just fourteen years old, her absent husband, her fretful attention to the hour, her sense of having always to hurry away, her coat not quite buttoned or her gloves pulled on. We also discuss endlessly, without a touch of darkness, the various ways each of us has found to circumvent our powerlessness. How to get cheap concert tickets, for instance. How to get on the pogey. Ways to ride the Métro free. How to break a lease, how to badger a landlady into repairing the water heater. Where to go for half-priced baked goods. Cecile Landreau is the one who tells us the name of the baked goods outlet. She has a large, clean ice-maiden face and comes from a little town out west, in Alberta, a town with a rollicking comical name. She gets a laugh every time she mentions it, and she mentions it often. A lively and obstinate girl – you remember – and highly adaptive. She moved to Montreal just one year before and already she knows where to get things cheap: discount shoes, winter coats direct from the manufacturer, art supplies marked down. She never pays full price. ('You think I'm nuts?') Her alto recorder, a soft pine-coloured Yamaha, she bought in a pawn shop for ten dollars and keeps it in a pocketed leather case that she made herself in a leathercraft course, also offered at the Y.

The poverty we insinuate is part real and part desire. We see ourselves as accidental survivors crowded to the shores of a cynical economy. By evasion, by mockery, by a mutual nibbling away at substance, we manage to achieve a dry state of asceticism that feeds on itself. We live on air and water or nothing at all; you would think from the misty way we talk we had never heard of parents or cars or real estate or marital entanglements. The jobs we allude to are seasonal and casual, faintly amusing, mildly degrading. So are our living arrangements and our live-in companions. For the sake of each other, out of our own brimming imaginations, we impoverish ourselves, but this is not a burdensome poverty; we exalt in it, and with our empty pockets and eager charity, we're prepared to settle down after our recorder lesson at a corner table in Le Piston and nurse a single beer until midnight.

But Mr. Mooney is something else. Hungry for membership in our ranks, he insists loudly on buying everyone a second round, and a third. Robert is his first name, Robert Mooney. He speaks illiterate French and appalling English. Reaching into his back pocket for his wallet, a thick hand gripping thick leather, he's cramped by shadows, blurred of feature, older than the rest of us, older by far, maybe even in his fifties, one of those small, compact, sweet-eyed, supple-voiced men you used to see floating around certain quarters of Montreal, ducking behind tabloids or grabbing short ryes or making endless quick phone calls from public booths.

Here in Le Piston, after our recorder lesson, he drops a handful of coins on the table and some bills, each one a transparent, childish offer of himself. My round, he says, without a shred of logic. He has stubby blackened fingers and alien appetites, also built-up shoes to give himself height, brutal hair oil, gold slashes in his back teeth. We drink his beer down fast, without pleasure, ashamed. He watches us, beaming.

All he wants is a portion of our love, and this we refuse. Our reasons are discreditable. His generosity. His age. His burnished leather coat, the way it fits snugly across his round rump. His hair oil and puttied jowls. Stubble, pores, a short thick neck, history. The way the beer foam nudges up against his dark lip. Any minute he's likely to roister or weep or tell a joke about a Jew and a Chinaman or order a plate of *frites*. The joke, if he tells it, we'll absorb without blinking; the *frites* we'll consume down to the last crystal of salt. Dispassionate acts performed out of our need to absolve him. To absolve ourselves.

Robert Mooney is a spoiler, a pernicious interloper who doesn't even show up until the third Wednesday when we've already done two short Mozart pieces and are starting in on Haydn, but there he is in the doorway, his arms crossed over his boxer's chest. A shuffling awkward silence, then mumbled introductions, and bad grace all around except for Madam Bessant who doesn't even notice. Doesn't even *notice*. Our seven stretches to eight. An extra chair is found, clatteringly unfolded and squashed between yours and Pierre's. (Pierre of the cowboy boots and gold earring, as though you need reminding.) Into this chair Mr. Mooney collapses, huffing hard and scrambling with his thick fingers to find his place in the book Madam Bessant kindly lends him until he has an opportunity to buy one of his own.

Layers of incongruity radiate around him: the unsecured history that begs redemption, rough questions stored in silence. How has this man, for instance, this Robert Mooney, acquired a taste for medieval instruments in the first place? And by what manner has he risen to the advanced level? And through what mathematical improbability has he come into contact with Mozart and with the gentle Madam Bessant and the YMCA Winter Enrichment Program and with us, our glare of nonrecognition? When he chomps on his mouthpiece with his moist monkey mouth we think of cigars or worse. With dwindling inattention he caresses his instrument, which is old and beautifully formed. He fingers the openings clumsily, yet is able to march straight through the first exercise with a rhythm so vigorous and unhesitating you'd think he'd been preparing it for months. He has nothing of your delicacy, of course, nor Pierre's even, and he can't begin to sight read the way Rhonda can – remember Rhonda? Of course you remember Rhonda, who could forget her? Mr. Mooney rides roughshod over poor Rhonda, scrambles right past her with his loud marching notes blown sharply forward as if he were playing a solo. '*Bon*,' Madam Bessant says to him after he bursts through to the end of his second lesson. She addresses him in exactly the same tone she uses for us, employing the same little fruited nodes of attention. 'Clearly you know how to phrase,' she tells him, and her face cracks with a rare smile.

The corners of our mouths tuck in; withholding, despising. But what is intolerable in our eyes is our own intolerance, so shabby and sour beside Madam Bessant's spontaneously bestowed praise. We can't bear it another minute; we surrender in a cloudburst of sentiment. And so, by a feat of inversion, Robert Mooney wins our love and enters our circle, enters it raggedly but forever. His contradictions, his ruptured history, match our own – if the truth were known. Seated at the damp table at Le Piston he opens his wallet yet again and buys rounds of beer, and at the end of the evening, on a slicked white street, with the moon shrunk down to a chip, we embrace him.

We embrace each other, all of us, a rough huddle of wool outerwear and arms, our cold faces brushing together, our swiftly applied poultice of human flesh.

It was Rhonda of all people, timorous Rhonda, who initiated the ceremonial embrace after our first lesson and trip to Le Piston. Right there on the sidewalk, acting out of who knows what wild impulse, she simply threw open her arms and invited us in. We were shy the first time, not used to being so suddenly enfolded, not knowing where it would lead. We were also young and surprised to be let loose in the world so soon, trailing with us our differently coloured branches of experience, terrified at presuming or pushing up too close. If it had been anyone other than Rhonda offering herself, we might have held back, but who could refuse her outspread arms and the particularity of her smooth camel coat? (Do you agree? Tell me yes or no.) The gravest possible pleasure was offered and seized, this hugging, this not-quite kiss.

Already after three weeks it's a rite, our end-of-evening embrace, rather solemn but with a suggestion of benediction, each of us taken in turn by the others and held for an instant, a moonlit choreographed spectacle. At this moment our ardour grows dangerous and threatens to overflow. This extemporaneous kind of street-love paralyses the unsteady. (The youth of today would snort to see it.) One step further and we'd be actors in a shabby old play, too loaded with passion to allow revision. For that reason we keep our embrace short and chaste, but the whole evening, the whole week in fact, bends toward this dark public commerce of arms and bodies and the freezing murmur that accompanies it. Until next week. Next Wednesday. (A passport, a guarantee of safe conduct.) *A la prochaine.*

One night in early March Rhonda appears in class with red eyes. The redness matches the long weepy birthmark that starts beneath her left ear and spills like rubbery fluid down the side of her neck.

You glance up at her and notice, then open your big woven bag for a Kleenex. 'It's the wind,' you say, to spare her. 'There's nothing worse than a March wind.' We're well into Bach by this time and, of all of us, Rhonda handles Bach with the greatest ease. This you remember, how she played with the unsupported facility that comes from years of private lessons, not that she ever mentions this, not a word of it, and not that we inquire. We've learned, even Mr. Mooney has learned, to fall back and allow Rhonda to lead us through the more difficult passages. But tonight her energy is frighteningly reduced. She falters and slides and, finally, halfway through the new piece, puts down her recorder, just places it quietly on the floor beneath her chair and runs, hobbling unevenly, out of the room.

Madam Bessant is bewildered – her eyes open wide behind her specs – but she directs us to carry on, and we do, limping along to an undistinguished conclusion. Then Lonnie H. goes off in search of Rhonda.

Lonnie H. is a riddle, a paradox. Her hair is as densely, dully orange as the plastic shopping bag in which she carries her portfolio of music and the beaded leather flip-flops she wears during class. That walk of hers – she walks with the savage assurance of the young and combative, but on Wednesday night at least she tries to keep her working-class spite in check; you can see her sucking in her breath and biting down on those orange lips.

Later, when we're doing our final exercise, the two of them, Rhonda and Lonnie H., reappear. A consultation has been held in the corridor or in the washroom. Rhonda is smiling fixedly. Lonnie H. is looking wise and sad. 'An affair of the heart,' she whispers to us later as we put on our coats and prepare to cross the street to Le Piston. An affair of the heart – the phrase enters my body like an injection of sucrose, its improbable sweetness. It's not what we've come to expect of the riddlesome Lonnie. But she says it knowingly – an affair of the heart – and the words soften her tarty tangle-haired look of anarchy, make her almost serene.

Some time later, weeks later or perhaps that very night, I see Pierre with his waspish charm reach under the table at Le Piston and take Rhonda's hand in his. He strokes her fingers as though he possesses the fire of invention. He has a set of neglected teeth, a stammer, and there is something amiss with his scalp, a large roundness resembling, under the strands of his lank Jesus hair, a wreath of pink plastic. His chin is short and witty, his long elastic body ambiguous. The left ear, from which a gold hoop dangles, is permanently inflamed.

It is Pierre who tells us one evening the truth about Madam Bessant's husband. The story has reached him through a private and intricately convoluted family pipeline: the ex-husband of a cousin of Pierre's sister-in-law (or something of this order) once lived in the same apartment block as Monsieur and Madam Bessant, on the same floor in fact, and remembered that the nights were often disturbed by the noise of crying babies and the sound of Monsieur Bessant, who was a piano teacher, playing Chopin, often the same nocturne again and again, always the same. When the piano playing stopped abruptly one day, the neighbours assumed that someone had complained. There was also a rumour, because he was no longer seen coming or going, that Monsieur Bessant was sick. This rumour was verified one morning, suddenly and terribly, by the news of his death. He had, it seemed, collapsed in a downtown Métro station on a steamy summer day, just toppled off the platform into the path of an approaching train. And one more detail. Pierre swallows as he says it. The head was completely separated from the body.

What are we to do with this story? We sit for some time in silence. It is a story too filled with lesions and hearsay, yet it is also, coming from the artless stammering Pierre, curiously intact. All its elements fit; its sequence is wholly convincing – Monsieur Bessant, swaying dizzily one minute and cut to ribbons the next, people screaming, the body collected and identified, the family informed, heat rising in waves and deforming the future. Everything altered, changed forever.

'Of course it might have been a heart attack,' Pierre says, wanting now to cancel the whole account and go back to the other, simpler story of an unfeeling husband who abandons his wife for a younger woman.

'Or a stroke,' Cecile Landreau suggests. 'A stroke is not all that unusual, even for a quite young man. I could tell you stories.'

Robert Mooney keeps his eyes on the chilly neck of his beer bottle. And he keeps his mouth clapped shut. All the while the rest of us offer theories for Monsieur Bessant's sudden collapse – heat stroke, low blood sugar – Robert keeps a hard silence. 'A helluva shock' is all he says, and then mumbles, 'for her.'

A stranger entering Le Piston and overhearing us might think we were engaged in careless gossip. And, seeing Pierre reach for Rhonda's hand under the table, might suspect carnal pressure. Or infer something flirtatious about Cecile Landreau, toying with her charm bracelet in a way that solicits our protection. And calculating greed (or worse, condescension) in our blithe acceptance of Robert Mooney's rounds of beer. Lonnie H. in a knitted muffler, pungent with her own bodily scent, could easily be misunderstood and her cynical, slanging raptures misread. A stranger could never guess at the kind of necessity, innocent of the sensual, the manipulative, that binds us together, that has begun as early as that first lesson when we entered the room and saw Madam Bessant tensely handing out purple mimeographed sheets and offsetting the chaos of our arrival. We were ashamed in those first few minutes, ashamed to have come. We felt compromised, awkward, wanting badly to explain ourselves, why we were there. We came to learn, we might have said had anyone asked, to advance, to go forward, something of that order. Nothing crystallises good impulses so much as the wish to improve one's self. This is one of the things that doesn't change.

After that first night, we relaxed. The tang of the schoolroom played to our affections and so did the heat of our closely drawn chairs, knees almost touching so that the folds of your skirt aligned with my thigh, though from all appearances you failed to notice. The fretfulness with which Madam Bessant regarded her watch put us on our honour, declared meanness and mischief out of bounds, demanded that we make the allotted time count – and so we brought our best selves and nothing else. Our youth, our awkwardness, our musical naiveté yoked good will to virtue, as sacredness attaches itself invisibly to certain rare moments.

I exaggerate, I romanticise – I can hear you say this, your smiling reproach. I have already, you claim, given poor Pierre an earring and a stammer, accorded Lonnie H. an orange plastic bag and a sluttish mouth, branded Rhonda with the humiliation of a port-wine birthmark when a small white scar was all she had or perhaps only its psychic equivalent, high up on her cheek, brushed now and then unconsciously with the back of her hand. But there's too much density in the basement room to stop for details.

Especially now with our time so short, five more weeks, four more weeks. Some nights we linger at Le Piston until well after midnight, often missing the last train home, preferring to walk rather than cut our time short. Three more weeks. Our final class is the fourteenth of May and we sense already the numbered particles of loss we will shortly be assigned. When we say good night – the air is milder, spring now – we're reminded of our rapidly narrowed perspective. We hang on tighter to each other, since all we know of consequence tells us that we may not be this lavishly favoured again.

Lately we've been working hard, preparing for our concert. This is what Madam Bessant calls it – a concert. A little programme to end the term. Her suggestion, the first time she utters it – 'We will end the season with a concert' – dumbfounds us. An absurdity, an embarrassment. We are being asked to give a recital, to perform. Like trained seals or small children. Called upon to demonstrate our progress. Cecile Landreau's eyebrows go up in protest; her chin puckers the way it does when she launches into one of her picaresque western anecdotes. But no one says a word – how can we? Enigmatic, inconsolable Madam Bessant has offered up the notion of a concert. She has no idea of what we know, that the tragic narrative of her life has been laid bare. She speaks calmly, expectantly; she is innocence itself, never guessing how charged we are by our guilty knowledge, how responsible. The hazards of the grown-up life are settled on her face. We know everything about the Chopin nocturne, repeated and repeated, and about the stumbling collapse on the hot tracks, the severed head and bloodied torso. When she speaks of a concert we can only nod and agree. Of course there must be a concert.

It is decided then. We will do nine short pieces. Nothing too onerous though, the programme must be kept light, entertaining.

And who is to be entertained? Madam Bessant patiently explains: we are to invite our friends, our families, and these *invités* will form an audience for our concert. A *soirée*, she calls it now. Extra chairs have already been requisitioned, also a buffet table, and she herself – she brings her fingers and thumbs together to make a little diamond – she herself will provide refreshments.

This we won't hear of. Lonnie H. immediately volunteers a chocolate cake. Robert Mooney says to leave the wine to him, he knows a dealer. You insist on taking responsibility for a cheese and cold-cuts tray. Cecile and Rhonda will bring coffee, paper plates, plastic forks and knives. And Pierre and I, what do we bring? – potato chips, pretzels, nuts? Someone writes all this down, a list. Our final celebratory evening is to be orderly, apt, joyous, memorable.

Everyone knows the fourteenth of May in Montreal is a joke. It can be anything. You can have a blizzard or a heat wave. But that year, our year, it is a warm rainy night. A border of purple collects along the tops of the warehouses across the street from the Y, and pools of oily violet shimmer on the rough pavement, tinted by the early night sky. Only Madam Bessant arrives with an umbrella; only Madam Bessant *owns* an umbrella. Spinning it vigorously, glancing around, setting it in a corner to dry. *Voilà*, she says, addressing it matter-of-factly, speaking also to the ceiling and partially opened windows.

We are all prompt except for Robert Mooney, who arrives a few minutes late with a carton of wine and with his wife on his arm – hooked there, hanging on tight. We see a thick girdled matron with square dentures and a shrub of bronze curls, dense as Brillo pads. Gravely, taking his time, he introduces her to us – "May I present Mrs. Mooney' – preserving the tender secret of her first name, and gently he leads her toward one of the folding chairs, arranging her cardigan around her shoulders as if she were an invalid. She settles in, handbag stowed on the floor, guarded on each side by powerful ankles. She has the hard compact head of a baby lion and a shy smile packed with teeth.

Only Robert Mooney has risked us to indifferent eyes. The rest of us bring no one. Madam Bessant's mouth goes into a worried circle and she casts an eye across the room where a quantity of food is already laid out on a trestle table. A cheerful paper tablecloth, bright red in colour, has been spread. Also a surprise platter of baby shrimp and ham. Wedges of lemon straddle the shrimp. A hedge of parsley presses against the ham. About our absent guests, we're full of excuses, surprisingly similar – friends who cancelled at the last minute, out-of-town emergencies, illness. Madam Bessant shrugs minutely, sighs, and looks at her watch. She is wearing a pink dress with large white dots. When eight o'clock comes she clears her throat and says, 'I suppose we might as well go through our programme anyway. It will be good practice for us, and perhaps Madam Mooney will bear with us.'

Oh, we play beautifully, ingeniously, with a strict sense of ceremony, never more alert to our intersecting phrases and spelled out consonance. Lonnie H. plays with her eyes sealed shut, as though dreaming her way through a tranced lifetime, backward and also forward, extending outward, collapsing inward. Your foot does its circling journey, around and around, keeping order. Next to you is Robert

Mooney whose face, as he puffs away, has grown rosy and tender, a little shy, embarrassed by his virtue, surprised by it too. Rhonda's forehead creases into that touching squint of hers. (You can be seduced by such intense looks of concentration; it's that rare.) Cecile's wrist darts forward, turning over the sheets, never missing a note, and Pierre's fingers move like water around his tricks of practised tension and artful release.

And Mrs. Mooney, our audience of one, listens and nods, nods and listens, and then, after a few minutes, when we're well launched, leans down and pulls some darning from the brocade bag on the floor. A darkish tangle, a lapful of softness. She works away at it throughout our nine pieces. These must be Robert Mooney's socks she's mending, these long dark curls of wool wrapped around her left hand, so intimately stabbed by her darting needle. Her mouth is busy, wetting the thread, biting it off, full of knowledge. Between each of our pieces she looks up, surprised, opens her teeth and says in a good-natured, good-sport voice, 'Perfectly lovely.' At the end, after the conclusion has been signalled with an extra measure of silence, she stows the socks in the bag, pokes the needles resolutely away, smiles widely with her stretched mouth and begins to applaud.

Is there any sound so strange and brave and ungainly as a single person clapping in a room? All of us, even Madam Bessant, instinctively shrink from the rhythmic unevenness of it, and from the crucial difficulty of knowing when it will stop. If it ever does stop. The brocade bag slides off Mrs. Mooney's lap to the floor, but she still goes on applauding. The furious upward growth of her hair shimmers and so do the silver veins on the back of her hands. On and on she claps, powerless, it seems, to stop. We half rise, hover in mid-air, then resume our seats. At last Robert Mooney gets up, crosses the room to his wife and kisses her loudly on the lips. A smackeroo – the word comes to me on little jointed legs, an artefact from another era, out of a comic book. It breaks the spell. Mrs. Mooney looks up at her husband, her hard lion's head wrapped in surprise. 'Lovely,' she pronounces. 'Absolutely lovely.'

After that the evening winds down quickly. Rhonda gives a tearful rambling speech, reading from some notes she's got cupped in her hand, and presents Madam Bessant with a pair of earrings shaped, if I remember, like treble clefs. We have each put fifty cents or maybe a dollar toward these earrings, which Madam Bessant immediately puts on, dropping her old silver snails into her coin purse, closing it with a snap, her life beginning a sharp new chapter.

Of course there is too much food. We eat what we can, though hardly anyone touches the shrimp, and then divide between us the quantities of leftovers, a spoiling surfeit that subtly discolours what's left of the evening.

Robert and his wife take their leave. 'Gotta get my beauty sleep,' he says loudly. He shakes our hands, that little muscular fist, and wishes us luck. What does he mean by luck? Luck with what? He says he's worried about getting a parking ticket. He says his wife gets tired, that her back acts up. 'So long, gang,' he says, backing out of the room and tripping slightly on a music stand, his whole dark face screwed up into what looks like an obscene wink of farewell.

Madam Bessant, however, doesn't notice. She turns to us smiling, her odd abbreviated little teeth opening to deliver a surprise. She has arranged for a different babysitter tonight. For once there's no need for her to rush home. She's free to join us for an hour at Le Piston. She smiles shyly; she knows, it seems, about our after-class excursions, though how we can't imagine.

But tonight Le Piston is closed temporarily for renovations. We find the door locked. Brown wrapping paper has been taped across the windows. In fact, when it opens some weeks later it has been transformed into a produce market, and today it's a second-hand bookshop specialising in mysteries.

Someone mentions another bar a few blocks away, but Madam Bessant sighs at the suggestion; the sigh comes spilling out of an inexpressible, segmented exhaustion which none of us understands. She sighs a second time, shifts her shopping bag loaded with leftover food. The treble clefs seem to drag on her ear lobes. Perhaps, she says, she should go straight home after all. Something may have gone wrong. You can never know with children. Emergencies present themselves. She says good night to each of us in turn. There is some confusion, as though she has just this minute realised how many of us there are and what we are called. Then she walks briskly away from us in the direction of the Métro station.

The moment comes when we should exchange addresses and phone numbers or make plans to form a little practice group to meet on a monthly basis perhaps, maybe in the undeclared territory of our own homes, perhaps for the rest of our lives.

But it doesn't happen. The light does us in, the too-soft spring light. There's too much ease in it, it's too much like ordinary daylight. A drift of orange sun reaches us through a break in the buildings and lightly mocks our idea of finding another bar. It forbids absolutely a final embrace, and something nearer shame than embarrassment makes us anxious to end the evening quickly and go off in our separate directions.

Not forever, of course; we never would have believed that. Our lives at that time were a tissue of suspense with surprise around every corner. We would surely meet again, bump into each other in a restaurant or maybe even in another evening class. A thousand spontaneous meetings could be imagined.

It may happen yet. The past has a way of putting its tentacles around the present. You might – you, my darling, with your black tights and cough drops – you might feel an urge to write me a little note, a few words for the sake of nostalgia and nothing more. I picture the envelope waiting in my mailbox, the astonishment after all these years, the wonder that you tracked me down. Your letter would set into motion a chain of events – since the links between us all are finely sprung and continuous – and the very next day I might run into Pierre on St. Catherine's. What a shout of joy we'd give out, the two of us, after our initial amazement. That very evening a young woman, or perhaps not so very young, might rush up to me in the lobby of a concert hall: Lonnie H., quieter now, but instantly recognisable, that bush of orange hair untouched by grey. The next day I imagine the telephone ringing: Cecile or Rhonda – why not?

We would burrow our way back quickly to those winter nights, saying it's been too long, it's been too bad, saying how the postures of love don't really change. We could take possession of each other once again, conjure our old undisturbed, unquestioning chemistry. The wonder is that it hasn't already happened. You would think we made a pact never to meet again. You would think we put an end to it, just like that – saying good-bye to each other, and meaning it.

Milk Bread Beer Ice

'WHAT'S THE DIFFERENCE between a gully and a gulch?" Barbara Cormin asks her husband, Peter Cormin, as they speed south on the Interstate. These are the first words to pass between them in over an hour, this laconic, idle, unhopefully offered, trivia-contoured question.

Peter Cormin, driving a cautious sixty miles an hour through a drizzle of rain, makes no reply, and Barbara, from long experience, expects none. Her question concerning the difference between gullies and gulches floats out of her mouth like a smoker's lazy exhalation and is instantly subsumed by the hum of the engine. Two minutes pass. Five minutes. Barbara's thoughts skip to different geological features, the curious wind-lashed forms she sees through the car window, and those others whose names she vaguely remembers from a compulsory geology course taken years earlier – arroyos, cirques, terminal moraines. She has no idea now what these exotic relics might look like, but imagines them to be so brutal and arresting as to be instantly recognisable should they materialise on the landscape. Please let them materialise, she prays to the grooved door of the glove compartment. Let something, *anything*, materialise.

This is their fifth day on the road. Four motels, interchangeable, with tawny, fire-retardant carpeting, are all that have intervened. This morning, Day Five, they drive through a strong brown and yellow landscape, ferociously eroded, and it cheers Barbara a little to gaze out at this scene of novelty after seventeen hundred miles of green hills and ponds and calm, staring cattle. 'I really should keep a dictionary in the car,' she says to Peter, another languid exhalation.

The car, with its new car smell, seems to hold both complaint and accord this morning. And silence. Barbara sits looking out at the rain, wondering about the origin of the word drizzle – a likeable enough word, she thinks, when you aren't actually being drizzled upon. Probably onomatopoetic. Drizzling clouds. Drizzled syrup on pancakes. She thrashes around in her head for the French equivalent: *bruine*, she thinks, or is that the word for fog? 'I hate not knowing things,' she says aloud to Peter. Musing. And arranging her body for the next five minutes.

At age fifty-three she is a restless traveller, forever shifting from haunch to haunch, tugging her blue cotton skirt smooth, examining its weave, sighing and stretching and fiddling in a disapproving way with the car radio. All she gets is country music. Or shouting call-in shows, heavy with sarcasm and whining indignation. Or nasal evangelists. Yesterday she and Peter listened briefly to someone preaching about the seven F's of Christian love, the first F being, to her amazement, the fear of God, the *feah of Gawd*. Today, because of the rain, there's nothing on the radio but ratchety static. She and Peter have brought along a box of tapes, Bach and Handel and Vivaldi, that she methodically plays and replays, always expecting diversion and always forgetting she is someone who doesn't know what to do with music. She listens but doesn't hear. What she likes are words. *Drizzle*, she repeats to herself, *bruiner*. But how to conjugate it?

In the back seat are her maps and travel guides, a bundle of slippery brochures, a book called *Place Names of Texas* and another called *Texas Wildlife*. Her reference shelf. Her sanity cupboard. She can't remember how she acquired the habit of looking up facts; out of some nursery certitude, probably, connecting virtue with an active, inquiring mind. *People must never stop learning*; once Barbara had believed fervently in this embarrassing cliché, was the first in line for night-school classes, tuned in regularly with perhaps a dozen others to solemn radio talks on existentialism, Monday nights, seven to eight. And she has, too, her weekly French conversation group, now in its fourteenth year but soon to disband.

Her brain is always heating up; inappropriately, whimsically. She rather despises herself for it, and wishes, when she goes on vacation, that she could submerge herself in scenery or fantasy as other people seemed to do, her husband Peter in particular, or so she suspects. She would never risk saying to him, 'A penny for your thoughts,' nor would he ever say such a thing to her. He believes such 'openers' are ill-bred intrusions. He told her as much, soon after they were married, lying above her on the living-room floor in their first apartment with the oval braided rug beneath them pushing up its rounded cushiony ribs. 'What are you thinking?' she had asked, and watched his eyes go cold.

The rain increases, little checks against the car window, and Barbara curls her legs up under her, something she seldom does – since it makes her feel like a woman trying too hard to be whimsical – and busies herself looking up Salinas, Texas, in her guidebook. There it is: population figures, rainfall statistics, a naive but jaunty potted history. Why at her age does she feel compelled to know such things? What is all this shrewdness working itself up for? Salinas, Texas. The city rises and collapses in the rainy distance.

Leaning forward, she changes the tape. Its absolute, neat plastic corners remind her of the nature of real things, and snapping it into place gives her more satisfaction than listening to the music. A click, a short silence, and then the violins stirring themselves like iced-tea spoons, like ferns on a breezy hillside. Side two. She stares out the window, watchful for the least variation. A water tower holds her eye for a full sixty seconds, a silver thimble on stilts. *Château d'eau*, she murmurs to herself. Tower of Water. Tower of Babel.

Almost all her conversations are with herself.

Imprisoned now for five long days in the passenger seat of a brand new Oldsmobile Cutlass, Barbara thinks of herself as a castaway. Her real life has been left behind in Toronto. She and Peter are en route to Houston to attend an estate auction of a late client of Peter's, a man who ended his life not long ago with a pistol shot. For the sake of the passage, admittedly only two weeks, she has surrendered those routines that make her feel busy and purposeful. (With another woman she runs an establishment on Queen Street called the Ungift Shop; she also reads to the blind and keeps up her French.) Given the confining nature of her life, she has surprising freedoms at her disposal.

We should have flown is the phrase she is constantly on the point of uttering. Driving had been Peter's idea; she can't now remember his reasons; two reasons he gave, but what were they?

He has a craning look when he drives, immensely responsible. And a way of signalling when he passes, letting his thumb wing out sideways on the lever, a deft and lovely motion. She is struck by the beauty of it, also its absurdity, a little dwarfish, unconscious salute, and silent.

There is too much sorrowful sharing in marriage, Barbara thinks. When added up, it kills words. Games have to be invented; theatre. Out loud she says, like an imitation of a gawking person, 'I wonder what those little red flowers are.' (Turning, reaching for her wildlife book.) 'We don't have those in Ontario. Or do we?'

The mention of the red flowers comes after another long silence.

Then Peter says, not unkindly, not even impatiently, 'A gully's deeper, I think.'

'Deeper?' says Barbara in her dream voice. She is straining her eyes to read a billboard poised high on a yellow bluff. IF YOU SMOKE PLEASE TRY CARLETONS. The word, *please*, it's shocking. So! – the tobacco industry has decided to get polite. Backed into a corner, attacked on all sides, they're hitting hard with wheedling courtesies, *please*. Last week Barbara watched a TV documentary on lung cancer and saw a set of succulent pink lungs turning into what looked like slices of burnt toast.

'Deeper than a gulch.'

'Oh,' says Barbara.

'Unless I've got it the wrong way round.'

'It's slang anyway, I think.'

'What?'

'Gully. Gulch. They're not real words, are they? They sound, you know, regional. Cowboy lingo.'

Peter takes a long banked curve. On and on it goes, ninety degrees or more, but finely graded. His hands on the wheel are scarcely required to move. Clean, thick hands, they might be carved out of twin bars of soap. Ivory soap, carbolic. He smiles faintly, but in a way that shuts Barbara out. On and on. Rain falls all around them – *il pleut* – on the windshield and on the twisted landforms and collecting along the roadway in ditches. 'Could be,' Peter says.

'Does that look brighter up ahead to you?' Barbara says wildly, anxious now to keep the conversation going. She puts away the tape, sits up straight, pats her hair, and readies herself for the little fates and accidents a conversation can provide.

Conversation?

Inside her head a quizzing eyebrow shoots up. These idle questions and observations? This dilatory response? This disobliging exchange between herself and her husband of thirty-three years, which is as random and broken as the geological rubble she dully observes from the car window, and about which Peter can scarcely trouble himself to comment? This sludge of gummed phrases? Conversation?

It could be worse, thinks Barbara, always anxious to be fair, and calling to mind real and imaginary couples sitting silent in coffee shops, whole meals consumed and paid for with not a single world exchanged. Or stunned looking husbands and wives at home in their vacuumed living rooms, neatly dressed and conquered utterly by the background hum of furnaces and air-conditioning units. And after that, what? – a desperate slide into hippo grunts and night coughing, slack, sponge-soft lips and toothless dread – that word *mute* multiplied to the thousandth power. Death.

An opportunity to break in the new car was what Peter had said – now she remembered.

Barbara met Peter in 1955 at a silver auction in Quebec City. He was an apprentice then, learning the business. He struck her first as being very quiet. He stared and stared at an antique coffee service, either assessing its value or awestruck by its beauty – she didn't know which. Later he grew talkative. Then silent. Then eloquent. Secretive. Verbose. Introspective. Gregarious. A whole colony of choices appeared to rest in his larynx. She never knew what to expect. One minute they were on trustworthy ground, feeding each other intimacies, and the next minute they were capsized, adrift and dumb.

'Some things can't be put into words,' a leaner, nervous, younger Peter Cormin once said.

'Marriage can be defined as a lifelong conversation,' said an elderly, sentimental, slightly literary aunt of Barbara's, meaning to be kind.

Barbara at twenty had felt the chill press of rhetorical echo: *a religious vocation is one of continuous prayer, a human life is one unbroken thought.* Frightening. She knew better, though, than to trust what was cogently expressed. Even as a young woman she was forever tripping over abandoned proverbs. She counted on nothing, but hoped for everything.

Breaking in the new car. But did people still break in cars? She hadn't heard the term used for years. Donkey's years. Whatever that meant.

A younger, thinner, more devious Barbara put planning into her conversations. There was breakfast talk and dinner talk and lively hurried telephone chatter in between. She often cast herself in the role of ingénue, allowing her husband Peter space for commentary and suggestions. It was Barbara who put her head to one side, posed questions and prettily waited. It was part of their early shared mythology that he was sometimes arrogant to the point of unkindness, and that she was sensitive and put upon, an injured consciousness flayed by husbandly imperative. But neither of them had the ability to sustain their roles for long.

She learned certain tricks of subversions, how with one word or phrase she could bring about disorder and then reassurance. It excited her. It was like flying in a flimsy aircraft and looking at the suddenly vertical horizon, then bringing everything level once more.

'You've changed,' one of her conversations began.

'Everyone changes.'

'For better or worse?'

'Better, I think.'

'You think?'

'I know.'

'You say things differently. You intellectualise.'

'Maybe that's my nature.'

'It didn't used to be.'

'I've changed, people do change.'

'That's just what I said.'

'I wish you wouldn't –'

'What?'

'Point things out. Do you always have to point things out?'

'I can't help it.'

'You could stop yourself.'

'That wouldn't be me.'

Once they went to a restaurant to celebrate the birth of their second son. The restaurant was inexpensive and the food only moderately good. After coffee, after glasses of recklessly ordered brandy, Peter slipped away to the telephone. A business call, he said to Barbara. He would only be a minute or two. From where she sat she could see him behind the glass door of the phone booth, his uplifted arm, his patient explanation, and his glance at his watch – then his face reshaped itself into furrows of explosive laughter.

She had been filled with a comradely envy for his momentary connection, and surprised by her lack of curiosity, how little she cared who was on the other end of the line, a client or a lover, it didn't matter. A conversation was in progress. Words were being mainlined straight into Peter's ear, and the overflow of his conversation travelled across the dull white tablecloths and reached her too, filling her emptiness, or part of it.

Between the two of them they have accumulated a minor treasury of anecdotes beginning with 'Remember when we –' and this literature of remembrance sometimes traps them into smugness. And, occasionally, when primed by a solid period of calm, they are propelled into the blue-tinged prehistory of that epoch before they met.

'When I was in Denver that time –'

'I never knew you were in Denver.'

'My mother took me there once . . . '

'You never told me your mother took you to . . . '

But Barbara is tenderly protective of her beginnings. She is also, oddly, protective of Peter's. Eruptions from this particular and most cherished layer of time are precious and dangerous; retrieval betrays it, smudges it.

'There's something wrong,' Barbara said to Peter some years ago, 'and I don't know how to tell you.'

They were standing in a public garden near their house, walking between beds of tulips.

'You don't love me,' he guessed, amazing her, and himself.

'I love you but not enough.'

'What is enough?' he cried and reached out for the cotton sleeve of her dress.

A marriage counsellor booked them for twelve sessions. Each session lasted two hours, twenty-four hours in all. During those twenty-four hours they released into the mild air of the marriage counsellor's office millions of words. Their longest conversation. The polished floor, the walls, the perforated ceiling tile drank in the unstoppable flow. Barbara Cormin wept and shouted. Peter Cormin moaned, retreated, put his head on his arms. The histories they separately recounted were as detailed as the thick soft novels people carry with them to the beach in the summer. Every story elicited a counter story, until the accumulated weight of blame and blemish had squeezed them dry. 'What are we doing?' Peter Cormin said, moving the back of his hand across and across his mouth. Barbara thought back to the day she had stood by the sunlit tulip bed and said, 'Something's wrong,' and wondered now what had possessed her. A hunger for words, was that all? She asked the marriage counsellor for a glass of cold water. She feared what lay ahead. A long fall into silence. An expensive drowning.

But they were surprisingly happy for quite some time after, speaking to each other kindly, with a highly specific strategy, little pieces moved on a chess board. What had been tricky territory before was strewn with shame. Barbara was prepared now to admit that marriage was, at best, a flawed and gappy narrative. Occasionally some confidence would wobble forward and one of them, Barbara or Peter, might look up cunningly, ready to measure the moment and retreat or advance. They worked around the reserves of each other's inattention the way a pen and ink artist learns to use the reserve of white space.

'Why?' Barbara asked Peter.

'Why what?'

'Why did he do it? Shoot himself.'

'No one knows for sure.'

'There's always a note. Wasn't there a note?'

'Yes. But very short.'

'Saying?'

'He was lonely.'

'That's what he said, that he was lonely?'

'More or less.'

'What exactly did he say?'

'That there was no one he could talk to.'

'He had a family, didn't he? And business associates. He had you, he's known you for years. He could have picked up the phone.'

'Talking isn't just words.'

'What?'

Barbara sees herself as someone always waiting for the next conversation, the way a drunk is forever thinking ahead to the next drink.

But she discounts the conversation of Eros which seems to her to be learned not from life, but from films or trashy novels whose authors have in turn learned it from other secondary and substandard sources. Where bodies collide most gloriously, language melts – who said that? Someone or other. Barbara imagines that listening at the bedroom keyholes of even the most richly articulate would be to hear only the murmurous inanities of *True Romance*. ('I adore your golden breasts,' he whispered gruffly. 'You give me intense pleasure,' she deeply sighed.) But these conversations actually take place. She knows they do. The words are pronounced. The sighing and whispering happen. *Just the two of us, this paradise.*

'We can break in the car,' Peter said to her back in Toronto, 'and have a few days together, just the two of us.'

Very late on Day Five they leave the Interstate and strike off on a narrow asphalt road in search of a motel. The cessation of highway noise is stunningly sudden, like swimming away in a dream from the noises of one's own body. Peter holds his head to one side, judging the car's performance, the motor's renewed, slower throb and the faint adhesive tick of the tyres rolling on the hot road.

The towns they pass through are poor, but have seen better days. Sidewalks leading up to lovely old houses have crumbled along their edges, and the houses themselves have begun to deteriorate; many are for sale; dark shaggy cottonwoods bend down their branches to meet the graceful pitch of the roofs. Everywhere in these little towns there are boarded-up railway stations, high schools, laundries, cafés, plumbing supply stores, filling stations. And almost everywhere, it seems, the commercial centre has shrunk to a single, blinking, all-purpose, twenty-four-hour outlet at the end of town – pathetically, but precisely named: the Mini-Mart, the Superette, the Quik-Stop. These new buildings are of single-storey slab construction in pale brick or cement block, and are minimally landscaped. One or two gas pumps sit out in front, and above them is a sign, most often homemade, saying MILK ICE BREAD BEER.

'Milk ice bread beer,' murmurs the exhausted Barbara, giving the phrase a heaving tune. She is diverted by the thought of these four purposeful commodities traded to a diminished and deprived public. 'The four elements.'

In the very next town, up and down over a series of dark hills, they find a subtly altered version: BEER ICE BREAD MILK. 'Priorities,' says Peter, reading the sign aloud, making an ironic chant of it.

Further along the road they come upon BREAD BEER MILK ICE. Later still, the rescrambled BEER MILK ICE BREAD.

Before they arrive, finally, at a motel with air conditioning, a restaurant and decent beds – no easy matter in a depressed agricultural region – they have seen many such signs and in all possible variations. Cryptic messages, they seem designed to comfort and confuse Peter and Barbara Cormin with loops of flawed recognition and to deliver them to a congenial late-evening punchiness. As the signs pop up along the highway, they take it in turn, with a rhythmic spell and counter-spell, to read the words aloud. Milk bread beer ice. Ice bread milk beer.

This marks the real death of words, thinks Barbara, these homely products reduced to husks, their true sense drained purely away. Ice beer bread milk. Rumblings in the throats, syllables strung on an old clothes-line, electronic buzzing.

But, surprisingly, the short unadorned sounds, for a few minutes, with daylight fading and dying in the wide sky, take on expanded meaning. Another, lesser world is brought forward, distorted and freshly provisioned. She loves it – its weather and depth, its exact chambers, its lost circuits, its covered pleasures, its submerged pattern of communication.